Silver Moon &

HAVE

OF 73

EROTIC DOMINATION

If you like one you will probably like the rest

A NEW TITLE EVERY MONTH

THE CONNOISSEUR
by
Francine Whittaker

This is fiction - In real life always practise safe sex!

For Martin

PROLOGUE

Greece

The mother of all storms had those girls who were not secured to their beds, or to some devilish piece of apparatus, huddling together in a subterranean room. Theo, known far and wide simply as The Connoisseur, had a well-stocked gallery of girls, each one special in her own way, and all a delight of sexual servitude. He was thankful there was no rain to mar the show, even though the lightning lit up the midnight sky dramatically for miles around. The flashes, mere seconds apart now, reached eerily into every crevice of what appeared to be an ancient Greek palace or temple.

On the balcony of his room in the living quarters, Theo sat like a prince in a royal box and used the naked, bound and gagged girl as a footstool. Every now and then he applied the heel of his shoe to ram the dildo that stuck from her arse further into her tight, secret channel. And when the tears streamed down her face as she whimpered into the gag, he reminded her with a crack of the dog whip across her buttocks of the purpose of her life.

"Your pain is my pleasure." Then, to further drive the point home, he gave a sharp tug on the chain that was fastened at one end to the arm of his chair, and the other to a crocodile clip that was attached to the girl's labia.

Below them in the centre of the marble expanse that in former days would have been used for ritualistic worship and was tonight unnecessarily floodlit, two naked girls were strung up, face to face, breast to breast. The wrists of each girl were secured together by means of leather cuffs around her wrists, and then fiendishly attached by a metal ring to the wrists of the other girl. Chains had been fastened to their cuffs, and by a series of pulleys which stretched the girls' arms tautly above their heads, the chains were themselves attached to the overhead bar of the wooden structure, erected hastily earlier in the day for the sole purpose of tonight's significantly private entertainment. But worse still were the painful nipple clamps that tugged the girls' cruelly extended nipples upward by other chains, also fastened to the overhead bar. Together, these restraints kept the girls balancing precariously on tip-toe, as too did the seething mass of snakes which slithered and coiled at their feet. While they were not venomous and could inflict no harm, both girls were piteously unaware of this fact. The overall effect was devastating and showed off the sensuous curves of their lithe, young bodies most pleasingly.

There was no doubt in Theo's mind that their pain, both physical and mental, was agonising, as indeed it had been designed to be. His thin lips twisted into a half-smile.

The black-hooded guards, wearing the leather harnesses that served as a uniform on this beautiful, decadent island, stood one behind each girl. With ferocious accuracy, they wielded their whips to strike in sadistic synchronization with each lightning flash, adding to the magnificent theatre of the occasion. Strike upon terrible strike had the girls writhing, and jerking on their chains like puppets on strings while the snakes coiled and uncoiled around their ankles; their shrill cries rang out and were lost across the Aegean.

Theo watched the scene with mounting excitement. Pumping his cock in his fist while holding the telephone receiver in his free hand, he gloried in the scene below him. Each ear-splitting scream and fall of the lash filled him with a lust that his caller in England could only begin to imagine.

"I had you installed there, Flynn, to do a job, not to procure pussy. What makes you think this... this temptress you've discovered will amuse me? I require at least a degree of subservience from new blood." He jerked on the chain and the girl beneath his feet screamed into her gag as the clip bit into her tender flesh. "If she's as sure of herself as you say, why should I give a fuck?"

Yet even as he said it, Theo's lust was sharpened. Surrounded by adoring slaves, he began to relish the idea of such a challenge, to turn a sexually confident woman into a subjugated slut. It was one thing to dominate a born submissive, but to break and enslave a cock-teasing seducer of men was another thing entirely. It might even have its compensations.

"Ok, the idea intrigues me. Have your own sport with her by all means, but don't damage the goods. I'll take control when I come to London in a couple of weeks-"Theo swallowed hard as the lash cut across the girls' breasts. When he spoke again, his voice came out in ragged gasps. "I'll want daily reports from someone I can trust... I'll have someone on a plane in the morning."

Theo kept his eyes rivetted to the two naked girls as they twisted and turned to evade the lash, and the thought of a new girl undergoing the same treatment made him pump his considerable shaft faster. He took a deep, steadying breath before giving his final instructions to the Englishman.

"Find out if this... what's her name?... Vivienne's got family- we don't want any extra baggage. Sever all her relationships. Don't do anything to alert her suspicions. You'll be rewarded if she lives up to expectations."

He slammed down the phone. In one frenzied moment of lust, the final blows crashed down on the two beautiful girls, he kicked at the half-obscured dildo and drove it deeper, the girl collapsed in a heap and Theo spurted his hot come over her trembling body.

Exhausted, having taken as much punishment as they could stand in one night, only the two girls' bonds prevented them from falling as they passed into the comforting blackness of unconsciousness.

Theo smiled and reached for his metaxas.

CHAPTER ONE

As her heart rate returned to normal, Vivienne splashed cold water onto her face. Her dusky-gold skin was positively glowing. Deftly applying fresh make-up, she told herself smilingly that no one save herself and Adrian, the eighteen-year-old "new boy" from Marketing, would ever know about their lunch time quickie in the new Divisional Manager's empty office.

Tiny arrows of elation caused her breath to catch in her throat as she remembered Adrian's virgin cock entering her hot, wet quim from behind. Her feline body had leaned over the photocopier, her full breasts flattened against the unyielding metal. Now she smiled as she looked back at his clumsy attempt to withdraw once he had come. She gave a little laugh and wondered if the cleaners would guess the cause of the stain on the new beige carpet.

In a characteristic gesture, she slipped her hand beneath her hair at her nape. First tilting, then throwing back her head, she flicked her thick, raven hair over her shoulder. Long and silky, she wore her hair brushed back from her face, and let it hang down her back like a shining curtain to her waist.

Her glowing, golden skin was unblemished. Blessed with high cheek bones, and almond shaped eyes that were an unusual shade of green, her appearance had often been described as "exotic."

After checking one final time in the mirror, she left the Ladies to return to her desk in Customer Services.

Smiling teasingly at the Credit Control supervisor as she passed his desk, she accepted his invitation for after work "drinks" with an almost imperceptible nod of her head. She had always felt an attraction for him, and now that he was free she would be quite happy to step into his wife's shoes, for a short while at least. In her way she felt quite sorry for him- it was common knowledge that his wife of twenty-five years had left him... for another woman! Vivienne bit into her bottom lip, unable to imagine what possessed one woman to fancy another. You certainly wouldn't catch me making love to a woman, she avowed silently.

What Vivienne wanted was a man, a real man. For fond as she

was of Nathan, her live-in boyfriend, there was something missing in their relationship. She wasn't sure when it had happened, but somewhere along the line, passionate fuck had turned into textbook copulation. That first night in his hotel room at the conference had been wonderful, and she had been more than willing when he had suggested moving in with her. He had been living with Vivienne for approximately six months now, but things had gone rapidly downhill after the first couple of weeks; she was already beginning to feel trapped.

For Vivienne, it had never been the same since he had declared his love for her, maybe that was what had killed it. She couldn't help but feel it was that nice, safe, dependable love, or the cloying love of an ill-suited marriage; there was no magic, no sparkle. It wasn't love that she was looking for- it was something far more potent than that.

Smoothing her short, black skirt that showed off her bare legs to an advantage, Vivienne settled herself behind her work station. She hit the mouse button and immediately the screen saver was replaced by a table of half-yearly sales figures. She checked her watch. There was just about time to study the figures and make a start on her report before Denise-something-or-other turned up for her interview.

***

Something made Vivienne swivel round in her chair to look out of the window. Flynn Pallister stepped from his BMW in the car park, seven storeys below. Now there was a real man!

Tall, suntanned and blond, Flynn was in his mid thirties. Vivienne found him sexy, in a well-groomed, well-spoken sort of way. Even the thought of him made her large nipples stiffen. Dark brown, they were clearly visible as they pushed against the flimsy fabric of her pale blue silk blouse.

Flynn had recently been flown in from the New York office by the powers-that-be. Now he was Divisional Manager of the South-eastern region at Head Office, twenty-five miles from London. It was all change since the company take over.

No one was sure where Flynn came from originally, though it

was rumoured he came from a well-to-do family somewhere in the North of England. He could have come from the moon for all Vivienne cared; it was his potential performance in bed that intrigued her.

A short while later Vivienne glanced up as Adrian flitted past her desk in Customer Services and scurried through the large, open plan office in the general direction of Flynn's. It was with a certain pride that she mulled over how he would always remember Vivienne Trevayne as the woman who had led him from youth to manhood in a single lunch time. While she had been delighted by his firm, young body, in truth it had been something of a kindness on her part. Adrian was pathetically shy of women, and had often been heard to complain that he had "never got anywhere with girls". And as he had been following her around like a lost puppy for the past couple of weeks, she had felt almost obliged to reward him.

Glancing up again, Vivienne was surprised to see two security guards on their way through the office. They were probably doing one of their periodical checks to make sure that everyone was wearing their ID.

When she received a phone call from Flynn requesting her presence in his office immediately, Vivienne left her table of figures and set off for his office. He had earned the reputation within the company as a hard task-master. He expected, and usually achieved, nothing less than complete efficiency and total commitment from his staff. While she had no intention of being at any man's beck and call, even Flynn's, it seemed unwise to upset him so early in their acquaintance.

Flynn's work station comprised two desks placed at right angles, one housing his computer and other equipment, while the second desk, running parallel with the wall, was covered in paperwork. Sitting behind his desk that faced the door, he sprawled sideways in his chair, one arm across the back. He gave her a broad, sexy smile.

She flicked her eyes to the photocopier, then the stain on the carpet, and smiled a secret smile.

"Hi, Flynn. If it's about the report, I was just about to start-" Vivienne began in her ususal, somewhat husky tones that men found incredibly sexy, while Vivienne thought it made her sound as if she were constantly suffering from laryngitis.

"Come in. Close the door." There was a note of authority in his urbane voice. "Draw the blinds." Sectioned off from the main office by floor to ceiling panels that could be easily taken down and re-erected elsewhere, there was one window that enabled Flynn to monitor most of the activities of the department. With the blinds drawn, as when Vivienne had been here earlier, it gave the illusion that Flynn's office was more private than it really was.

"I know you're conducting an interview in a few minutes, so I'll keep this brief-" his eyes travelled upward from her ankles to her thighs "as is your skirt."

Vivienne smiled. She knew she had good legs, and if a man wanted to eyeball them, it was fine by her. It gave her a thrill when a man looked at her the way Flynn was looking at her now, and she couldn't resist the temptation to flirt. Using the tip of her tongue to wet her lips, she looked at him coquettishly from beneath her long eyelashes. Transferring her weight from one leg to the other, she took up a provocative pose with her hand on her hip.

Flynn beckoned her towards him. Taking a metal rule from his desk drawer, he used it as a school teacher might to point to the floor beside his chair, indicating the spot where he wanted her to stand. What made Flynn different? When he said "jump" Why did she want to take up pole vaulting? It never occurred to her to refuse. Instead, she savoured the feeling of contentment that washed over her as she took up the required position beside him.

Facing him, she could see an assortment of objects scattered among the paperwork on his desk, including a collection of bulldog clips of various sizes, a wide leather belt and the leather tip of something sticking out from underneath a file. Following the line of her gaze, he slowly pushed back the file, to reveal a riding crop.

"I might go riding," he said by way of explanation.

"Oh. Have you got your own horse?"

"Who said anything about horses?" He picked it up, flexed it, then brought it swishing down across his open palm. Replacing it on the desk top, Flynn selected one of the large bulldog clips and held it up to her eyes. He opened it and held it poised within inches of her eyes, then snapped it closed. There was a menacing undertone to his voice as he said "I find these quite useful, too."

He lowered his hand and brushed it against her skirt, pushing the fabric against her mons. She smiled down at him, happy to feel his light touch at last. Hoisting up her skirt, she guided his hand toward the elastic of her flimsy, pink panties, intending to steer his fingers towards her hairy mound. Her heart sank as he pulled her hand away.

"We'll do this my way or not at all." He brought the bulldog clip down between her legs and held it against her nylon covered crotch. He opened it, then snapped it closed.

Instinct made her jump backwards.

Flynn merely laughed, let her skirt fall back into place and dropped the clip on the floor. He held out his hand and gently pulled her back into position.

Feeling stupid, she smiled down into his suntanned face. She could see the hunger there in his eyes- she could also see the huge bulge in his trousers.

"You're beautiful, Vivienne," he reached out and cupped her full breast in his hand, kneading it gently through her blouse "but you already know that. And you want every man in the place to know it, too, don't you? It gives you a thrill to know that men lust after you and can scarcely control their desire to master your body."

Vivienne had always rejoiced silently in the knowledge that hers was a body that could drive a man insane. After all, if you had been blessed with good looks, you could hardly fail to notice, could you? And hers were exceptionally good looks.

Of medium height, she had narrow shoulders and a long, elegant neck; her full breasts gave emphasis to her narrow waist and sensual, rounded buttocks, and her hips and thighs narrowed to long, shapely legs. The whole, stunning effect gave the illusion that she was taller than her five feet four inches.

Releasing her breast, Flynn ran his fingers up the insides of her thigh, making her quiver deliciously. Already she could feel her sex moistening as the familiar stirrings of arousal coiled and uncoiled in her belly. Then he repeated the process, except this time he scraped his fingernails into the soft, yielding flesh.

"Ouch!"

He dug his nails deeper, making her gasp.

"Turn around, Vivienne."

Well, if he wanted to play games that was fine by her. Besides, she thought it might turn out to be fun. She turned so that her back was towards him. A delicious warmth spread from her breasts to her pussy as she imagined how much he wanted her.

Using the tip of the metal rule, he hoisted up her skirt at the back to reveal the pink thong of her panties that separated her rounded buttocks. She felt the cold, hard edge of the rule as he used it to force her thighs apart. He rubbed it back and forth, back and forth against her pussy lips, which to her shame were already leaking juice and making her panties damp.

He withdrew the rule and she waited with a smile on her lips as she wondered what he would do next. But nothing had prepared her for the sudden shock and she screamed out at the blaze of pain as he slapped the rule sharply across her thigh. Then with lightning speed, he caught hold of her right wrist and wrenched her arm backward. Startled, she tugged to free herself, but he held it securely with one hand, level with her narrow waist.

"What are you doing, Flynn? That hurts!"

"Really? What about this?" He struck her again with the rule and again she screamed.

She gave a sharp cry as he yanked her arm upwards so that her hand was between her shoulder blades. He made no move to release her. Nor did she make a move to pull away.

Flynn's fingers dug into her wrist as he held her tightly, while the fingers of his free hand found her labia lips as they pressed against her fine, damp panties. With finger and thumb, he gave them a sharp pinch. Then she heard a sharp snapping sound and was lacerated by sudden pain as the bulldog clip closed over her panties.

"Argh!"

"Be quiet-" once again the rule cracked against her thigh "or I'll put it on without your panties."

"God no! Take it off! Please, it hurts. Let go of me, Flynn, or I'll scream."

"Go ahead- no one will hear you. I've arranged for a special showing of the safety at work video to be shown in one of the conference rooms on the second floor. People should be leaving about now."

Even as he squeezed tightly on her other wrist and yanked her arm upward, her lips curved of their own accord into a kitten smile. She didn't know why he was being so spiteful, nor did she care. She guessed it was nothing but some sort of power game he was playing.

But more was to come. She felt something touch her wrists, then to her horror he began to bind them together. The belt! She tried to pull her hands free, but he had bound them tightly.

"You may lower your arms now, Vivienne."

Only slightly relieved, she stood trembling with her secured hands resting on her bottom and the bulldog clip dangling from her labia, only slightly protected by the nylon. The metal cut into the tender flesh, bringing tears to her eyes. Never had she known such pain, nor so spiteful a man.

"Okay Flynn," she began bravely, "you've had your fun. Now let me go."

She made to turn round, but his hand shot out at once to stop her.

"It's come to my attention, Vivienne that you have something of a reputation", he admonished her. "In fact, you're something of a slut."

The allegation stung her. "That's a bit strong! How dare you bring me in here to discuss my sex life. I really can't see that it's any of your business. I don't need your approval as to how I should conduct my private life. I would have thought a man like you would know better than to listen to idle gossip."

Vivienne knew that her sex life had been a subject of tittle-tattle among work colleagues. She had heard herself referred to as "the fuck-patrol" and "cock chaser" by some of the men in the office, notably those who hadn't made it to her bed. But as Flynn's fingers began to swirl in tiny circles over her soft flesh, she was unable to tell from his tone whether he was taking disciplinary measures into his own hands, about to issue a formal warning or merely trying it on. To make matters worse, she knew her golden-toned features were beginning to turn rosy, not a usual occurrence since she was seldom embarrassed.

"For that reason, I've had Security remove your little friend, Adrian, from the premises. Thanks to you, he's now out of a job."

"Bastard!" Her heart set up an erratic thumping in her chest as her anger took hold. "You can't do that!"

"Oh, but I can. And I'll go on doing it. So unless you want anyone else to face life on the dole, I suggest you keep your favours to yourself."

Thunderstruck, no words came to her. But even as her blood rebelled through her veins, she slowly became accustomed to the virulent pain of the metal that imprisoned her burning labia. His madness and uncertain temper left her little choice- she must get out of here. Yet somehow, she couldn't find the will in her legs to make a run for it. Instead, she stood stock still, and vowed to report him to the authorities. Until then, she would play him at his own game.

His fingers left a feathery trail across her buttocks. His breathing became heavier as he reached between her legs and cruelly twisted the clip, forcing another cry from her lips. He laughed, twisted again, and on the third twist he yanked it off. Before she could react his hands were at her waist. Gripping hold of her panties, he pulled them down around her knees. His forefinger traced a line along the deep crease of her buttocks, then pressed against the tightly puckered hole of her anus. She swallowed hard. No one had ever entered that private place, and every nerve in her body stiffened at the very thought of it. She would die if he-

"Tell me, Miss Trevayne ... is your pussy as tight as your nerves?"

The formal use of her surname, along with his curious line of questioning caused an uncharacteristic bout of nerves that set her trembling. Yet afraid as she was, she heard herself respond as if instead of hurting her, he were merely setting out to seduce her.

"There's only one way to find out," she whispered foxily, looking at him over her shoulder.

Flynn raised an eyebrow questioningly. "We understand each other?"

Even as she silently cursed him, she revelled in the knowledge that he wanted her. All she had to do, she reasoned, to get back at him was to lead him on a bit- it wouldn't hurt him to wait a bit longer, would it?

"I hate to rush things, Flynn- perhaps another time, another place- I have an interview, remember. And I still have that report."

Flynn's attitude seemed to change. He withdrew his fingers and with a quick movement, released her hands. He flicked the belt in the air- it made a terrible cracking sound- and every part of her body tensed as she waited for it to come cracking down on her flesh. But Flynn seemed to have lost interest and pushed her away roughly. With her panties around her knees, she lost her balance and stumbled. To her shame, there was juice trickling down her thighs.

"Oh yes, the interview." He pointed to the vacant chair opposite him, on the other side of his desk. "Sit."

For some reason that she couldn't fathom, she didn't flee from his office, but after pulling up her panties and flicking her hair over her shoulder, she did as he asked and sat.

"The name of the young lady you're about to see is Denise." The glittering, white hot hunger in his eyes burned holes in hers, even as his brusque tone stung her. "There's nothing else you need to know, except that you will employ her."

The spark of defiance hadn't quite been extinguished. "There are several other candidates, Flynn. I haven't seen them all yet."

"Nevertheless, you will employ Denise. You're aware that the interviews were set up before Denise applied, and should therefore also know they are mere formalities. For the sake of appearances, you'll conduct all the interviews professionally, but ultimately turn everyone else down. I repeat, you'll employ Denise-" his voice took on a new, worrying tone as he straightened in his seat, "or lose your own job."

Vivienne's mouth opened wordlessly. Any sexual feelings she felt for him melted away as if they had never been.

"Do I make myself clear?"

"Crystal!" she said, scathingly.

"Then get to it. Denise is waiting in reception."

Vivienne stood up and marched angrily to the door. Who the

fuck did he think he was to threaten her? She had a good mind to tell the bloody girl that the job had already gone.

"Oh, Miss Trevayne?" Flynn waited until she turned to face hm. "I'll be away for the next few days. You're to take next Thursday off. Make up whatever story you like, but don't come into work. Here-" He delved into his pocket and drew out a wad of notes, which he held out to her. "Go do some shopping."

She nodded towards the money, now lying on the desk top. "What's that, Mr Pallister, some kind of reward for toeing the line? I haven't given her the bloody job yet. I don't need your money."

"Just take the fucking money! I've heard that, as well as your other... dubious talents, you've a penchant for shopping." He held up the bulldog clip in a silent threat. "So, go shopping next Thursday-buy yourself some decent shoes that flatter your ankles and ditch those things you're wearing. They may be the height of fashion, but they're atrocious. Meet me, at 6.30, next Thursday evening, at the Midway Hotel."

"Piss off"

"You'll find life easier if you do as you're told, Miss Trevayne. Be there!"

"Get stuffed!"

So what if he was her boss? No one had ever treated her like that before. No one had even spoken to her like that and got away with it. She flicked her hair over her shoulder, held her head high and marched from his office. He knew where he could stick his money.

Flynn watched her flounce off down the corridor. His lips formed a smile as he wondered what Vivienne would make of Denise. Would the delectable Denise's subservience rub off? His thoughts went one step further and he imagined Vivienne writhing under the whip. Personally, he couldn't wait to see the haughty bitch brought low.

***

Paston Communications was now part of the huge Zortac empire, which had branches throughout Europe and the US., and it was hoped that Zortac would breathe new life into the town, for this was a town where jobs weren't that easy to come by. Paston Wick had been going through something of a local depression lately; two large companies had cut their work force dramatically; a small, family run engineering works had been forced to close, while the promised "new" jobs at the Petrochemicals plant in a neighbouring town had failed to materialize.

Vivienne loathed the idea of the repetitive questioning of a seemingly never-ending line of hopeful candidates, especially now that she knew the whole thing was rigged. How could Flynn be so heartless? Yet perversely, his very heartlessness sent a thrill of arousal directly to her tortured sex. Subconsciously, she rubbed her thigh. The redness had faded now, yet she could still feel the sting of the rule, or perhaps she only thought she could. Never one to shirk her duties and by nature an affable, outgoing young woman, Vivienne painted on a smile as she led the dewy-eyed girl into the office on the second floor that was used for board meetings.

Vivienne took an instant dislike to the unassuming redhead. Her CV proclaimed her age to be eighteen, and she certainly had a youthful appearance. But Vivienne had the feeling that she was older than she appeared by several years- nearer twenty-eight, and that would make her older than Vivienne by about two years.

"Denise, isn't it?" With her labia still sore and throbbing, Vivienne sat down on one side of the long table and gestured for Denise to sit opposite. "Please, take a seat." In her characteristic gesture, Vivienne slipped her hand underneath her mane of sleek, shining hair and flicked it over her shoulder. "Would you like a coffee?"

The redhead smiled prettily. "No, thank you."

Denise smoothed her long, flowing skirt before sitting, and Vivienne made a mental note to tell her that she would have to wear something more appropriate in the office. While Vivienne had no objections to smart, calf-length pencil skirts, floor-length frills and flounces were definitely out. And there was something about the high-necked, tightly cuffed blouse that made Vivienne uncomfortable.

God, she was so cringingly fragile and girlie! The Titian hair that frothed around her shoulders wouldn't look out of place in plaits, tied with huge bows of ribbon. Even her voice sounded squeaky clean, while Vivienne's own husky tones gave a clue to her sensual nature.

She had a fleeting mental image of the milky-white skinned creature in ankle socks, sucking a lollipop. Vivienne herself could think of much nicer things to suck- Flynn Pallister's cock would do for starters. But he had lost his chance! she reminded herself. Pulling a face, she wondered how she could ever have fancied a rat like that. Her hand slipped beneath the table and clutched her mound as if that would stop the hurt, and instead felt the heat raging there like a furnace between her legs. The pain had been excruciating...so why had she been so wet?

"Thank you for seeing me at such short notice," Denise said in a barely audible voice that was sweet as saccharin.

Gritting her teeth, Vivienne began her usual speech. "The company is going through a transitional period at the moment. You may have read about it in the national press-"

"There was a piece on TV-" Denise supplied a little too eagerly, "on Business Matters. Apparently, Paston Communications has been the subject of a take over, and has been absorbed into the Zortac empire. But the real mystery is, who owns Zortac? No one, it seems, can supply the answer to that little conundrum."

OK, so she's not as dumb as she looks! Vivienne thought tetchily. Irritated, she drew in a deep breath.

That trouble with Flynn had really got to her, and now she felt her temper beginning to bubble on the back burner. She brought her hand up again and clasped the other tightly in front of her on the table, and watched her knuckles turn white.

She took another deep breath, while mentally trying one of the techniques in The Little Book of Calm to compose herself. Often short tempered and tense lately, perhaps she should follow up the idea of one of her colleagues and seek out a yoga class, or maybe t'ai chi, anything to help her learn to relax.

Pushing the thought aside, Vivienne drew in another steadying breath and gave Denise one of her pleasantest smiles. If she was to take the bitch on as Flynn demanded, then it would best all round if the girl understood right now who her immediate superior was. The last thing Vivienne needed was a smart-arse in her department. She had been supervisor for three years now with ever more responsibilities, and wasn't about to be seen losing her rag to some simpering, five-foot-nothing new girl.

"There's been speculation, of course." Vivienne stamped her authority on the interview. "But for the meantime, it's business as usual. We're one of the largest Internet Providers, and we're heavily into digital technology. There heave been one or two immediate changes since the take over, one of which is our new Divisional Manager, Flynn Pallister." Not even a flicker of recognition crossed the girl's features at the mention of his name, and Vivienne wondered what exactly was going on here. "He's only been here with us a few weeks, since the takeover became public knowledge. The man he replaced had been with the company for several years, so it was a bit of a surprise to us all that he left so suddenly."

That was an understatement- the whole place had been thrown into disarray when he had announced that, after fifteen years, he'd had enough and was taking an early retirement, to "spend more time with my family." Vivienne had been surprised, too, since she had been having an on-off affair with him for the past two years. He had always told her how he found her demanding lovemaking a breath of fresh air after his wife's lay- back-and-let-it-happen attitude.

"Mr Pallister has taken over," Vivienne continued, "and is making sweeping changes. You know the kind of thing, reorganising the place, changing the computer system, etc...." And sacking anyone he doesn't like the look of, she added silently. "Now, if you could fill me in on your details, previous experience-"

The girl indicated her CV which had been faxed though that morning. "It's all in there", she breathed smilingly. "I think you'll agree that my experience is vast. I must say how excited I am to be joining the work force at this crucial stage in the company's development."

Vivienne turned her head and rolled her eyes heavenward. Denise's enthusiasm was a tad overblown, to say the least. She eyed the redhead suspiciously. It was true that her CV was faultless, if anything, she was over qualified for the job. She was the ideal applicant, yet there was something not quite right; it all seemed a bit too good to be true.

"I see you've been working abroad. What made you come back to England?"

Denise smiled. "I have commitments..."

The door burst open as the vigorous Flynn Pallister came striding into the room. He took up a position standing behind Vivienne, who momentarily forgot her dislike of him, tilted her head and gave him one of her come-and-play smiles. But to her annoyance, he didn't seem to notice her. Instead, he held out a long, slender hand to the bloody redhead.

Vivienne found herself staring at his long fingers, those same fingers that had stroked her so sensuously, only to inflict pain seconds later. She felt a dampness between her thighs as she recalled the dual sensations of pain and pleasure, and began to fidget in her seat.

"Ah! Denise, glad you could make it." Flynn's mouth set firmly. Denise smiled coyly. Meeting Flynn's eyes for a brief moment, she breathed a sugar-coated "Hello" before quickly averting her eyes downward.

Sensing there was something more than a friendly greeting passing between the two, Vivienne was aware that the air had suddenly become electrically charged. She was sure the two had met before.

Immediately, she was on her guard. Could it be that these two were more than casual acquaintances? Had they met in New York? Her fertile imagination threw up a mental picture- this time she saw the sexy Flynn and the innocent Denise in bed together. The image was so sudden and well-defined that she almost laughed aloud at the absurdity of it. Flynn was a highly sexed man who would be interested only in a woman of equal ardour, a woman who could impassion and inflame a man- a woman like herself.

Vivienne said pointedly "I didn't realize that you knew each other."

"Oh, we've...we've met once or twice," Denise answered breathlessly without raising her eyes, "during our..."

"Careers", Flynn supplied obligingly.

At first, Vivienne thought she must have imagined it but no, there it was again, a definite movement in Flynn's trousers as he ran his eyes over Denise's slight, frippery- encased frame.

How on earth could a man like Flynn be turned on by a pseudo teenager, Vivienne wondered churlishly, when she herself had more than enough to offer him? Maybe she would keep the appointment next Thursday, if only to show him what he was missing when she told him to go to hell.

Flynn cleared his throat. "Well Denise, I'm sure Vivienne has filled you in on the situation here, but if you'd like to come along with me now to my office, I'll outline your duties. You'll start right away, of course?"

"Of course", Denise said in a tone that Vivienne could only think of as obedient.

Fighting to keep the bile from rising, she watched as Denise, eyes cast downward, fell into step behind Flynn, following six paces behind him as if he were a sultan and she a slave, as he led the way through the busy office. Why did some women behave like that, Vivienne wondered, as if men were in some way superior, the more dominant species? She was thankful that she had never felt that way, and she was damn sure she wasn't about to start acting like it now, however bossy and spiteful Flynn Pallister may be.

Yet there was something about Flynn that got the juices flowing. And the more she thought about it, the more turned on she became- and the more she despised the little redhead. She wasn't usually prone to jealousy, but then even she wasn't usually prone to feeling this horny.

CHAPTER TWO

Vivienne was awoken from sleep by the sound of the phone ringing. She reached across to answer it, then realized that she wasn't in her own bed. Right now she was in a double bed, in a room at the Midway Hotel.

Flynn Pallister's voice came to her through the fog of drowsiness as he spoke to his caller.

With a smile on her lips, she turned on her side and closed her eyes, trying to recall the details of the previous evening's lovemaking. Though passionate and immensely enjoyable, for much of the time Flynn had kept her pinned on her back by holding her hands tightly above her head, rather than allowing her to take up her more usual, preferred position astride a man. She had also spent much of the night on her knees, a position she positively hated, while being pounded into doggie fashion. But Flynn's superior strength, as well as his unspoken threat of pain, had kept him firmly in control.

Flynn's hoarse, hushed voice caught Vivienne's interest at once.

"Yeah, the bitch is here with me now, sleeping. I knew she'd turn up. She's hot and horny, but got a lot to learn before she becomes a fully-fledged member of the 'spread me and bed me' brigade."

Vivienne was stunned. She had never heard him use such language before, and was struck by the incongruous nature of the coarse words, spoken with such a well-bred accent.

"She's a great lay for all that. She'll be fucking perfect, once she's been brought to heel."

Shocked to hear herself discussed in such a way, by a man with whom she had spent a terrific night of hot sex, Vivienne sat up. She turned her head in the direction of the small sitting room, where Flynn, hidden from her view, was taking the call. Staggered, she would never have credited him with a kiss-and-tell mentality; would never have thought it possible that a man of such apparent culture would gain sexual satisfaction from recounting the lurid details of his affairs. And over the phone! Yet here he was, loquaciously telling all, like a youth in a pub boasting to his mates.

Disturbingly, Vivienne found herself listening with more than astonishment. In fact, she was rather enjoying it.

"I caught her looking at herself in the mirror once or twice, watching herself being fucked; it turns her on. And no wonder, she's got a hell-of-a sassy body, great tits and arse! And not a blemish on her."

Vivienne felt the warm glow that came with the knowledge that she turned men on. She listened intently as Flynn continued, his excitement growing.

"Not even pussy-eating. No rough stuff either, not this time. I thought I'd leave that to you. Yeah, I've got the gear with me, but what's the point? I don't want to scare her off. In the event, I decided to stick to straight sex."

Having almost convinced herself that the events of over a week ago in his office had been a one-off, she was alarmed by this seemingly new twist. So, Flynn really did favour kinky sex- and he'd had the nerve to call into question her reputation! At least hers didn't include anything perverted, she told herself smugly; she had never indulged in anything other than straight, vaginal sex and cock sucking. Anything else struck her as unnecessary, even distasteful. She was in no doubt that there were women who enjoyed being sprawled over the table and fucked, but she wasn't one of them.

It was time she got out of here, before she became involved in things she definitely didn't like the sound of.

"Of course she'll be worth the trouble! Sure, a real hot number, with a sopping cunt that cries out to be fucked, and a body that begs abuse."

Now things were sounding nasty. Yet in spite of the sirens that resounded loud warnings inside her head, Vivienne stayed exactly where she was. She held her breath as she listened, became horrifyingly aware of a dampness between her parted thighs.

"She can't get enough of it; a real fuck freak. Give her a good seeing to, and she'll agree to anything." Horror-struck, her hands shot to her mouth to stifle her cry. Who on earth could he be talking to? Her heart thumped wildly as she craned her neck toward the doorway to try and hear more. There was a long pause before he spoke again, and it seemed she was no longer the topic of conversation. And his next words sent a chill through her.

"It wasn't just the kid from Marketing I had to get rid of- it seems she's been fucking a guy from Credit Control. 'After work drinks' she calls it."

Vivienne gulped. How could Flynn possibly know about that? He had been out of the office for a week.

"Hey, I'm working on it- he'll be gone, ok?"

Flynn was using his position to kick out anyone who got too close to her. Why? What made her so special? What was going on?

"Denise? She's doing fine. The company's on target, so shouldn't present any major problems. When would you like to take delivery of the goods?"

Panic rose in the pit of Vivienne's stomach. What goods? Drugs? Was Flynn caught up in drug trafficking or what? She had a definite feeling of unease. Not only did Flynn have a propensity towards kinky sex and dirty conversation, but now that she thought about it, his appointment at work had been a bit odd, too. Who was he? Why would he give up a home, as well as a good job in New York, to come and work in a quiet corner of Hertfordshire? It didn't make sense.

A shiver passed through her as she heard Flynn returning to the bedroom. Feeling inexplicably guilty, for a moment she was at a loss as to what to do; she opted to stay out of trouble and dived beneath the duvet. She had never been any good at intrigue, and pushed the whole episode to the back of her mind. And as Flynn appeared in the doorway, Vivienne gave what she thought was a rather convincing performance, as if awaking form a deep and satisfying sleep. She yawned, and stretched her arms in the air.

"Ah, you're awake." Flynn's usual demeanour had returned, and he was again the urbane, incredibly sexy individual who made her heartbeat quicken its pace. He treated her to a sexy smile as he strutted naked into the room. His fair hair was still wet from his shower and his sun-tanned body glistened with little beads of perspiration. His penis hung limply between his legs, bobbing temptingly as he walked.

Vivienne turned her head on the pillow. Her thighs parted beneath the duvet, aching to feel his cock inside her again, filling her completely.

"You're going to be late for work if you don't move yourself." There was no mistaking the tremor of arousal in his upper-class voice.

Propping herself up on one elbow, she looked at him archly from under her eyelashes. She slipped her free hand under her hair at her nape, to lift it upward in her characteristic manner.

"Come back to bed, Flynn, and fuck me again." Her permanently husky voice came out as a seductive purr as she reached out to him, pushing back the duvet invitingly to reveal her golden body, already flushed with arousal. Her large, dark brown nipples were already beginning to harden. "I could take the morning off, and you haven't any meetings until this afternoon; we've plenty of time. We could travel into work together. I could come back here with you this evening, and-"

"Set all the tongues wagging", he drawled as he settled himself to lie beside her on the bed.

The veins in his neck stood out like cords of rope as he swallowed hard. He spread one hand on her belly, and while his thumb toyed with her belly button his signet-ringed little finger sought out her clitoris, eliciting a purring sound from deep in her throat. He applied pressure, then more, then taking the hard nub between thumb and forefinger, he pinched it until she cried out. At last he released it.

"I'd prefer to keep our liaison a secret."

So, it was one rule for him and another for her! She wrapped her hand around his flaccid prick and tugged him towards her. Thanks to her eavesdropping, she was incredibly turned on. And despite her aversion to what she thought of as kinky sex, she had a shockingly lurid mental picture of herself spread face down over a table, with Flynn thrusting into her from behind. For the first time in her life, her heart beat erratically at the thought of boudoir fantasy games.

"Make love to me now," she whispered throatily, "and I promise I won't breathe a word." Yet even as she said it, she knew that something had changed. The room had become charged with an air of authority that she could almost reach out and touch.

Before she had time to register what was happening, he had pushed her down onto the pillow and clamped his hand across her mouth. Shaken, she stared wide-eyed into his face, and found all traces of tenderness had gone.

"Tell anyone, bitch, and you'll wish you'd never been fucking born. Understand?"

Stung by his abusive words, she was beginning to feel frightened. She nodded.

"I'm going to take my hand away. Scream, and I'll give you something to scream about."

Her brain screamed threats of her own, but none made it past her lips. Nevertheless, as he removed his hand, words of defiance came tumbling from her mouth.

"What are you, Flynn, some kind of control freak?"

Suddenly she cried out, more with shock than pain, as his hand delivered a stinging blow across her cheek. Dizzy with starbursts that danced in front of her eyes, she closed them tightly, as if that would make things right again. It didn't, and she cupped her hands round her burning cheek.

"Shut up and listen! When you leave here, you're to go back into work as if nothing had happened. You'll say nothing about our time here to anyone, nor will you meet anyone after work. You're to go straight home."

"Yes, Sir!" she said sarcastically.

That brought a sharp slap across her other cheek, and once again she cried out. She nursed both cheeks and stared up at him, hurt and incredulity registering in her eyes.

"There's more where that came from", he threatened. His fingers, punishing and cruel now, ran over her sinuous curves with the roughness of unbridled lust. "Afterwards, you'll shower. Meet me at an address I'll give you later, and make sure you look your seductive best. You're going to help me close a deal with a friend of mine who's in England on business. He's wealthy, important and very influential, so I suggest you're on your best behaviour. Got it?"

Opening her eyes she nodded mutely, still cupping her reddened cheeks. For the first time in her life, she felt a sense of fragility as it dawned on her that Flynn was the kind of man who could, and would, hurt her. What kind of madness had made her keep the appointment with him, anyway?

Slowly, he lowered his head and his lips covered hers in a ravenous, bruising kiss. She was almost unable to breathe. Her traitorous body arched in invitation. As if everything that had gone before had never happened, she longed to feel his shaft penetrate her pussy in the same way his tongue probed her mouth. Despite the roughness with which he began squeezing her firm, rounded breasts, she felt them tighten, and her quim quivered in sweet anticipation. And the rougher he became, the more her nipples hardened painfully.

His lips slid across her face and kissed her neck. His fingers seemed to lose their aggression as he took her turgid nipples between finger and thumb and tweaked them skilfully. She felt herself melting. When he was like this, he was an accomplished lover who knew how to press all the right buttons, and she moaned with delight as he pressed all of hers.

Whilst it was true that she'd had a few affairs and had read accounts of women who had multiple orgasms, she hated to admit, even to herself, that she wasn't one of them. Sometimes orgasms eluded her completely; she often faked it. Of course, she would rather die than admit it to anyone - she had her reputation to think of, and thankfully she'd had no need to fake it with Flynn, who had brought her to climax time and time again during the night.

Strangely, she always enjoyed sex more with her casual partners; it had become something of a chore with Nathan. Yet she had faith that one day she would meet the man of her dreams who would satisfy her completely, and bring her to the perfect orgasm. She gave a little laugh at the notion.

"What's funny?"

"Nothing. I...."

"Then be quiet! Don't make a sound without permission, and only speak to answer a question. Otherwise I'll gag you."

Nervous and confused she lay back and enjoyed the sensations as his fingers swept over her body.

After a while, Flynn's breathing became lower and his words hoarse with the intensity of his passion. "You're a very sexy lady- real fuckable- the kind of woman that men fantasize about."

Vivienne lapped up the compliment gladly... and silently.

"I swear I've never seen eyes that shade of green before. How is it that a girl from deepest Hertfordshire has such unusual features?"

With slowly returning confidence Vivienne raised herself on her elbow. The fingers of her free hand moved in tiny circles across his hard abdomen as she explained languorously "Mixed ancestry." She ran her tongue teasingly over her soft, pliant lips. "Although my father's side of the family were all English, it seems all the men liked foreign women- my mother was Irish, her mother Arab, her mother French- there's Indian way back."

"That explains it, then."

"Explains what?"

"Your exotic looks, the colour of your skin. Your parents- they're both dead?"

"Yes." Shaking her head, she looked at him mournfully and said in a little-girl voice intended to mimic Denise "I've no one in the world to care for me."

"Except your boyfriend- Nat or something, isn't it?"

With a light touch, she began to stroke his semi-limp penis, starting at his balls and working upwards to its bulbous head. She loved the feeling of power it always gave her when a limp cock began to stir and grow beneath her caress, just as Flynn's was doing now. Now it was her turn to be in control.

"Nathan," she corrected, "he prefers to be called Nathan."

"Ah yes, Nathan. Tell me, are you happy with him?"

The question threw her for a minute and she gave a slight squeeze on his prick, summoning a groan from his lips.

"Of course I'm happy," she lied. "Why wouldn't I be?"

"Because if you were-" he bent towards her and kissed the top of her head "you wouldn't be here with me now. I think you should dump him."

She couldn't find an answer, even for herself, so she didn't try. Momentarily, the "L" word raised its profile as she considered her relationship with Nathan. There was no point in saying she loved him, because she knew it was a lie. She cared for him but love, if that's what it had been, had disappeared long ago, along with the passion.

"I want you to get rid of him, Vivienne. Otherwise," he flipped her onto her back. "I'll do it for you. In fact, I think I'll give him a ring when you've gone."

Before she had time to answer, he shifted position and made a grab at her legs. With a hand clasping each of her ankles, he pushed her feet towards her, thus raising her knees. Moving them outwards now to part her thighs, he lowered his head between them and began to lap at her sweet juices.

Despite her earlier warning, again she laughed."What's the matter, Flynn? Have you lost something?" she quipped. "I doubt you'll find it in there."

Once again, she cried out at the sudden sting as his hand slapped her thigh. While she rubbed the reddened patch, from somewhere he produced a ball gag and thrust it in her mouth, forcing her tongue down and almost making her choke. He fastened it behind her head and her eyes bulged in shock. Her hands flew up to remove it but he grabbed them and wrenched them away, lying one either side of her body.

"Don't move your hands, and don't even think of removing the gag. I warned you, bitch! I tried to go easy on you, to break you in gently. But no, you want the rough stuff. And that suits me fine! If I'd had my way, I'd have taken you home and laid into you. But my orders were to make sure you're unblemished and in one piece when I hand you over." He paused, and the coldness she saw in his eyes froze her blood. "And be in no doubt that I will hand you over. But first -" He gave her one final, brutal slap across her right breast that brought tears to her eyes and a silent scream into her gag. "I'm going to do to you what I should have done in the beginning."

Madness was in his eyes as he straightened up and swung himself off the bed. Her heart beat furiously as she realized he was out of control. Heaven only knew what he was about to do, but she knew it was imperative that she made a run for it, before he did something that they would both regret. Before she had time to yank off the gag, he grabbed her arms and tied her wrists together in front of her, using a silk scarf he found in her handbag. Then he hauled her to her feet by her hair and had her stand with her face against the wall, so that her nose touched the peeling wallpaper.

Suddenly her consciousness was filled by blinding light and pain as his belt cracked across her back. Though the blow had been deadened by her thick hair hanging like a protective shield down her back, she whimpered into her gag as the aftershocks made her tremble. She screamed into her gag as she heard the swish! Crack! The second blow struck just above the first. The pain cut into her in a blaze of fire. Never in her life had she been subjected to a beating, and the terror shone in her eyes. And a vivid picture built up in her mind, in which she could see herself, sensuous in her bonds, with Flynn viciously beating the contours of her golden body. Swish! Crack! The third blow wiped the vision from her mind as it crossed the other two. Swish! Crack! Vivienne hardly felt the fourth, for she had crumpled down onto the floor.

Flynn kicked her. "Get up, Vivienne! Don't worry, your hair will have protected you- this time. I'll have kept my part of the bargain and you'll be unblemished when I hand you over. You'll also be wiser. Now get up and get out- I have a couple of phone calls to make."

***

Vivienne's strappy, spiked heels made no sound on the carpet as she hurried down the hallway. And as she flew down the stairs, she reflected on how sometimes Flynn seemed to be one of the sexiest men she had ever known, while at others he was simply malicious. Yet even now she found it hard to believe, he was involved in any kind of industrial skulduggery, not Flynn. It was all a dreadful mistake.

But if that was the case, what was all that about handing her over? She didn't understand, and wasn't at all sure that she wanted to.

But perversely, she didn't regret one moment of their liaison, even though it had left her feeling afraid and confused. Never before had a man made her feel so wanted, so sensual, so alive.

Never before had her body responded so readily to a man's touch. Even now, as she thought about him on the way to the car park, her nipples stiffened, rubbing sensuously against the cotton of her low-cut blouse. Tiny ripples of arousal began to spiral through her, and she longed to be caressed once more by those skilled fingers.

Vivienne hurried across the car park toward her shiny, red sports car, a recent acquisition out of the money her parents had left her. Slithering into the front seat, she smoothed down her black mini skirt. As the cool air wafted up between her naked thighs and stroked the hot bud of her clitoris, she remembered she wasn't wearing any panties, and felt a sneaking feeling of wantonness. She smiled a secret smile, and wondered what the hell had happened to her panties, anyway? She had left them on the chair with her other clothes, but when she had dressed, there had been no sign of them. She drew in a breath as a thought struck her. Flynn was most probably one of those men that collected women's panties.

She gunned the engine, and joined the M25. Thankfully, it wasn't far to Paston Wick; it wouldn't take long if she put her foot down. She was almost halfway back to Paston Communications when her mobile rang.

Vivienne sighed, knowing instinctively that it was Denise on the other end of the line. Although the redhead had proved to be reliable, conscientious and willing to do anything that was asked of her, there was a subservience about her where men were concerned that Vivienne found irritating. And she still wore those awful frilly skirts that flapped around her ankles. Sometimes Vivienne found herself wondering what the girl wore underneath - probably a lace-up corset with several layers of thick underwear over the top. And it struck Vivienne then that she had never seen Denise wearing any other kind of blouse but one that fastened tightly around the neck- very prim and proper. She didn't belong in this new millennium, but was stuck very firmly in the early part of the previous one. Denise's voice leached saccharin down the line.

"Vivienne, I've been trying to get hold of you all morning. Where've you been? I rang your flat and spoke to Nathan. He said you'd stayed over in Birmingham last night."

There was a hint of amusement in her tone, giving Vivienne the impression that Denise knew very well where she had spent the night. But how could she know?

"I didn't know there was a conference in Birmingham yesterday. It's not entered in your desk diary."

It was hard to miss the mocking undertone to the pathetic little-girl-home-alone voice she employed so effectively as she added "Flynn Pallister's missing, too- I don't suppose you've seen him? Is everything ok, Vivienne?"

Vivienne took a deep breath. She hated lying, and only did so when she felt it absolutely necessary. She made up a thin story about having forgotten the conference until the last minute and having forgotten to put it in her diary.

Denise put the boot in with honeyed venom. "Your Nathan seemed quite upset. He doesn't like you going away, does he? I don't know what he imagines you get up to."

Thinking of Nathan again gave rise to a pang of guilt. She daren't even imagine what crushingly dependable Nathan would say if he ever discovered she had spent last night with Flynn, in a hotel room, a mere fifteen miles from home.

"The conference broke up later than I expected, and I didn't relish the idea of the drive home at that time of night. So I stayed over, no big deal. I rang him. Anyway, what's the problem that can't wait fifteen more minutes, time for me to arrive?"

"Oh, nothing really. Security just brought a package up for you. Some guy left it in reception."

"A package? What sort of package? Who's it from? Is there a name on it?"

There was a slight pause on the other end of the line. Vivienne thought there was something peculiar about Denise's tone when she finally answered, but couldn't quite put her finger on it; it was almost as if Denise knew more than she was saying, was keeping something back.

"The Connoisseur."

"Connoisseur? What the hell's that supposed to mean? Leave it on my desk and I'll sort it out when I get there. I'm on my way into the office now. 'Bye."

***

Vivienne pulled into the car park at Paston Communications, and parked beside a silver Mercedes with blacked-out windows, all of which were tightly closed. All, that is, except for the driver's window, which allowed her a near-perfect view of the fair-skinned chauffeur. Young and handsome, with high Slavic cheekbones and a square jaw, he adjusted the angle of his shades and his grey, peaked chauffeur's cap to shield his eyes.

Sashaying across the car park Vivienne turned, looked over her shoulder and winked at the chauffeur. Then she headed straight for the Ladies before going to her office.

On her desk was a package, about seven inches square, wrapped in black tissue paper. A plain white card with gold edging, bearing the words 'To Vivienne, regards, The Connoisseur' in black, hand written script, was attached to it by a gold-coloured thread.

"I suggest you open it."

She glanced up. "Flynn!" For a moment she was lost for words. She hadn't expected him in to work so soon. She was unnerved, he seemed so calm, so normal now.

"I don't know who this is from; it's an odd signature."

"Open it, Vivienne", he said on a half whisper. "All you need to know is that he is Greek."

Something in his voice told her not to question it further. Carefully, she unwrapped the package, and opened the box inside.

"Oh my God!"

"It's a choker," Flynn explained, "rather expensive, too. It's made from solid gold. It's a gift, to keep." Flynn smiled. "He thinks gold flatters the neck."

His smile didn't reach his eyes, Vivienne thought as she lifted the choker from its box.

"What's this ring for?" she asked, gently lifting up the gold ring at what she presumed was the front.

"Charms-" he said too quickly, "to attach charms and things to."

"And these smaller rings at the back?" She lifted the padlock from the box. "And this?"

"The clasp."

"But there's no key!"

"That's because it doesn't need one."

"Oh." Vivienne was sceptical. Something didn't ring true. Why would a man she had never met send her such a bizarre gift? She had no doubt that it was gold; it was very heavy.

"If you please him," Flynn continued easily, "you'll get the other bits later. No, don't close it!" he said as she looped the padlock between the two rings at the ends of the slightly flexible golden band.

"But I can't see how it undoes."

"Stop it, Vivienne," he hissed, "it doesn't matter. Don't fetch it out here in the office. Wear it tonight, when you'll be able to thank The Connoisseur personally. You'll be meeting him tonight, when I hope you'll help me to close that... business deal we spoke of."

She stalled for time as a feeling of unease began to uncurl inside. "I'm not sure I can make it tonight" If she were to go with him, she may be a party to whatever it was he was up to, be it drug trafficking or industrial espionage. If that were the case, why did he intend taking her, and not Denise, who was obviously caught up in it all to a greater extent? She wondered if the mysterious overlord and the Greek Connoisseur were one and the same. Maybe if she went along with Flynn, she reasoned, to meet his contact and witness the exchange of goods, then she could blow the whistle on him later.

"What sort of deal, Flynn?"

"One that will affect your life. We'll talk no more about it now, but be at Burridge's Salesrooms at 7.30 sharp."

CHAPTER THREE

"You look like a whore!"

Stunned by Nathan's sudden outburst, Vivienne swung round to see him leaning drunkenly against the bedroom doorjamb, with a glass of whiskey in one hand, obviously not his first of the day, and his tie in the other.

"Where are you going this time?" Nathan demanded as he threw his tie on the bed. "Don't tell me 'a conference' because I bloody well won't believe it."

One look at his face told her he hadn't had a good day at the office; he had come home expecting love and sympathy in equal measure, dinner on the table, followed by a stiff drink, a stiff cock and a warm bed. What Nathan really needed was a wife who was besotted with him.

Nevertheless, she wished she didn't have to lie; despite everything, she didn't want to hurt him. But if she were to uncover any wrong doing on Flynn's part, then she would rather that Nathan knew nothing about it. The last thing she wanted was for someone else to be involved. Besides, he was in no fit state to listen to the truth.

"I'm sorry, did I forget to mention it?" Vivienne's expression was one of wide-eyed innocence as she began window-dressing her alibi. "I have to meet a prospective client at Burridge's. He's rather an important customer and has flown in especially for this meeting. It seems Burridge's have some kind of exhibition on. It looks as if I'm in for a tedious evening. Don't wait up- I'll probably be home quite late; we'll be discussing business over dinner."

"And I can tell exactly what sort of business! You're barely decent."

She drew in an exasperated breath and turned back to the mirror. Flynn had stressed that she should look sexy, so she had chosen her outfit with care. Her slinky mini dress was made from a stretchy, leopard print fabric that clung seductively to every curve of her sensuous body; there was little disguising the mound between her legs- the hemline was barely an inch or two below her sex. The bodice was close fitting and fashioned like a bra, thus doing away with the need to actually wear one, pushing up her firm, rounded breasts and inviting the onlooker to caress them. The shoe-string shoulder straps were black, and there was a long zip up the front that started at the hemline and ended at a point between her breasts. Underneath, she wore a thong, made from the same kind of leopard print fabric.

Vivienne wet her bright red lips with the tip of her tongue, rather liking the change from her usual, understated peach lipstick. Her vivid green eyes were emphasised by kohl and extra layers of mascara. With her golden skin and her black hair hanging over her bare shoulders almost to her waist, she could have passed for someone from a more exotic climate.

To finish off, she had fished out a silver necklace with one sapphire in the centre that her parents had bought her on her eighteenth birthday. There was no way she was going to wear the choker, even if it was solid gold. She had the strangest feelings of foreboding when she touched it.

She snatched up her small black bag, popped the choker inside and marched across the room, to where Nathan was still leaning in the doorway. His eyes raked over the curves of her body.

"It's the first I've heard about this dinner", he said scathingly. He downed the last of his whiskey and staggered across to the bed, seizing her arm as he passed. He reached across to plonk his glass on the bedside table, then sat down heavily on the edge of the bed, pulling her down with him. He gripped her shoulders and turned her round to face him as he spoke, and she recoiled at the reek of whiskey on his breath.

"How many have you had, Nathan? I've never seen you like this before."

"We're discussing you, not me", he slurred. Nathan turned back the duvet in an invitation."It's Friday bloody night - I was hoping we could spend some time together. That company doesn't own you, you have a right to time off. We could drink a little wine, make love-"

Once she would have been tempted, but not now, somehow she felt as if she were set on a course that made turning back impossible.

"I've told you, I have to go out. It's not my fault that my Head of

Division set this up."

"All you care about is 'furthering your career', any way you can. You don't want a lover, you want an entire work force, preferably between your legs."

"That's a terrible thing to say!"

"Tell me about Birmingham - why Birmingham, I wonder- why not London, or maybe Bishops Hill? Where are you really going tonight? I'm beginning to think the stories I've heard about you are true. Who is it this time, Flynn bloody Pallister again?"

Vivienne froze at the mention of his name.

"Don't bother to deny it, I know all about you and Pallister, and your sordid hotel room. Take that wounded look off your face! I had a phone call from your Flynn Pallister- he couldn't wait to brag about all the weird little games you and he play." His eyes mirrored the derision of his smile. "He says he knows every inch of your body intimately."

With lightning speed, Nathan pushed her backward. His hands pinned her down so that she lay on her back with her legs dangling over the edge of the bed. Before she knew what was happening, he had repositioned himself so that he sat astride her waist, peering down at her. Panic and anger did battle within her as she struggled, without success, to push him off and sit up.

"Nathan! What are you doing? Let me go."

"Your friend Pallister also told me that the best way to fuck you is when you're restrained, preferably by a belt tied around your wrists." He watched as the colour drained from her face. "Well, I haven't got a belt handy, but I thought I'd give it a go anyway. What do you think, Vivienne?" He snatched up his tie. "Or shall we do it the other way?"

"What are you talking about?" She felt the heat in her face.

"Your precious Mr Pallister said you're real hot for bedroom bondage. Funny really, I should have known. He said the other way you like it is spreadeagled over a table."

"How could you believe such a thing. It's true he tied my hands, but I had no choice in the matter. But he never tied me over a table."

She recalled her own mental picture of herself stretched over a table, with Flynn taking her from behind. She remembered the ill-treatment she had suffered at Flynn's hands, and suddenly became aware that her nipples were hard, and knew from Nathan's face that he was also aware. Her shoulders shook with the effort of holding back her tears.

"After all the months you and I have been together, you should know I'm not into that sort of thing! If I was, don't you think I'd have mentioned it? It's true I love sex, straight sex. Flynn goes in for that sort of thing but I don't."

"How do you know, if you've never done it?"

She lashed out at him, pounding his back with her fists. "I don't have to do it to know I won't like it. What sort of woman do you think I am?"

"I'm beginning to wonder."

Again she hammered against his back. "Let me up. You're hurting me."

To her relief, he suddenly let go of her shoulders and rolled off her. He sat on the opposite side of the bed, with his back towards her. Vivienne pulled herself up and tucked her legs underneath her, tugging at the hemline of her dress. Taking a deep breath to gain purchase on her temper, she spoke as calmly as possible.

"I should have told you before. It's over between us. I know it's my fault, and for what it's worth, I'm sorry. I haven't been faithful."

"You mean you've been getting laid like a common whore."

"All right have it your own damn way!" Her anger escaped her grasp. She stooped to pick up her bag from where it had fallen on the floor and marched across to the bedroom door.

His caustic voice followed her. "There's still the matter of the table."

She spun round, eyes glittering with rage. "I've never been fucked over a bloody table. But perhaps you're right- maybe I should try it!"

Despite her outrage, a picture of herself, naked and helplessly bound by ropes, stretched out over her own dining table flashed into her mind, and she was horrified by the reaction the vision generated. It was as if her blood had turned to liquid fire as it surged from her breasts to her aching quim - and its very intensity frightened her, leaving her panting.

Repulsed, yet at the same time inexplicably excited by the thought, she turned to leave, before her own traitorous body forced her to stay.

"You're pathetic, Nathan."

"And you're nothing but a whoring slut! I ought to take you now; show you how a real man fucks his woman."

"A real man wouldn't need whiskey to get a hard-on."

He rose from the bed and strode round the room towards her, his body taut with anger. Vivienne turned to face him in the same instant as he raised his arm. For a moment, she thought he would strike her and shrank back; she raised her arm to shield her face, but the fight drained out of him slowly, and he let his arm fall to his side.

"You're not fucking worth it!"

That, she realized, was the difference between Nathan and Flynn - Flynn would have struck her.

Curiously, there was a moistness trickling down her inner thigh.

Feeling the effects of the drink, Nathan put out a hand to steady himself. "There's a good chance that I'll be gone when you get home."

"I won't be coming home tonight! So just close the door on your way out. 'Bye."

***

Situated in the old part of town, nestling among the antique shops, craft shops and hairdressers, Burridge's Salesrooms was a well-established, well-respected gallery. Tucked away as it was in this part of Hertfordshire, it went largely unnoticed by the locals, though its reputation was worldwide.

There was no sign of Flynn when Vivienne arrived at the gallery, so she made her way inside. She was trembling slightly, partly from anger and partly from a kind of excitement at meeting the Connoisseur. Flynn had indicated that this meeting with the anonymous Greek businessman would somehow change her life, though by how much she was only to find out later. Now that she had put distance between herself and the intense depth of emotional snarl-up back at her flat, she looked forward to the evening that lay ahead, whatever it might bring.

She decided to kill time, to say nothing of trying to erase the whole sordid episode with Nathan from her mind, by wandering among the paintings. There were already a few other people there, but she paid no attention to anyone else, not even the sprinkling of celebrities, the rich and the famous who had been tempted by the "bargains" on display at the illustrious Burridge's Salesrooms.

She came to a halt in front of a large, strangely disturbing picture, Andromeda Waiting by Miles Meredith, painted around 1851, in oils in the style of the Pre Raphaelites.

"If you like the painting-" came a heavily accented, deep-timbered voice behind her "I'll buy it for you."

"Sorry?"

Vivienne turned. On seeing the Greek for the first time, she dissolved into a mishmash of heat, water and jelly. She wasn't sure what she had expected, probably someone like Aristotle Onassis, but what she hadn't expected was anyone like this; he looked as if he had more in common with a gangster than the smooth tycoon Flynn had described earlier in the day.

Tall, broad shouldered and arrogant, he was in his mid-forties- and breathtakingly sexy. With a darkly dangerous glint in his eye, there was no doubting his masculinity; it was almost as if he had contrived to emphasise it.

No, not merely sexy, she corrected herself, more of a drop-dead-gorgeous sex machine. It was obvious he was a horny individual on account of there being a substantial bulge in his trousers. And, having been in an on/off state of arousal for most of the day, Vivienne's throat went dry as she imagined herself undoing his fly and taking out his engorged cock. Once again, she felt ripples of excitement reverberating through her.

The atmosphere was suddenly charged with sensuality; her heart quickened its tempo and, oblivious to her surroundings, she felt the blood rush to her head. Heat suffused her cheeks, not from embarrassment but from sexual arousal. She had always been a woman with a healthy sexual appetite, but this was something different- this was new- and dangerous, eclipsing anything she had felt for Flynn.

"I said that I'd buy you the painting."

"It's... an extraordinary picture..." she breathed, staggered by both his generosity and his apparent wealth, "but I couldn't possibly accept such a gift."

"I want you to have it." There was an edge to his voice that startled her.

It took Vivienne great effort to pull her face muscles into line. She was immediately engulfed by a strange sense of respect, almost fear- it was as if his very presence demanded reverence. Who was this guy, some kind of Greek Mafia Godfather? There was something tantalizingly exciting about him, leaving her in no doubt at all that he was a powerful individual, just as Flynn had told her.

"Look, I'm no art expert, but if this is an original, can you imagine what sort of price tag's attached?'

"Nevertheless, it's yours."

There was something in his tone that unsettled her. And the look that crossed his face warned against further argument.

His deep set eyes, the colour of smooth, dark chocolate, came to rest on her generous, shapely breasts that strained to be free from her bodice. Uncharacteristically, she was still blushing under his ravishing scrutiny as they continued to check each other out. Standing beside her with his hands in his pockets, first impressions were that he hadn't a care in the world. Nonetheless, there was something deliberate about his casual manner, something about his unhurried ease that told her his laid-back attitude was a sham; he was far from being the easy-going character he appeared, and he did indeed have a great deal on his mind!

What she was less sure of was what it had to do with her. What, exactly, was she supposed to do to help Flynn close his deal? Sleep with the man? She found herself smiling- nothing would give her greater pleasure.

He wore no tie and the navy blue, silk shirt he wore with arrogant sensuality was open-necked to reveal his olive-skinned throat, with wispy black hairs that curled enticingly upward from his chest. His jet black hair that touched his collar was swept back from his forehead. A shadow of stubble covered his square chin and angular jawline, giving the impression that he was in need of a shave, but like the stray lock of hair that had fallen forward in a loose curl over his right eyebrow, she felt sure the look was contrived.

"Thank you, Mr... I'm sorry, I didn't catch your name, and I can hardly call you 'Connoisseur' all evening. That is who you are, The Connoisseur?"

"You may call me Theo if you wish."

Theo's dark, smouldering eyes met Vivienne's in a moment of electrifying need as his fingers glided down her arm, making her skin tingle. Without hesitation, she offered up her soft mouth to be kissed. As his dark-shadowed jaw grazed her tender skin, his lips touched hers. She closed her eyes and melted into the moment. She felt his tongue penetrate the warmth of her mouth, and longed for his shaft, solid as he pressed it against her, to enter that other warm, moist place. He put his hands on each of the rounded cheeks of her buttocks and squeezed. Breaking the kiss, he squeezed them harder, so hard that she gave a little cry. She thought she heard him chuckle, but dismissed the idea almost at once. Not everyone was as spiteful as Flynn, she reminded herself.

"It's settled then," Theo's smooth voice made her think of honey poured from a jar, but his dark eyes carried a warning as he spun her around to look at the painting again.

"Do you know the story of Andromeda?"

"Not really, I'm afraid", she confessed.

"No," his hand stayed her as she moved to turn around to face him again, "don't turn around." Again, there was that hard edge, the note of authority.

Vivienne let out a sudden gasp as Theo's hand dipped beneath the hem of her short dress. Heat seared her flesh as his fingers worked their way up her smooth thigh, manoeuvred their way to the front, and burrowed between the front of her thong and her fleece-covered sex.

Longing blazed through her veins as her body responded, even as she tried to tell him to keep his hands to himself until later; tried to remind him there were other people milling around. But somehow, the words that were well-ordered in her brain became a mere tangle of incoherent sounds that choked on her lips. She whimpered softly as his fingers tugged sharply at the thatch of tight curls that frothed around her throbbing quim. Slowly, he traced the line of her concealed opening with his forefinger, stroking the lips of her most private parts with a touch as gentle as silk on bare skin..

Vivienne drew in a tremulous breath as he slowly worked open her tumescent lips. A bolt of sexual delight ricocheted through her; she jumped visibly as his finger shot up inside, probing deeply into her moistness.

"Theo-" she whispered, only half-complainingly.

"Don't you like it, Vivienne?"

Like it? She was almost dying with pleasure.

Theo's finger slid tantalizingly back and forth as he stimulated her, gradually increasing speed until she squirmed on his finger, in time with his rhythm. She bore down as he inserted a second finger, and again cried out his name as the squelching sounds announced just how deeply aroused she really was. She tried again to tell him to stop, but she didn't move away. Instead, she allowed herself to melt into the rapturous thrills of need. Forgetting the world around her, nothing else existed beyond the fervour of the moment; she saw nothing but Andromeda Waiting before her, heard nothing save the sounds of her pussy-juices as he continued to excite her wet cunt. Aghast to feel tiny trickles of sweetness dribble down her thigh, she drew in an agitated breath.

She felt his hot, animal breath on her neck. Her husky voice wavered through gasps of pleasure. At last she murmured the words she knew she should have spoken before.

"Theo! Stop it- someone might come at any moment."

"I think it might well be you." His voice, dark with persuasion, urged her on. "Now, Vivienne, now-"

Her muscles tensed. Then the first tremors swept through her. She groaned softly as her muscles clenched. Then, with a volcanic explosion, she was almost swept away on a warm tide of elation. Her head fell back against the rigidity of his chest. Finding it difficult to stand, Vivienne rested against him as other emotions crowded in on her; she was shocked at her own licentiousness, racked by the exertion- but most of all, she was disappointed to have come so soon.

But her ordeal wasn't over yet. He placed a proprietorial hand on her shoulder as his fingers slid ever deeper into her sex, continuing to excite her.

"I admire your enthusiasm," his rich tones were shadowed by mockery, "but surely you can do better than that. Shall we try again?"

As if in reply, her muscles tightened around his probing digits. She tensed. To her shame, the lower part of her body responded of its own accord, gyrating shamelessly as she pushed down hard. She was helpless; could do nothing to stop the primeval urges that seized her. But, even as her body responded to his most intimate caress, her mind was racing, desperately afraid someone might see them.

Vivienne let out a deep sigh as a wave of desire pulsated through her body. She was on the very verge of a second, potentially ferocious orgasm. Panting deliriously, she tried to tell him that she was about to climax again.

"I'm...I'm com-"

She broke off as, with total indifference to her needs, he abruptly withdrew his fingers from her inflamed pussy. Sharp pain, red hot in its intensity, sliced through her as he pinched her clitoris hard between finger and thumb, making her cry out. Seemingly unconcerned by her discomfort, he pinched her again, this time even harder, causing tiny shock waves to dart through her body as the echo of pain seared her.

Theo's voice remained frighteningly calm.

"Talk to me, tell me about Andromeda."

The realization that he had intended to hurt her filtered into her brain, with a mix of cold horror, and hot arousal.

"You hurt me!"

"It excited you, didn't it? Now your cunt's crying out to be filled. Now," again his punishing fingers slid inside her quivering pussy, "stand straight, and tell me about Andromeda." There was a severity to his tone that chilled her, and his accent became stronger. "If you stay in line, you'll get your first- what do you call it?" he paused as he recalled the expression "Brownie point! If not, well, life might just get a bit tougher....." He let the words hang menacingly between them.

She was out of her depth, and suddenly was more afraid than she had ever been in her life. So why didn't she just turn tail and run, she wondered. Hardly able to stand, her hunger for him was so strong that her brain hardly registered that his demand was for obedience. However, she raised no more objections, and did as she was bidden. She felt shockingly indecent, yet strangely elated as she relished his fierce caress as she began to discuss the painting, with people thronging around them.

To her horror, a man and a woman came and stood beside them to look at the painting. Surely they would see what Theo was doing to her! She bit into her bottom lip as her juicing pussy squelched loudly. God, they would hear it! Desperately afraid, she tried to pull away but Theo held her firm, unconcerned or more likely, she realized, enjoying her distress. She felt his fingers jab sharply inside, in a silent demand that she was to continue.

"Wasn't... Andromeda some kind..." she found it difficult to talk under such circumstances and had to force herself to carry on, "of sacrifice to the gods?" As he worked her with more fervour she found it difficult to concentrate. There was no respite from his long, frenetic fingers as they plunged deep, up to his knuckle, inside her tormented quim. Spirals of desire ricocheted through her body. And, at the same time, she imagined herself being hauled off to the Police station for indecent behaviour.

Desperately, she willed him to stop, yet longed for the moment to go on and on forever. Blushing crimson with humiliation, she wanted to crawl into a hole and quietly fade away.. Never had she felt like this, so violated, so wildly excited, so out of control. She would do anything he asked, anything, only please don't let him hurt her.

As if totally unconcerned about her predicament, Theo continued in a matter-of-fact voice, as if it were the most natural thing in the world to have his fingers up a woman's cunt openly at such a venue.

"Andromeda was chained to a rock, a virgin sacrifice to the great sea monster. Tell me about the painting, Vivienne, tell me what you see."

"I see a woman, a beautiful, sensual woman..."

To her relief the couple moved away. She knew they must have known what was going on and feared they were even now heading for the authorities.

"Yes, my sweet, a real hot bitch," Theo rammed his fingers hard up her achingly sensitive channel, eliciting another cry from her lips, "a bitch on heat, like you." Again he hammered his fingers deeply into her, and her treacherous muscles closed tightly around them in response.

"I... I... I find y...your mastery of... the English l... language... amazing!"

He ignored her sarcasm. Using the forefinger of his free hand to indicate the girl in the painting, while the fingers of his other hand continued to work her exquisitely tormented pussy, he said "See how windswept her hair is. It's the same colour as yours. How would you look with yours unkempt, I wonder."

Theo lowered his hand from the painting, and dragged his fingers through her hair. He took a step backward, then pulling it sharply into a bunch he wound her hair around his fist. He yanked it hard towards him; she fell backward as she let out a cry. With her body once more pressed close against his, she felt the iron hardness of his shaft against her buttocks. With one hand entangled in her hair, the other continued to work her to a frenzy.

Shamelessly, Vivienne's lower body reacted to his abuse by taking on a life of its own, bucking and swaying as she bore down on his hand. With her head resting against his hard chest, her eyes closed and she moaned softly.

Slowly, Theo withdrew his fingers from her soaking, burning sex, leaving her bereft, as if a light had gone out in the world. She so badly wanted- needed- to come again. If only they could be alone.

"Why don't we go now, Theo? We could skip Flynn's business deal and go straight to your hotel."

"I've got business well in hand." Rejecting her, Theo's hand dropped from her hair. He placed his other hand flat against the small of her back, and propelled her forward, away from him.

"Open your eyes, bitch! Look at the painting." When she didn't comply, his voice took on a chilling note of command. "I said 'look at the fucking painting, Vivienne!' You had better learn, and fast my sweet, that I don't like repeating myself."

She opened her eyes and fixed them on the painting, and in particular the girl's garment that clung to her body, doing little for modesty.

Theo's accent seemed thicker now. His tone was a harsh whisper that betrayed his arousal, as surely as his stiff cock had done moments earlier. As if reading her mind, he said "The garment was called a chiton, and was merely a rectangle of cloth, pinned at the shoulders. However, Andromeda's has come unfastened, and has slipped to reveal her breasts." His hand travelled to Vivienne's, where perspiration already beaded. Clasping one breast, ripe as a peach, firmly in his powerful hand, he kneaded it surprisingly gently after his spitefulness, a fact that confused, thrilled and delighted her. He found her nipple, hard and erect, and rolled it between finger and thumb through the fabric of the dress. Again she moaned, hardly able to stand the unbearable ecstasy of it all.

"Look at her, Vivienne. She looks terror-stricken, wouldn't you say?"

It seemed to Vivienne that Theo was getting even more turned on by Andromeda's fear. And, as his excitement increased, so too did the pressure with which he manipulated her breast. When he spoke, his words were heavy with lust and punctuated by ragged breaths. And she realized that she didn't know which excited him more, herself or the painting.

"Or is she in the throes of sexual arousal? She knows that the men watching from the cliff lust after her, the same way men lust after you, my sweet. She's hot for it, and knows that every man there wants to ram his cock up her. On the other hand, she knows she's helpless to defend herself against the sea monster to whom she has been abandoned. She can't escape- from death or desire. It's making her come just thinking about it- the same as you, Vivienne. All you can think about is what you'll do to my cock when we get out of here. Andromeda was punished," there was a steel edge underlining each word, "perhaps it's time to punish you..."

Things were getting serious now and she froze with terror. Flynn had hurt her, but she somehow knew that this man was capable of real cruelty. Her bottom lip quivered as her tiny voice forced the words out between parched lips.

"Punish me? What have I done?" Her heart beat so rapidly that it thumped in her temples.

"You've teased men, led them on. But there doesn't really have to be a reason, other than- " he laughed, and for the first time uttered the words that were to become etched on her very consciousness, "your pain is my pleasure."

His hand fell away from her breast, but not before he had dealt a vicious, electrifying pinch to her nipple that left her in no doubt that here was a man who had no qualms abut carrying out his threats. And as Theo turned away from the painting, she tried to collect her thoughts; tried to put her emotions into some kind of order as she stood for a moment gazing up at Andromeda.

Whatever was she doing letting a man like Theo into her life? Flynn wasn't here to close his precious deal, so she could walk away now and never see Theo again. Of course, Flynn would probably see to it that she lost her job at Paston Communications. But if she were to stay here with Theo, who knew what kind of trouble she would land herself in? There was a cruel streak that ran though him, and a tantalizing sexuality that she had never known before.

"Take a last look, Vivienne. See how the sea rages below her." He took a few steps across the room. "It reminds me so much of the sea around my home." Without looking back, he said "Come- I've reserved a table, but they won't keep it all night."

She caught up with him as he reached the doorway.

"Where are we going for dinner? The Bowl and Platter?" She smiled in anticipation as she remembered the intimacy of the muted lights at the restaurant up the road. If he could frig her so deliciously in such public surroundings, whatever would he do to her in a more secluded setting? A smile danced on her lips as she considered.

Theo took her hand in his own and raised it to his lips; first he kissed each fingertip seductively, then one by one he put each into the wet warmth of his mouth, up to the knuckle. He sucked it, curled his tongue around it, then slowly, teasingly, withdrew it, except for the last finger; he bit down hard causing her to draw in a sharp breath. And the more pain that showed in her kohl lined eyes, the longer and harder the bite went on, until at last she could stand it no more.

"Please, Theo... Argh!... no more." Yet even as she said the words, she trembled with erotic fascination.

Releasing her finger at last, he told her "I'm taking you somewhere more appropriate."

"What about my car?"

"Give me the keys, and I'll see it's brought safely to the hotel."

It never crossed her mind to refuse. She delved into her handbag and handed over the keys. Clutching them in his palm, he led her through to another room, where an auction was in full swing. He nodded to a man at the back of the room, then tossed him her car keys. Again he smiled down at her, and his midnight eyes burned savagely.

"After we have eaten," he told he, "I will begin your instruction."

Her mouth dropped open. "Instruction?" For a moment she thought the worst, then realizing why she was here, she asked "Concerning what, Flynn's deal? I thought he was going to meet us here."

"Perhaps we'll meet up with him later."

Outside, the uniformed, tall, fair-skinned chauffeur opened the passenger door of the silver Mercedes.

"Incidentally, I'm disappointed that you decided to disobey my wishes by not wearing the gift I sent you." His censuring tone followed her as she slithered across the back seat. He settled himself beside her.

"Ouch!" she yelled as he ripped her necklace from her neck. "That was a gift from my parents."

"Who are both dead, while I'm very much alive. I will forgive your transgression this time, providing you can produce your collar now."

The use of the word 'collar' momentarily threw her. "Oh, the choker? I've got it here." She raked through her bag and produced the collar.

He snatched it from her. “Lift up your hair”, he commanded. When she did so, he placed the cold metal around her long, elegant neck. “Padlock?” he held out his palm, into which she placed the padlock, which was about three quarters of an inch in size. He slipped it through the two rings at the back, and Vivienne tensed nervously as the padlock closed with a click.

“How does it come undone?” she asked as she dropped her hair back into position.

“You’ll need this,” he said, with a twisted smile as he drew the end of his chain from his waistcoat pocket and held up a small golden key for her inspection. He watched with an amused expression as she ran her fingers around the collar, fingering first the padlock at the back, then the ring at the front. His voice, demanding and cold, informed her as the implication became clear to her “You’ll wear the collar always, until I say otherwise.”

CHAPTER FOUR

They travelled in silence. Keyed-up and frightened, Vivienne ran her finger around the inside of her collar. If only there were some way that she could get it off! The full horrors of her plight began to dawn on her- she could hardly believe that she had been stupid enough to get into a car with a man she knew virtually nothing about- a man who had threatened to punish her to boot. He could be taking her to some dive in the back of beyond, a place from which she had no means of escape.

There was an imperious aura around Theo as he sat immobile, deep in thought. His unshaven features and faultlessly-styled stray lock of hair gave him the look of a delinquent. His worried frown was like that of an unscrupulous businessman working on the finer points of a shady deal, or a gangster plotting a daredevil heist.

Vivienne slipped her finger through the heavy ring at the front of the collar. Afraid to pursue the thought of the possible uses of such a device, she was certain that it wasn’t to attach charms to as Flynn had told her. She had always considered herself a woman of the world, but she realized now that there was a gaping hole in her knowledge- she was still very much an innocent when it came to the shadowy underworld that Theo inhabited. Aware of the horrors that permeated her brain, Theo gave her a malicious half-smile that froze her blood. His eyes travelled the length of her zip, conveniently running from the hem of the dress to the bodice. She blanched as he focussed his attention on the two, satin-skinned, golden-toned globes that were barely contained. Rising and falling temptingly with each trembling breath she took, Vivienne felt them tighten under his licentious gaze.

Even through her fear, her nipples hardened painfully.

He produced a pair of nail scissors from a briefcase and, reaching across, cut through the shoestring shoulder straps of the bodice before locating the zip's metal clip that nestled between her juicy breasts. He gave it a sharp tug, yanking it downward. Peeling back the fabric as if it were the skin of an orange, he pulled it down to her waist so that her bare breasts swung free.

She drew in a startled breath as his hand closed over her left breast, squeezing it savagely. Suddenly, his mouth was upon the other. He took her nipple, then much of her breast into the moist warmth and sucked noisily.

Then she felt incising pain as his teeth sank into the soft flesh.

"Argh!"

With a hand on each shoulder she tried to push him off. But that only made him bite all the harder.

"Bastard! Let go of me!" She swung her eyes to the mirror that reflected the chauffeur's eyes. "Help me-" she entreated, "stop the car! Please. Can't you see that he's hurting me?"

The chauffeur could see all right- the same as she saw his reflected smile.

Un-clamping his teeth, Theo took her head between his huge palms and splayed his fingers. He pressed so hard that she thought he would crush her skull. His ragged breath warmed her face as he said something in Greek.

She shuddered as he repeated the words in English..

"You must learn to embrace pain, drink it in as if it were the very elixir of life". then brought his crushing lips down upon hers. His tongue snaked deeply into her mouth, depriving her of air.

She tried to convince herself that everything was all right, letting herself believe that this was the deep, passionate kiss of a man who at least had some feelings for her, a man who cared. But he broke away and pushed her aside as if she were nothing but a toy he had outgrown.

Vivienne glanced up and caught the chauffeur's lascivious expression as their eyes met in the mirror. Panic spiralled from the pit of her stomach upward towards her throat. They were heading away from town in the opposite direction to the motorway and all the major hotels in the area, heading further and further into the countryside. With a jolt she realized that, by forsaking the motorways to which she was so accustomed in favour of the narrow county lanes, Theo was deliberately trying to get her lost. They crossed from one county to another.

The Merc was too wide and brushed the overhanging trees and hedgerows either side as it sped along.

"I want to go home, Theo."

"What you want is no concern of mine." His accent seemed stronger now, so too were the brutality of his words as they sliced through the night. "I have the upper- hand and unlimited rights, while you have none at all. You're nothing and have nothing- not even a name- Vivienne Trevayne ceased to exist the moment you stepped into the car."

Her mouth dropped open to protest but no sound came out.

"You're going to receive the treatment a slut like you deserves. You will be subdued - by force if necessary. You'll be forced to acknowledge that men are not your equals but your superiors."

She managed a croak of incredulity.

"Make no mistake - it's no idle threat. This is merely the beginning. If you slake my very particular needs, you'll spend the weekend finding out what it means to be enslaved. If not, when I've finished with you- well, we'll cross our bridges when we come to them."

He wound a hank of her glorious, long raven hair round his hand and yanked her head backward. At the same time, his free hand flicked open a penknife. He brandished the wicked blade inches from her face, making her quake with terror. Yet even his cruelty couldn't diminish the warmth of arousal that swelled through her.

"I have one girl in my collection with no hair on her body. I removed it all with this very knife. Unless you want to go the same way - I suggest you learn fast."

Her hand flew to the door. She tried the handle.

"Central locking is such a... what do you English say?... such a boon, don't you think?"

"You're mad, Theo. Let me go!"

His lips twisted into a mockery of a smile. "There's no escape. The deal is done- I own you now, and you're mine to do with as I please."

Realization sliced through her- Flynn's deal, the 'goods' he had spoken of all referred to her. He had even told her that she was to be handed over.

Defiance blazed in her green eyes. "This is illegal." Her words cracked on her lips. "It's against the law to deal in human flesh. Human beings can't be bought and sold like cattle."

"Nevertheless, I paid a great deal of money for you, and I intend to extract my money's worth before I return to Greece. Whether or not I take you with me has yet to be decided. As the owner of Zortac and therefore Paston Communications, I might get better value from you in the office, and use your other charms solely on my trips to the UK. Then again, I may sell you on. But all this is in the future."

He snatched up her hand and placed it on his hard cock, which throbbed to life beneath her fingers. She shrank back, afraid that if she touched him it would somehow legitimize everything he had told her. But such was her own wantonness that once again, her body betrayed her with its flush of arousal that tinted her naked skin from the waist upward to her hairline. She longed to caress his shaft, have it fill her completely; to finish what he had started back at Burridge's. All she had to do was undo his fly...

Her fear was stronger than her need. Besides, she preferred privacy, and with the damned chauffeur watching everything in his mirror, things were far from ideal.

Withdrawing her hand, she challenged irritably "I'm hungry. You promised me a meal- or are you going to starve me into submission?"

He gave a bitter laugh. "Perhaps later. But tonight you'll eat well, to keep your strength up. When we arrive at my hotel-"

"So where is this bloody hotel? Where exactly are we going?"

He raised a mocking eyebrow and gave her a half smile. "To a hedonistic world full of pleasure and pain... pleasures beyond your wildest imaginings, and torments beyond anything you've yet encountered."

She felt like a butterfly trapped in a jam jar. She glanced out of the black tinted window, just in time to read the signpost.

"Bloody hell! How far do you intend taking me?"

He hooked his finger though the ring of her collar, and pulled her roughly towards him so that his face was within inches of her own.

"All the way! Relax while you have the chance." Laughing, he released her collar and told her coolly "You'll need all your energy later."

How the hell could she relax! Her mind shifted skittishly between fear, the aching between her legs and the memory of Theo's licentious fingers as they had plunged deep inside her pulsating quim. He seemed to exude sexual power the way other men exude sweat. She couldn't deny the excitement his very presence aroused within her. If his finger-fucking was anything to go by, the real thing would be sensational. She found herself smiling in anticipation of a night of terrific sex.

Trying to think more coherently, she told herself that his threats were just that- threats. If he got off on scaring her half to death, what did it matter? After all, no one could or ever would own her; she was a free agent to do as she pleased.

He broke the silence with a low, harsh whisper that sounded remarkably like an order.

"Take off your panties and open your legs."

"What!"

"Quiet! Don't ever question my authority. Take off your fucking panties and open your legs."

The underlying menace in his tone somehow made disobedience unthinkable. Ignoring the dissenting voice in her head along with her rising panic, her trembling fingers crept beneath the hem of her short dress. Keeping her feet on the floor, she raised her rounded buttocks an inch or two from the seat. Slipping her fingers beneath the elastic, she eased the insubstantial scrap of fabric that masqueraded as her thong over her backside, before lowering it again.

She was already wet, and as her soft skin made contact with the seat, hot shards of arousal thrilled through her, and a necklace of moisture dampened the leather. She eased the thong down her long, shapely legs to her ankles. As she disentangled one spiky- heeled foot from the opening, Theo held out his hand.

"Give it to me."

"But-"

"Now!" he barked sharply.

Extricating her other foot, she handed over the damp, animal print thong. She watched horror-stricken as he tossed it over the front seat, where the chauffeur lifted it to his nose to breath in the musky essence of her arousal as he drove.

Theo opened a well-stocked drinks cabinet and poured himself a glass of the Metaxas that he had brought with him from Greece. Without offering her a drink, he closed the cabinet again. With the glass to his lips, he pulled open the drawer beside the drinks cabinet, from which he took an oblong box, about six inches in length, covered in scarlet velvet. Sipping his Metaxas, he passed the box to her. Again the malicious half smile as he patted a spot in the middle of the seat.

"Sit here, with your feet on the seat and your knees apart."

Raising her eyes to the chauffeur's mirror, she realized at once the implications of such an act. "But your chauffeur-"

"Will have a view to die for, won't you, Valentin?"

The chauffeur's low-toned voice was tinged with an eastern European accent, and a hint of amusement. "Yes, Master."

Vivienne caught the lustful glint in Valentin's eyes in the mirror. She wondered how often he had witnessed such reflected acts. Her pussy muscles clenched in excitement, causing a swell of wantonness to rise upward to the very tips of her erect nipples.

"Open the box. Inside you'll find a little gift, a diversion, which you'll drive deep into your gaping, wet cunt. Make sure that Valentin's view isn't hindered, accidentally or otherwise. In fact you'll do this exclusively for Valentin's enjoyment. Understand?"

She wasn't at all sure that she did, but she nodded anyway. "Why do you torture me like this?"

"An odd choice of words."

"Please, no more games. I came here in good faith-"

"Bitch!" His hand gave her a resounding slap round the face that brought a red patch to her cheek and a shriek from her throat. "You came here to get laid. The box!" he prompted.

She took a moment to rub her smarting cheek and steady herself. She stared down at the box in her hesitant hands, fearful of what it contained. Then, with her heart battering against her rib-cage and her fingers shaking visibly, she removed the lid.

Her eyes sprung open wide and her mouth gaped. Inside were two golden balls, each one about the weight of a golf ball and only slightly smaller in size. Joined together by a length of gold coloured silk cord, one of them had a long, matching tassel, maybe three or four inches long, attached to it. She held the objects in the palm of her hand, staring at them suspiciously. She couldn't put these things into her sex- they were too heavy and would fall out. Besides, she could never bring herself to do such a shameless thing. But if she refused.....

She caught the look in Theo's eye. He was watching her as an owl watches an ill-fated mouse, with nothing more than the sound of his ragged breathing to indicate that he was living flesh and blood.

Vivienne flicked her eyes back to the mirror, and Valentin's met hers with an unwavering, brilliant blue gaze.

Fingering the balls now as if they were nothing more than a string of worry beads, she raised her legs and rested her heels on the edge of the seat. She opened her thighs.

"Wider!"

She opened them as wide as she could, stretching them outward to reveal her glistening sex. Once again, her treacherous body betrayed her aching need, and her cheeks flushed crimson as she realized that Valentin could see the sweet juices that positively oozed from the deep pink lips of her sex as it hungered to be filled. With hands that trembled with lustful expectation, she nudged the first ball against the moist folds, and recoiled slightly as the object struck cold against her burning, turgid labia lips. Then, parting of their own accord to admit the golden sphere, her nether lips swallowed the first hungrily, taking it deep inside her secret passage.

The second sphere followed effortlessly, sucked in by the very force of her desire. They felt strange at first, hard against the delicate membranes of her insides. But they were cold no longer as they absorbed the heat from her scorching sex.

Valentin's eyes returned to the road, while Vivienne's own eyes swung downward to the thatch of black hair between her open thighs. The golden tassel hung tantalizingly between her labia lips. Several inches long, it dangled over the edge of the sumptuous leather seat.

Theo fixed her with a cool gaze while his fingers trailed a blaze of flame down the side of her face as they glided over her fevered skin from her hairline to her chin. He said something in Greek, then continued in heavily accented English.

"You'll not remove them until I give you leave to do so. I want to keep you hot and wet. Also, it will give me a hard-on knowing you can feel the balls moving inside you, stimulating your cunt every time you move." He gave her a shove that almost made her topple over. "Get back to your corner. Sit quietly. You'll not speak again until my permission is granted."

Afraid to move for fear of the balls falling out, she closed her thighs tentatively and put her feet on the floor. She raised her buttocks; her skin had stuck to the seat again and she was suddenly bombarded with all kinds of sensations as she shifted across the leather upholstery. The balls moved deliciously inside as they knocked against each other, sending spirals of pure pleasure rippling through her.

She took up a decorous pose with her hands in her lap. What a sight she must make, she thought, sitting demurely with the hem of her short dress covering her black bush of wiry curls modestly, while the silky tassel brushed against the soft skin of her inner thighs, betraying the presence of the balls. Her bodice was still bunched around her waist, so that her naked breasts bobbed temptingly as the car sped over the rough roads.

Theo had been right about one thing- the balls stirred teasingly with every movement she made. What's more, she was actually getting wetter as she pictured the mental image of herself. She smiled. Craving release, her fingers strayed to her clitoris. With a light touch she began to stroke the hard bud.

In an instant, there was a click as cold metal touched her wrists. Chill horror filled her as she realized that he had handcuffed her.

"If you can't refrain from touching yourself, your hands will remain shackled."

"But-"

Whack! His hand came down and slapped her breast. The soft flesh quivered beneath his huge hand. Immediately, a red patch appeared. That seemed to incite him more and once again his hand came down. Whack!

"Quiet, Bitch! It would give me the greatest pleasure to have Valentin stop the car so that I could flog you by the roadside."

***

"Tidy yourself," Theo ordered as they pulled into the car park of a large, well-known, Country House hotel. "Tonight we'll eat in one of the most elegant dining rooms this side of London. Afterwards, we'll go up to my suite. If you make the grade- satisfy me, then I'll keep you as my trained bitch. If not- " he waved his hand dismissively.

Too late she remembered she wasn't supposed to speak.

"Oh, I guarantee satisfaction", she quipped, earning her another stinging blow across her breast. She pulled up her severed bodice. Her breasts were burning, though whether from pain or something more carnal she couldn't tell.

"I will have obedience, Slut, one way or another."

Theo opened the drawer again and took out a long chain. It had a leather loop at one end and a clip at the other, like a dog's lead. Vivienne looked on in disbelief as he leaned across and attached it to the ring at the front of her collar. He gave it a sharp tug that brought her golden-toned face close to his olive one. An electrical charge passed between them as his dark, plundering eyes locked onto hers in a intense battle of wills. Her heart sank as her eyes swerved away, admitting defeat.

"I'm well-known here, so no one will be surprised to see me with a nameless piece of nothing in tow."

The red stain of shame burned her cheeks as for the first time in her life, Vivienne knew real humiliation. Theo led her by the chain, with wrists still handcuffed in front of her, from the relative safety of the Merc to the hotel. She felt as if she were a slave on her way to market. All she needed was a ring through her nose, she thought sullenly as she followed Theo up the granite steps.

Suddenly, she was afraid to be alone with him, and looked around for some means of escape. A black car pull into the cark park. She wasn't sure if she felt safer or even more afraid when two huge, beefy men that she took to be guards climbed out and fell into step a short distance behind her.

The doorman, impressive in his dark green uniform, held the door open for them with a "Good to see you back, Sir" and looked her over. His lecherous eyes travelled down her body from the golden collar to the tassel that was clearly visible dangling between her legs as she walked.

Once inside the lobby that had more in common with a Victorian drawing room than a hotel reception area, any remaining dregs of confidence drained away as other guests noted her arrival. Seen alternatively as an object of curiosity, loathing and sexual exploitation, some nudged their companions conspiratorially, while others openly stared. Others still looked at her with disdain, while one man approached Theo and made him an offer of a substantial amount of money.

"Just one night of fucking, and you can have the slut back."

To her relief, Theo declined the offer. He gave her another sharp tug that had her tottering on her spiky heels.

Wanting to die with shame, she had no choice but to follow meekly as he led her toward the busy dining room. She could hardly believe this was happening to her as the Head Waiter conducted them through the elegant room. Any hopes she had of being tucked away in a corner were dashed as he escorted them to a table at the heart of the room, surrounded by other tables. Many pairs of eyes speared her when the Head Waiter pulled out her chair for her.

This was so absurd it couldn't be happening. This was England at the dawn of the new millennium, not some remote, middle eastern state at the beginning of the last one. This couldn't be happening!

Dear God, it was!

Theo turned her collar around so that the ring was at the back, with the chain hanging down between her bare shoulder blades. Taking the leather loop in his hand, he tied it to the back of her chair, so that she was obliged to sit upright with her back straight and her head held high, exposing the vulnerability of her beautiful, golden throat.

Her manacled hands immediately found the padlock which was now at the front. How was she supposed to eat? Surely he didn't expect her to sit here like this.

***

The removal of her handcuffs did nothing to improve Vivienne's appetite. While the food and wine were excellent and would have been welcome at any other time, she merely picked at each of her courses. The restrictions forced on her by the chain made it impossible for her to relax, as did the humiliating circumstances. There was an embarrassing chink of the links every time she moved. Her back ached. And the collar, though neither excessively tight nor obstructive, was nevertheless uncomfortable.

Theo's two guards stood one either side of the doorway, with their hands clasped in front of them. Their eyes remained fixed on Theo and Vivienne throughout her strange ordeal.

Vivienne knew she was way out of her depth with Theo. Since their arrival, he had made no reference to the collar, chain or the golden balls she still wore inside her inflamed pussy. In fact, he hadn't spoken to her at all. Neither had the waiter. She could almost have believed she had ceased to exist if were not for the stolen glances and continual low whispers from other diners, and the occasional muttered obscenity as someone passed their table. It must be obvious, she thought, to everyone in the place that she was being held against her will, yet no one raised the matter with the waiters. No one offered assistance or called for the management. Was it merely the famed British reserve at work, the desire not to become involved, or was something more sinister going on?

Theo's attitude remained phlegmatic. There was an undercurrent throughout the meal, like a smouldering heat before it explodes into an all-consuming blaze.

There was something about him, Vivienne thought as she looked at him from under her long lashes, like a caged wildness. The blaze in his eyes assured her that he wanted to make love to her every bit as much as her traitorous body wanted him to, so why did he persist with the game? She wished he was just a normal guy, instead of an arrogant bastard who got off on intimidation and cruelty- why couldn't he just cut the crap, go to his suite and fuck her? If only she had met him under different circumstances, she would have shown him how a woman likes to take the initiative.

Theo raised his wine glass to his lips.

"You seem to have lost your delightful sparkle."

When she found her voice, her tone was one of virtuous outrage. But with a heat in her loins, a throbbing in her quim and an ache in her throat, her usually husky voice became positively rasping.

"I thought I wasn't allowed to speak! I'm sorry I'm not the perfect dinner companion, but it's hard to shine when you're chained to a bloody chair. Have you any idea how humiliated I feel? First, there was that despicable business at Burridge's, then those- those filthy things you made me insert. If this is all some kind of humiliating game..." She broke off as the waiter appeared and began to clear away the dirty dishes. Fighting to suppress her sudden fury, she gulped down a mouthful of wine as if it would somehow wash away the bad taste of Theo's treachery.

Paying no heed to the proximity of the waiter, Theo said "I promise you it's no game. On the contrary, I take humiliation very seriously. However, I find your sudden attempt at chastity rather exciting, if somewhat misplaced, and something of a charade. Correct me if I'm wrong, but I thought you rather enjoyed having your cunt frigged."

Aghast, her hand shot up to cover her mouth, while the waiter, obviously enjoying the titillation tremendously, raised his eyebrows and began to fiddle with the flower arrangement in the centre of the table.

Theo's expression told her that he was enjoying Vivienne's embarrassment. He nodded to the waiter, actually encouraging him to eavesdrop.

"It's more potent in public, don't you think?" Theo paused long enough for the waiter to find another task, namely blowing out their candle and pilfering a lighted one from a near-by table, "Face the truth, you're nothing but an exhibitionist slut. You enjoyed flashing your dripping cunt to my chauffeur."

He watched as her face pinkened with shame.

The wild mix of embarrassment and anger that pounded through her veins was fanned by her own mad desire. "That's not true."

"How easily the lies fall from your lips. For that you'll be doubly punished. From this moment on, you exist merely as an instrument of my pleasure." His voice was edged with malice as he hammered the point home. "If it gives me pleasure, be assured that I will punish you- savagely."

"You won't get away with this! I'll scream."

"How very delightful. There's little I enjoy more than hearing a woman scream."

"Go to hell, Theo!"

There was a smirk on his face- he genuinely did enjoy humiliating her, she realized. And, in that moment she knew she hated him. The message from her brain, however, didn't reach the rest of her body, which was reacting to the situation with its own brand of treachery; her nipples hardened unbearably, and there was a furnace between her thighs.

The waiter, having run out of time-wasting chores, finally removed the dishes.

"Have a drink," Theo refilled Vivienne's wine glass, "it will help you to relax."

"Are you trying to get me drunk?" she challenged caustically.

He gave her a constricted smile. "Far from it; I want you fully conscious when- and if- I fuck you." He clicked his fingers and the waiter re-appeared instantly. "More wine."

Realising she was defeated, Vivienne sat with her eyes downcast and her fingers picking at the napkin in her lap. The waiter hurried back with a new bottle of wine. As he refilled their glasses, she felt the toe of Theo's shoe work its way up her leg under the cloaking protection of the tablecloth. She drew in a sharp breath as it caught against the tassel. With a quick flick of his toe, as skilfully as if he had used his finger, Theo brushed the tassel aside, which in turn stirred the balls inside her juicing love channel.

Theo said something to the waiter, who was immediately spurred into action. He put down the bottle. Then, walking round the table he lifted the side of the tablecloth as he went, laying it on the top of the table so that their legs were now visible. When one side slipped down again, he weighted it with a heavy ashtray seconded from the neighbouring table, where a young couple were enjoying a romantic meal.

"Don't be fooled by their apparent innocence", Theo told her, "she has little more worth to him than you have to me. The difference is that he once thought himself in love with her, whereas I shall never love you. Now he has grown tired of her and is selling her on. This is, in effect, their farewell."

"Is everyone here as perverted as you? Are they all friends of yours?" she asked accusingly.

"Not at all. It's merely a coincidence that they're here tonight. My guests are not due until tomorrow."

The waiter took up a position ramrod straight beside the table. In the same moment, the hard toe of Theo's shoe forced open her naked thighs. He rubbed his shoe in the coarse black hairs that curled protectively around her quim, then pressed his shoe tip against her pulsating, bare sex.

She drew in an audible breath, which caught the attention of several other diners who turned their heads to see what was going on. Obligingly, the waiter stepped aside to give them a better view.

"I see I've hit my target." Theo pressed harder, eliciting a purring sound from deep in her throat.

Even now she didn't realized the peril she was putting herself in. She flicked out her tongue teasingly and wet her lips that curved into a salacious smile.

He jabbed his toe viciously against her quim, making her jerk against her chain as instinctively she tried to pull away.

"I'm Master here, Bitch! Never attempt to win my favour with your flirting." He nodded to the waiter who began to untie her leash. "It's time to prove your worth. Get on the floor and show me what you can do with your mouth."

The warm thrill of arousal that coursed through her veins was checked by cold Realization. He wanted her to give him a blow-job, here and now- in public! She swallowed hard, shaking her head from side to side, her lips forming a silent denial.

"You dare to refuse me?" Removing his toe, he deliberately spoke in a voice loud enough to be overheard, pronouncing every word as if he were an officer commanding his troops. "I expect total obedience. Get up from your chair and move under the table. Kneel before me as if in homage. Take out my prick. Get down on all fours and take it between your lips. Suck it as if were the very first cock you've ever sucked; suck as never before, until you feel it throbbing in the deepest recess of your throat."

The waiter hauled her to her feet. Thoughts of taking flight instantly began to form in her brain, until she remembered the goons in the doorway. Any further thoughts of leaving were dashed when the waiter placed his heavy hand on the top of her head and pushed her downward, under the table.

"So," she said bravely, the pieces of the jigsaw beginning to fit together, "you're working together."

In an undertone meant only for her hearing, the waiter hissed through clenched teeth. "Let's just say I'm an interested party."

How interested she wouldn't discover for some time yet.

She could have protested, even fought him off; she could have run, thrown herself on the mercy of the hotel management- instead she rested back on her knees. A tear of humiliation leaked form her eye as she tugged self-consciously at the short hem of her dress which had risen upward. She pressed her thighs tightly together, trying without success to obscure both the golden tassel that dangled from the moistness of her distended lips, and her black thicket.

Horribly conscious that Theo's power extended far beyond her imaginings, she was shocked and ashamed at her own speed, her own willingness, to allow him to take control of her life. Her heart palpitated in her breast. Was she really a slut, an exhibitionist? No, she told herself, never!

Yet even as the thoughts crowded in on her, clamouring for her to regain her dignity, her trembling hands reached inexorably for his fly.

Somewhere, a cry went up. "Whore!"

Vivienne turned her head in the direction of the hysterical, female shriek. God! There was a little group of other diners congregating around their table, all transfixed.

"Whore!" cried the voice again, followed by others.

"Get the manager! Call the Police!"

"Suck the come from his balls, Babe!"

"She can go down on me when she's finished!"

Overcome by the indignity of it, she sat back on her haunches and froze. Paralysing fear filled her head with Police and prison cells. But her instincts told her that the penalty for disobeying the sadistic Greek would be far worse than anything the authorities could do to her.

She took out his magnificent, hard shaft and, with both hands gripping it tightly, she drew it towards her pliant lips. Her tongue found the weeping eye in its centre, then she drew it into her hot, wet mouth. Her hands dropped away as she knelt with her palms on the floor. Her rocking motions as she sucked his cock, accompanied by the chink of the chain that still hung down her back, caused the golden tassel to swing tantalizing between her legs, sensually brushing her inner thigh. Spilling out of her now strapless bodice, her rounded breasts with their hard, dark brown nipples, swayed voluptuously as her hands supported her weight.

She sucked noisily on his deliciously hot, throbbing flesh as if experiencing the sensation for the first time. Not knowing, or even caring if the little group still watched, or whether the management had been alerted to the licentious scene, she sucked ever harder, taking his cock deep into her throat.

Suddenly, he jerked forward, ramming it deeper. He gave a strangled cry. His hot seed gushed against the back of her throat. She gulped and spluttered and tried to pull away, but strange hands held her firm and she was obliged to gulp down the fiery liquid of Theo's lust.

She made herself a silent vow- it would be the last time he humiliated her!

CHAPTER FIVE

There was to be no respite even in the lift. Even before the door had fully closed behind them, Theo was making demands.

"On your knees."

"Wha-?"

"Obedience!"

With his powerful fingers gripping the back of her neck, sharply he drove her down on to her knees. The lift lurched and she fell forward so that her head touched the floor. Theo raised his foot, bringing it down to rest heavily on the back of her neck. Grabbing the hem of her short dress, he yanked it upward until it was bunched around her waist. With her unblemished naked rump thrust upward, the humiliation of the position filled her with a nauseating dread- how much worse could things get before she was free of him and his perversions?

Theo was quick to seize the opportunity that the proffered golden-toned behind presented him. He gave it a hearty slap, followed by a grunt of approval as the soft flesh quivered beneath his hand, while the poor girl struggled to catch her breath. Then, as if he were a vet examining a horse's mouth, he bent down and prised the juicy buttocks apart to peer at her tight anus.

"You've got an irresistible arse hole. I wonder, has it ever been fucked? I suspect not- I've got a scrumptious, virgin hole to deal with."

Fighting to hold back tears of shame, anger flared her nostrils.

"You bastard! Why do you hate women so much that you have to degrade them?"

Theo merely laughed and kicked her legs apart, exposing the deep red slash with the golden tassel that still dangled between the desire-swollen lips. When he spoke, his accent seemed stronger, his words came out thicker.

"For a girl of your reputation, you seem remarkably ignorant of what is required of you. I thought I had made it plain, but I'll endeavour to clarify your condition and your standing in the scheme of things. You're nothing, and what I require from nothing is silence and obedience. From now on, any breach of the silence rule will be dealt with harshly. As for hating women, on the contrary, I adore women, especially when they squirm. And I will make you squirm, for your pain will be my pleasure."

He bent down and reached between her thighs. Skilfully, he manipulated the tassel so that its swaying movement caused the balls to knock against each other inside her, sending tiny, erotic sensations sparking through her. Inflamed almost to the point of detonation, Vivienne's body tensed in an instinctive response.

Suddenly, Theo gave the tassel a sharp tug that drew a cry of anguish from her lips. The first ball was removed, causing her muscles to twitch involuntarily. Her lips parted as her moans of discomfort, frustrated longing and yes- pleasure- tangled with groans of shame in the small confines of the lift. Then, with the force of a bullet exploding from a gun, the second was ejected, leaving a gaping vacuum that longed to be filled.

She managed to turn her head sideways and struggled to get up. Theo, however, had other ideas and forcefully kept her face pressed against the floor. The pressure he exerted on the back of her neck made rising impossible, and her upper lip caught on the carpet so that it was uncomfortably pulled upward. Her features crumpled and she had to fight back the tears.

Afraid to protest further against the humiliating position of submission in which she found herself, Vivienne closed her mouth and bit into the inside of her lower lip.

"I'm going to move my foot now. You won't stand up, but raise yourself to your hands and knees. When the door opens, you'll stay on all fours and follow me down the corridor. I'll rid you of every last shred of dignity before you leave this hotel."

He removed his foot and threw the golden balls into the corner of the lift. Unsure if he expected her to retrieve them, she said weakly "My balls..."

"Will make a nice souvenir for someone-" he finished for her.

She heard the whistle of air as he swung the end of the chain lead, then a crack! as the leather loop struck her bottom.

"Ow!"

"That's for questioning my motives."

The door opened and he stepped out into the carpeted corridor. He gave the lead a sharp tug, slapped the side of his leg with his hand and called out brightly "Here, girl" in a way that put her in mind of Lassie, which she knew had been his intention all along.

The friction caused between the contact of the carpet and Vivienne's knees burned horribly as she followed him. And to make matters worse, her long hair trailed on the floor so that she kept trapping it beneath her hands as she crawled along. Holding the chain taut, Theo didn't slow down his pace even when she stumbled and almost fell. He gave an impatient jerk on the lead so that she had to scurry along.

Her dress was still bunched around her waist, exposing her naked flesh from the waist down. All at once she became aware of footsteps coming up fast behind her. A warm glow of shame crept upward from her neck to her hairline, thankfully hidden by her mass of black hair. Images of being hauled off by the authorities again filled her mind. But almost instantly these images were replaced by others, and she could see herself as the person following could see her, with her bare bottom swaying temptingly.

Theo stopped outside one of the doors. Without looking at her he pressed her head downward with his foot so that she was staring at the floor, as the stranger following walked past.

"Ah, your new slut, I presume." It was a man's voice, deep and gravelly. "Any good?"

"The party that I acquired her from assured me that she's a good fuck, although I haven't tried her out myself yet."

Again, Vivienne felt the now familiar burning sensation as her cheeks reddened with shame. It struck her as odd that, as a woman not usually prone to blushes, she seemed to be colouring-up all the time since Theo had entered her life.

Theo opened the door and she followed him inside the darkened room.

"Tonight you'll sleep on the floor."

This was too much for her and the words tumbled out before she could stop them.

"The floor? Oh, come on! Even you wouldn't be that-"

His cold, sharp rebuttal hurt her as much as the kick in the ribs that toppled her to the floor.

"Remember your place."

Her place? The needle-pointed stinging behind her eyes grew more acute and her temper was fizzing dangerously close to the surface. As she lay on the floor, she had to bite hard into her bottom lip to stop herself from yelling at him and earning herself another boot in the ribs. Instead, she just curled into the foetal position, welcoming the darkness of the room. He unclipped her lead and she felt the cold metal of the handcuffs as they clicked closed around her wrists.

Somehow his words seemed more serious in the dark, and more chimerical at the same time.

That was it! she thought, she was in a dream; real-life had come to an abrupt end when she had entered Burridge's.

"Think of this as a training course, like the ones you've been sent on at work. Except you're not here to learn about management techniques or team building, you're here to absorb the requirements of a submissive. However, your learning period will be extremely unpleasant unless you learn to obey the silence rule."

She heard his footfalls as he crossed the room. She also thought she heard a muffled sigh, but concluded she must be mistaken.

"You won't speak again unless spoken to directly. You'll keep your eyes lowered at all times- from now on it's forbidden for you to look into my face. Any violation of that particular rule will be severely dealt with."

Theo flicked on a light and as her eyes adjusted from darkness to light, painful reality came crashing down around her. Theo was sitting on what was clearly an antique daybed, with an overabundance of sumptuous cushions piled at each end of the ornately carved, scrolled ends. Behind him, old masters hung on the walls, while a pretty, tawny haired, ivory skinned girl, knelt at his feet, with her eyes downcast.

Theo laughed at Vivienne's shocked expression. He said something in Greek, and the girl lifted her hands. She also was handcuffed, and there was a chain attached to the cuffs, which was wound round the leg of the coffee table and drawn back on itself and clipped to one of the links.

Drawing herself up to a kneeling position, Vivienne watched in disbelief as Theo's hand worked the girl's ivory, pink-tipped breasts. She also wore a slave collar with a ring at the front. But unlike Vivienne's, this one was made of some kind of black metal, that stood out starkly against her pale skin.

Theo took a short chain, with a small device at each end, from the coffee table. Horrified, Vivienne watched the girl's face contort in agony as he attached a clamp tightly to the nipple of her left breast. He then attached the second to the other nipple. Pinched painfully, the nipples darkened peachily. Theo manipulated both breasts from underneath, every now and then seizing the chain that swung between them and tugging it downward, elongating the hard nipples. She screamed as Theo turned little screws in the clamps that had the effect of tightening the clamps, squeezing the blood from them.

As she watched the poor girl's suffering, Vivienne grew more and more agitated as she realized she was powerless to help the girl. If only there were something she could do, but handcuffed as she was, there was nothing she could do but watch. And shame lashed her as she felt the first trickles of moisture between her thighs. Deeply ashamed, she realized that she rather enjoyed watching the girl suffer.

"My room is through that connecting door," Theo indicated a door with an antique cupboard alongside, looking incongruous with a computer mounted on top, "but you'll share a room with this other bitch." He gave the girl's thigh a vicious kick.

The sob that escaped Vivienne's lips was a bitter groan that shook her shoulders with the effort of keeping back the tears of his betrayal, but no way would she ever give him the satisfaction of seeing her cry! Instead, she kept her wide eyes fixed on the scene.

"Escape is impossible. There are guards outside the door." Again he tightened the screws on the nipple clamps.

"Argh!"

Ignoring the girl's cries, Theo continued to address Vivienne matter-of-factly.

"Staying on your hands and knees, go through to the bathroom. Strip and take a shower. Then, still naked, come out here again on all fours. Crawl through that other door" again he indicated a door, "sit on the floor beside the bed and wait to be tied down for the night."

Vivienne drew in a horror-stricken breath. Her eyes bulged and her mouth gaped- but no sound passed her lips. Silently she turned, and headed for an open door through which she could see a shower cubicle. Though how she was supposed to shower she couldn't begin to imagine. Undressing would be easy, since all she was wearing was the vandalized dress.

As he watched her go, Theo allowed himself a smile of satisfaction. The taming of Vivienne was turning out to be everything he had hoped it would be, and more. The harder she found it to comply with his commands, the more opportunities she unwarily presented him for chastisement. Tomorrow, her training would begin in earnest.

But one thought was uppermost in his mind as he watched her sensuously crawling figure disappear into the luxurious bathroom and kick the door closed behind her- while all his girls lived in fear of him, they also loved him, adored him as their master- it was time to work that particular spell on Vivienne.

***

Vivienne woke often during the night, each time surprised that she had slept at all. She had spent the night lying flat on her back on the floor, with her ankles tied together with some kind of cord that bit into her ankles. Lying across the foot of the two single beds in the room, she had looked up longingly at the beds with their lavishly frilled bed coverings, wondering what possible pleasure Theo could derive from the girls' hardship. Positioned side by side, the beds had matching antique, brass bedsteads, with a row of vertical bars along the foot and head, and ornate knobs at each corner.

Theo had fitted a wide, black leather belt that cinched her narrow waist tightly, sensuously accentuating the flare of her hips. It was terribly uncomfortable and made breathing somewhat difficult until one got used to it- if one could ever get used to it. There was a ring at the front, similar to the one on her slave collar. Using a clip, Theo had fastened her handcuffed wrists to the ring, so that she was compelled to sleep all night with her hands resting awkwardly on her stomach, making it impossible to touch herself intimately to relieve the frustration that had been building since the art gallery.

The other girl, also stripped naked, had already been similarly prepared when Vivienne had returned from her shower.

Both girls had been made to lie on their backs on the floor, with each girl's feet touching those of the other girl. Theo had bound the two girls together, sole to sole. By means of leather straps passed over their toes, he had secured Vivienne's right foot to the other girl's left foot, wound the strap a couple of times round both their insteps, then passed the ends of the strap round Vivienne's ankle to buckle it at the side as if it were a shoe. He had then repeated the procedure with their other feet, this time buckling the strap around the other girl's narrow ankle.

As a further refinement, Theo had made the poor, pale skinned girl wear the painful nipple clamps all night. Tightening them one final time before leaving, he reminded her how fortunate she was to have been chosen to undergo such suffering for him, and that he was indeed a bountiful Master for not having attached a crocodile clip to her clitoris.

While speaking to each other was strictly forbidden without Theo's express authorization, inevitably the two girls had risked urgent whispers when left alone. The girl told Vivienne that if Theo bothered to call her anything at all, it was Clitty.

After having introduced herself, Vivienne mentioned, not unkindly, that while she had never expected to be the only female in Theo's life, it had come as something of a surprise to discover that she wasn't the only female in his hotel suite. Anticipating Vivienne's question, Clitty told her that they were fortunate that there were only the two of them present.

"Is that supposed to make me feel better?" Vivienne hissed back, suddenly angry.

"It means the Master will give all his attention to us."

"Can we cut all this 'Master' crap?" Her hatred for Theo grew as each second ticked past. "As for having his attention, quite frankly I'd rather spend the night in a pit full of snakes."

Clitty smiled knowingly- there were some things best left unsaid.

"What's going to become of us, Clitty? I don't how old you are, where you come from or how you ended up being treated like this, but-"

"Everything's fine, you're in good hands."

"Theo's hands?"

"You're lucky, Vivienne , because he chose you himself. I, on the other hand, was merely a gift."

Vivienne's shock registered in her voice. "A gift? You mean someone actually gave you-"

Clitty had come to Theo via Japan, she said, about a year ago when she was just nineteen.

"We aren't allowed to remember what out lives were before coming to Theo, let alone discuss them,"she said, but did tell Vivienne that she had been a parting gift from her Japanese master to Theo, and was then taken to his Greek island.

"I've served him there ever since. Theo likes the effect of my slave collar against my skin so much that he sent word to Japan to have another device made of the same metal, which I also wear and cannot remove. This is the first time I've accompanied Theo on a business trip, and I've not been allowed to leave this suite since we arrived. I've been kept naked and chained.

"But don't feel sorry for me, Vivienne, I'm not unhappy; I'm happier now than I've ever been in my life. And you will be too, if you learn to follow the rules.'

"So what are the bloody rules?"

Clitty's laugh was a pretty, tinkling sound. "Rule number one: don't question everything."

"Listen, Clitty. Theo is nothing but a brute, a sadistic savage, and we must escape-"

"You've so much to learn! Theo is our Master, we're his slaves and that's the end of it."

With that, despite the painful clamps, Clitty had fallen asleep almost at once.

***

Both girls woke slowly. There was no way of knowing what the time was since the heavy red drapes that hung at the windows on the right hand side of the beds and at the windows along the adjoining wall facing the beds,were still drawn.

Vivienne had never been much good at sit-ups, and therefore it took all her strength to struggle to a sitting position. Theo was standing beside her and, with a slow smile that lacked mirth, he raised his foot. With a kick to her breasts that momentarily knocked the wind from her, he sent her crashing down again.

"Bastard!" she ground out through gritted teeth.

Once more flat on her back, she assessed him with cool hostility, through sparkling eyes that expressed a different emotion entirely, something far more basic that made a mockery of her avowed hatred.

She conceded he was handsome in a harsh, brooding sort of way. His tousled, jet hair curled around his neck and his unshaven face gave him a rugged, outdoor look that belied his businessman image.

Remembering that she wasn't supposed to look him in the face, she averted her eyes downward, running them over his naked body. He had the kind of physique that she would have described to friends as 'in-shape', with a fine covering of curling black hair over the rigidity of his chest.

Her eyes travelled onward, down to his impressive shaft that was already stiffening. And, hating herself as much as she hated him, she found herself longing to open her legs to allow him entry. If only he would untie her!

He lowered himself onto Vivienne's tethered body. Sitting astride her, one leg either side of her thighs, he straddled her shapely, golden legs with his hair-covered, olive ones.

She drew in an apprehensive breath; with her secured hands still attached to the belt, she was completely at his mercy.

My God! Surely he wasn't going to fuck her with Clitty in the room. She would die of shame.

"How dare you leave me like this all night!" Emboldened by the fact that she didn't immediately receive a slap round the face, she continued bravely "Take those horrible things off Clitty's breasts. They'll stop her blood!"

"Only to her nipples. And the pain will be exquisite once it starts flowing again. She'll feel it for days to come, and her nipples will remain agonizingly hard."

Reaching an arm behind him, his fingers raked provocatively through the thick, black thatch of hair that adorned Vivienne's prominent pubis. She felt his fingers creep further down, prising open her heated, satin-skinned thighs enough for two fingers.

"I'm sorry you've had to endure such discomfort," he whispered as he began his silky, treacherous seduction. His other hand brushed the hair from her face as gently as if she were a rare piece of porcelain. His fingers found her clitoris. Stroking it skilfully, he continued

"You, my sweet-" his fingers moved in feathery motions over

her hardening bud, "you deserve everything it's within my power to bestow upon you." His mouth twisted into that half-smile that should have warned of atrocities to come. His fingers continued to excite her, eliciting sighs of rapture from her parted lips. "In time, you'll forgive me for the harsh treatment I've meted out to you. Say you forgive me."

Somewhere at the back of her mind, she heard the warning voice that told her to be strong, not to give up her will, to fight against his spurious tenderness. But his fingers were too knowledgeable, and his soft voice too seductive.

With the skill of a true master, he eased her into a state of relaxed happiness.

"I forgive", she breathed through lips that craved the taste of him.

"Tell me you give yourself to me, of your own free will."

Even tied and helpless, she could do nothing to prevent the bucking of her abdomen or the hardening of her nipples. Soft and yielding, her body was out of her control and responded to his touch instinctively. His huge palm cupped the rounded cheek of her behind, his caresses soothing away any remaining doubts.

Vivienne allowed herself the joint luxuries of daydream and self-delusion. This man in whose magnetic aura she bathed was a long way from being the lascivious, stony-hearted Greek who had degraded her so publicly; his treatment of her then had been an aberration, a curious phenomenon caused by a build-up of unrequited need that was unlikely to occur again since she would attend to his every desire.

Sweet reason seemed to have deserted her and she heard herself answer dreamily as her eyes misted over with nameless emotion.

"I give myself.... do with me as you wish..."

Relinquishing her clitoris, his fingers reached for her breasts. Entranced by his anodyne touch, her nipples stiffened brazenly, until they stood erect like hard, brown acorns. She offered up her mouth and he inclined his head towards hers and her soft, pliant lips parted as if by magic beneath his. As his hot, moist tongue tangled with hers, he tantalizingly explored the wet depths of her mouth. His kiss became more demanding, luring her into an emotional whirl of care-free inattentiveness. Her mouth yielded to his satin seduction as surely as her will began the inexorable course of yielding to his.

The atmosphere in the room was one of grave need so that everything else, like fear, caution, even hate was overridden, making her disregard the warning voice in her head. As surely as she could feel her own desire, she could taste his savage lust. Nevertheless, she wanted him- in that moment he was as vital to her as the very air she breathed- she would do anything he asked of her.

He returned his attention to her hard clitoris. Now his fingers were more frenzied, bringing moans and incoherent words from her lips. Juicing freely, her quivering pussy burned with desire while her clitoris throbbed beneath his expert touch. Her muscles clenched and her legs stiffened. Working her clitoris relentlessly, Theo smiled a satisfied smile as the force of Vivienne's bucking body sent shock waves through her, down her legs to her feet, causing Clitty's body to jerk also since the girls were still joined at the feet.

And as Vivienne screamed in glorious abandon as she came, so too did the other girl, without ever being touched.

With a mocking laugh, Theo adjusted his position, turning so that he was facing Clitty.

"What a charming pair of whores. I think that maybe I should keep you strapped together permanently. It saves so much time and effort when you both come together."

He laughed again as, still straddling Vivienne's hips, he unfastened the straps that held the two girls bound together. He leaned forward and tugged spitefully on Clitty's nipple clamps. Her face crumpled in pain, and that seemed to satisfy him. He then untied the cord from Clitty's ankles, leaving Vivienne's still tethered with the cord.

He stood up and, easing his hands beneath Vivienne's body, still bound cruelly with the biting cord and with her handcuffed hands attached to the belt, he carried her across to one of the beds. He dumped her on the bed nearest the window, then unceremoniously propped her up in a sitting position with her back resting against the brass bars of the bedhead. In this position, Theo told her with a sadistic smile, she could reach her clitoris if the need arose.

He took out a length of narrow rope from a drawer in the bedside cabinet, and suddenly Vivienne was back in the real world - Theo's world.

"Theo!" Her voice rose in panic as she feared the worst. " Please, let me go."

He gave a derisive, hollow laugh. "What happened to 'I give myself. Do with me as you wish'?" he mimicked cruelly. "Make no mistake, Slut, though it was so charmingly given I neither want, nor need your consent- it merely amuses me to hear you say the words. As I repeatedly tell you, you're already mine. I will do to you whatever I want, when I want."

Staring into her green eyes, bright with fear and some other nameless emotion, he spat the words that curdled her blood.

"It's time you learnt the truth about your condition. Just like that filthy whore-" he jabbed a finger to where Clitty still lay bound on the floor, "you exist solely for my pleasure. Never forget that I'm your master, and as such I have the right to fuck you or beat you, as the mood takes me. You've angered me greatly with your insolence, and now you'll see how I deal with my slaves. Watch carefully, for this time someone else will take your punishment. She'll have one stroke of the lash for each time you've displeased me."

Vivienne cried out, "No!" but his dark, hungry eyes showed no mercy.

"That's another lash you've earned her. I suggest you shut that delicious mouth of yours, or the girl will hate you as much as she adores me."

He crossed the floor back to where Clitty lay trembling. With one hand grabbing each ankle, he dragged her roughly across the few feet to what Vivienne took to be the facing window, beside which they had both slept. He made Clitty stand with her slender back facing the beds and her head lolling against the heavy red drapes.

"You do adore me, don't you, Whore?"

"Yes, Master." Clitty's voice was a soft, terrified whisper that filled Vivienne with pity and remorse.

"Louder!"

"Yes, Master."

Theo un-clipped her handcuffed hands from the belt. Still leaving the clamps in place, with a flourish he pulled back the drapes, to reveal several iron rings set in the wall at varying intervals and heights.

"You must understand," Theo said, addressing Vivienne while he worked, "that this is no ordinary hotel suite - it's my hotel suite-" his laugh was like the roar of some animal, "in fact, it's my hotel. It's extremely handy for my trips to London. The suite's very well equipped. It's sound proofed of course, and put to excellent use by like-minded people who, for a considerable fee, use it in my absence."

Theo retrieved a footstool upholstered in red velvet from underneath the oak dressing table and dragged it over to the drapes, where Clitty waited impassively, her head bowed. Vivienne watched open mouthed as, climbing on to the stool, Theo proceeded to attach one end of the rope to Clitty's handcuffs, and the other end to a ring set high above her head. He then pulled on the end of the rope, which had the effect of stretching her pale, slender arms upward above her head and hoisting her upward, until she was teetering on tiptoe. Theo then climbed down again, kicked away the stool and wound the end of the rope round a hook in the wall to secure it.

Vivienne watched in dismay as, still on tiptoe, poor Clitty struggled to ease the terrible ache in her arms by shifting from one foot to the other. And she couldn't help but notice the elegant curve of Clitty's back, and the way she tossed her head as she fought to retain her balance.

Theo picked a cruel-looking whip from a selection in a wall-rack, then positioned himself one side of Clitty's slight, rather frail-looking body. Glancing across to where Vivienne gaped in horror, and, to her shame- fascination, Theo told her coldly "Watch and learn. Next time it might well be you under my lash."

Clitty's body tensed, and Vivienne found that her body tensed in sympathy. She drew in a breath-

Theo raised the whip, there was the sound of it whizzing through the air, then a Crack! and a scream as it came down across the back of Clitty's thighs, turning the pale skin red almost instantly.

Whizz! Crack!

"Argh!" Clitty's flesh quivered as the second strike hit below the first.

Whizz! Crack!

"Argh!"

Theo addressed Vivienne mockingly. "See how she suffers for you? I remind you that each strike is one that you have earned."

Whizz! Crack!

"Argh!"

Unable to stand it any longer, Vivienne screamed out. "For God's sake, no more!"

Theo smiled cruelly. "One more to be added to the final tally."

Whizz! Crack!

"Argh!"

Vivienne's body, uncomfortably propped up against the brass bars that hurt her back, shook uncontrollably now as she fought to keep herself from crying out again as the blows rained down across the soft flesh of Clitty's exquisite, ivory thighs. But it was not only the cries of anguish she stifled, but also the clamour of her own climax as the rapid movements of her finger brought her to orgasm.

CHAPTER SIX

Leaving Clitty sobbing as she hung helpless in her bonds, Theo strode across the room, whip in hand. Close up, Vivienne could see that the fearsome scourge was made of one long, tapering cable of plaited leather that had been coated with varnish.

Her slightly parted lips quivered as his intentions became chillingly obvious.

"So, a good whipping makes you come, does it?"

Instinct made her shrink back against the bars on the bed as if they could offer protection. Cold and unyielding as her back pressed against them, they made deep impressions in her flesh. But the discomfort was short lived as he seized her by the ankles and dragged her down until she was prostrate on the bed. Grabbing her shackled wrists, he uprooted her hands from her dripping sex and unclipped them from the belt. She thought that he was about to release her, and her spirits lifted, only to plummet again when he raised them above her head. Adjusting her position so that her arms were stretched tautly, he anchored the handcuffs to one of the bars.

"Let's see what happens when it's you that's getting the thrashing."

Soft and vulnerable, her body trembled in terror. There was a wildness about him that warned against pleading for mercy- she had learned enough by now to know that merely incited him to further brutality. She closed her eyes tightly as he raised his arm. She froze as she heard the whip swish through the air, and then a second later, blinding red filled her head as the first blow struck across the soft flesh of her upper thigh. Her body jerked in response.

"Argh!"

"Open your eyes, Bitch! Watch the lashes come down as eagerly as you watched them strike the other slut."

Obediently her eyes flicked open. Her mouth fell open too as she stared up at his raised arm, her body tensing. She flinched, and he laughed as he aborted the strike in mid air. She drew in a breath as he again raised his arm. In the split second it took to whizz through the air, she saw it curl and flick as it came down to strike.

Lightning filled her brain as the blow struck directly over the path of the first, but she didn't cry out. She wouldn't give him that satisfaction.

"I will make you scream!" He raised his arm. She tensed. Whack! Whack! Whack! Three vicious strokes in rapid succession soon had her screaming in total abandon.

"Aaarrghhh!"

Her body spasmed as fire blazed across her thighs where the lash had struck, criss- crossing her flesh with deep red stripes that were already forming ridges.

"What's the matter?" he said mockingly, his accent heavy with the urgency of his lust "not coming yet?"

Ice met fire as his cold gaze met her burning green eyes.

"Is your cunt wet yet?" His hand squeezed between her hot thighs.

Again she tensed as his finger shot up inside her moistening sex.

Her face burned with shame as he withdrew it again, slick with her juices and held it up for her to see.

"So, the bitch does like it after all." His lip curled menacingly.

She braced herself, knowing instinctively that the worst was still to come. Her mind was in a whirl as he laid down one red stripe over another, loud sobbing punctuating her shrieks. The tears flowed as her pussy grew wetter. She neither counted, nor cared any longer how many times the whip struck, all she knew was that her supple, tethered body was writhing in agony, and for some reason she couldn't fathom, her insides were glowing. Consumed by pain, white light and shame, she felt something akin to exhilaration spread through her loins.

Beads of sweat ran down the golden valley between her breasts. Drowning in a strange mix of emotions, the extreme pain gave way to one of extreme need.

It took a moment for her to realize that not only had the blows stopped coming, but that Theo had untied the cord that had bound her ankles for so long. Taking one ankle in each hand, he spread her legs.

Settling himself on his knees between her legs, now wide open and outstretched as if in invitation, Theo brushed his shaft back and forth against the black hair that swirled around her pussy, then ran its tip along her swollen labia provocatively. Then, unbearably slowly, he inched his way between the delicate folds.

Manipulating her emotions with breathtaking mastery, Theo ran his fingers soothingly over the tortured flesh of her thighs. He lowered his head and brushed his lips tenderly over the angry weals.

With a sudden intake of ragged breath she felt his thick rod of hot flesh plunge deep inside her sex, filling her completely, more completely than she had ever been filled before. Her inner muscles clutched greedily at his shaft as his powerful thrusting increased. She cried out his name as wild sensations leaped through every part of her being.

Overflowing with glorious, hitherto unknown tingles and shudders as his brutal impaling increased in intensity, she moaned incoherently. Her body arched to meet each new thrust, each one deeper, stronger than the last.

Joined in the rhythm of erotic fascination, she and Theo became one essence of passion. The heavy weight of his body covered hers, as she arched beneath him. His fingers twined in her raven hair, and she writhed in rapture. Between hoarse words spoken in Greek, Theo whispered her name breathlessly, then threw back his head. With a bestial howl, he gave one last, powerful thrust as his scalding liquor shot deep into her quim. In almost the same moment her own body tensed with the first spasms of orgasm. Every muscle in her body stretched and tightened in painful ecstasy. She let out a shriek of exultation and rode her own climax like a woman possessed, and came out the other side like a woman reborn.

As her own peak ebbed away on a tide of hedonistic euphoria, she watched through half closed eyes as Theo's contorted features resumed their former composure. Warmth flowed through her, enfolding her in the warm bliss of fulfilment. Like a kitten that's just tasted its first saucer of cream, she smiled up at her benefactor, and it was a smile of radiant delight.

There was a strange a look in his dark eyes, almost tenderness, that she knew he didn't want her to see. Lingering somewhere between delicious afterglow and erotic shame, she told herself that, for the moment at least, the hard-hearted savage had disappeared.

He climbed off her sensuously glowing body and stood looking down at her.

"Rest now. You'll need all your strength later."

"What's happening later?" she asked coquettishly, her lips repeating the mischievous sparkle in her eyes, the pain of her beating already erased. But to her bitter disappointment, the fleeting look of tenderness in his eyes had passed, and there wasn't even a suggestion of a smile on his thin lips.

"I'm going to turn you from temptress - " he fixed his eyes on the angry red ridges that criss-crossed her golden thighs, "to obedient slave."

"Big talk!"

"No-" he corrected, grabbing the whip again and lifting his arm, "a guarantee."

"Argh!"

The whip caught her across the insides of her thighs, where the quivering flesh was most tender.

"That was for breaking the Silence Rule. If you continue to defy me, I'll have you gagged- permanently. As I told you before, you deserve everything it's within my power to bestow upon you- and that means as much pain as I see fit."

With that, he re-tied the cord around her ankles, threw the whip to the floor, and strutted from the room, leaving Vivienne paralysed with fear and gasping for breath, and Clitty still hanging by her wrists.

***

Vivienne heard rather than saw the door open. She stiffened in cold apprehension as two men entered the room. One she recognised immediately as being the waiter from the restaurant, while the other...

God no!

Mortified, she watched as Flynn Pallister strode towards the bed. The scarlet flush of humiliation was on her. She would rather die than let him see her like this. How the hell would she face him at work on Monday morning?

"Ah, Miss Trevayne," mockingly, he bowed his head to kiss the tip of her nose. Then, as his mouth closed over hers in a bruising, stifling kiss, his hands reached for her nipples. He gave them a sharp pinch, then straightened up.

Even now, his urbane tones excited her. "I'm afraid I didn't bring any bulldog clips, but I did bring you these..." With unhurried arrogance, he slipped his hand into his pocket, and took out two lengths of fine cord, each with a loop at one end.

He slipped the loops one over each already stiffening nipple, then slid a small metal toggle in place to tighten the loops.

Calling out to the waiter to come and help with this "lusting little whore-bag", he unfastened her handcuffs from the bed. Together, the two men hauled her back to a sitting position. They turned her belt round so that the ring was at the back. Unlocking one handcuff, they pulled her hands behind her back, re-fastened the cuffs, and attached them to the ring on the belt.

"Theo gave us permission to use you both in any way we wanted for the next hour or so, provided we stop you from frigging yourself, and then follow his further instructions to the letter when we're through with you."

The men each took one end of narrow cord and yanked it upward, elongating her nipples painfully so that she cried out. For the first time she noticed a heavy ring set in the wall about three feet above her head, and it was to this ring they attached the ends of the cords, stretching her nipples upward and ensuring that she would not move from the sitting position. Flynn pulled open a drawer in the bedside cabinet.

"As you know, I prefer my women-" he took out a device and dangled it teasingly before her eyes, smiling delightedly as she recognized its use "gagged."

He fitted the ball gag that differed from the one he had used before, only in the fact that the actual ball was slightly bigger, and stood back to admire his work.

"You see, Miss Trevayne, I have the best of both worlds. Not only did I make a great deal of money from your purchase, for which, incidentally-" he paused to laugh, "I thank you, but as one of Theo's most trusted personnel, I get to use you from time to time. Yet I can't help but wonder how I'm ever going to manage at work without you! I can only hope that he soon tires of you and kicks you all the way back to the office. Still, I have you now- why not sit back and enjoy the show?"

Laughing raucously, the two men swaggered across the room to where Clitty hung like a rag doll by her wrists. Fearing now for her new friend's safety, Vivienne watched with mounting horror.

"We'll have some sport with this one since we're here."

While Flynn tore off the nipple clamps, the waiter grabbed Clitty by the hair and yanked her head backward, exposing her vulnerable, ivory throat with the black metal slave collar.

Theo had been right, Vivienne conceded - the black metal did indeed have a pleasing effect against Clitty's skin, and she found herself wondering what the other device could be that he'd had made of the same metal. Clitty had said she was forced to wear the device all the time, yet so far Vivienne had seen no evidence of it. Her curiosity aroused, she cursed the fact that so far her own bonds had kept her from seeing Clitty's entire body.

Without checking on Clitty's well-being, the waiter thrust his fingers deep into her sex, making her moan. Working her furiously, he gave a sudden whoop of delight, kissed her rakishly on the lips, then released her hair. Without a murmur of complaint, she slowly raised her head to let it loll on one side.

Removing his fingers, shining with Clitty's fragrant juices, he shoved them in her mouth and made her lick them clean.

As if on some unseen command, both men unzipped their flies and pulled down their underpants. The waiter positioned himself behind Clitty's swaying body while Flynn dropped to his knees between Clitty and the wall. Burying his face in her thick, curling fleece, he held her firmly round the waist with his suntanned hands to steady her, then clamped his mouth firmly over her sex. There was a soft clanking of metal.

The waiter now stood behind her. He took out his impressive penis and, without either lubrication or warning, thrust it up Clitty's back passage.

Clitty cried out, and immediately received a sharp slap across her already inflamed thigh. Still on tiptoe, she tried to shift position to better accommodate him.

As Flynn slurped noisily, lapping up Clitty's sweet sap, still accompanied by the strange clanking of metal, the waiter grunted and groaned earthily as he buried his cock deep inside Clitty's back passage.

Vivienne had never seen anyone fucked up there before, and shuddered repeatedly as fear and revulsion did battle within her. With her hands secured behind her back, there was nothing she could do but watch as Clitty was savagely violated.

Except that, as she watched, Vivienne became aware of a spreading warmth within her as some other emotion began to uncurl deep inside. Ashamed she realized that, just as before, she was becoming incredibly turned on by witnessing the brutal debasement of the helpless girl. Her clitoris pounded and, driven crazy with desire, she wriggled her hands in the tight cuffs to try and remove them, so urgent was the need to satisfy the demands of her body. Her nipples swelled and hardened, making the thin cord bite deeper into the tender, puckered flesh around her nipples, and unable to cry out she whimpered against the ball gag.

Grabbing Clitty's legs, Flynn lifted her from the floor and placed one leg over each of his shoulders, thus giving him greater access to her pussy. As the pale skinned girl groaned in near delirium, the force of the waiter's cock ramming into her drove her quim even harder against Flynn's face, causing his head to knock against the wall, though Flynn seemed not to notice the discomfort. Lost in his own kind of delirium as he continued licking Clitty out noisily, Flynn's fingers gripped her so tightly round her slender waist that he made little indentations in her soft skin.

Suddenly, with a series of violent jerks and loud, guttural cries, the waiter shot his come up Clitty's tight hole. She wiggled her bottom prettily in response as he emptied himself fully. When he had completely finished, he wiped his cock clean on her buttocks. Reluctantly, Flynn pushed her away from his face. Grabbing her legs again, this time he lifted them upward to extricate himself, leaving Clitty swinging on the rope as he stood up.

At last the two men loosened off the rope and let her down. As she tottered on the end of the rope, swaying and weak form the harsh treatment she had repeatedly received, Flynn unhooked the rope and let her down. The waiter untied the rope from her handcuffs and scooped the exhausted girl up into his arms.

Vivienne just caught sight of something that looked like black metal hanging between her legs.

***

Once he was alone with Vivienne, Flynn hurriedly rid himself of his clothes. Naked, he strode towards the bed. Without a word, he positioned himself kneeling with one leg either side of Vivienne's sore, angry-looking striped thighs. With one fluid movement he removed the ball gag and stuffed his hard erection in Vivienne's mouth.

"Suck me off, Baby."

Tied as she was, Vivienne had little choice. She gagged on the swollen flesh as he pistoned in and out. Almost choking as he forced his prick deep into her throat, she tried to pull her head away, but he slipped his finger through the ring of her collar and roughly drew her closer.

The cord around her nipples tightened painfully. She whimpered in distress, but oblivious to her agony- or more likely encouraged by it, his thrusting became more frenzied. She spluttered on the first drops of semen.

"Are you hungry, baby?" he yelled as he shot his scalding come down her throat, forcing her to swallow the thick, salty liquid.

Half choking, the tears began to flow, first as a gentle stream, then a torrent that shook her body.

"Save your fucking tears, Slut, you'll need them later."

Once again struck by the incongruity of the coarse words spoken with such a well- to-do English accent, she could almost convince herself that the nightmare wasn't happening at all. Humiliatingly dribbling from the corners of her mouth as he pulled out of her, she sobbed loudly.

"There'll be plenty of time for blubbering. You don't have a clue what's happening here, do you? You, my pretty little trollop, are about to become one of the most abused lumps of flesh it's ever been my pleasure to screw." Seeing her shocked expression, he laughed and continued cruelly, "Provided, of course, Theo doesn't get bored with you and throw you out with the garbage!"

Loosening the loops from her nipples, he at last removed the cords, leaving them hanging from the wall ring as a callous reminder. Dressing quickly and leaving her with her hands secured behind her back, he left the room, to return moments later with a cup of coffee and a bowl. After placing the bowl on the bedside cabinet, he held a cup for her to drink the hot, strong coffee that burned her mouth as she gulped it down greedily.

Hauling her from the bed, he made her stand by the wall, beside the array of whips as he re-hung Theo's whip in its correct position.

He removed the handcuffs and belt, and made her get down on her knees.

Her hair fell haphazardly over her face. She put her hand under her hair, and in her characteristic gesture, threw back her head and shook her head so that her hair tumbled sensuously over her shoulders.

"How does it feel to be sold into slavery, to be nothing more than a chattel to be bought and sold like any other commodity? I knew from the first moment I set eyes on you that you'd be a real fuckable addition to Theo's collection."

She was about to ask what collection, but thought better of it. While her opinion of him hadn't changed inasmuch as she still thought of him as incredibly sexy, she knew from experience how cruel he could be. The last thing she needed now was another thrashing.

He made her hold her arms out in front, then attached leather straps about three inches wide to each wrist. Each had two metal rings attached and a buckle which he did up tightly. Then he fastened similar straps to her upper arms, buckling them tightly also. With unnecessary roughness, he kicked her ankles apart and secured matching straps snugly.

"Almost ready for breakfast", he announced.

Confused, for a moment her eyes held his. He fingered her crotch, prising open her tumescent lips. She shuddered with arousal as her pussy sucked his fingers in, a tide of wantonness sweeping everything from her mind but the pleasure of his tantalizing touch.

"What a delicious hot, hungry cunt!" Withdrawing his fingers, he wiped them in her shining, raven hair.

He clipped her right wrist strap to the one on her right upper arm, then did the same with her left. With his hand on the top of her head, he pushed her downward, ordering her to lie on the floor. Without complaint she did as she was bidden, laying her cheek against the thick carpet while Flynn attached long chains to each ankle strap. Giving them a sharp tug that raised her legs and pulled them towards her head, he laid a long metal pole across her shoulder blades. Winding the ends of each chain round the pole, he used a clip to join the two ends together and attached them to the centre of the pole, thus keeping her ankles raised. Taking a shorter length of chain, he secured it across the undersides of her firm, rounded buttocks. Then, as a final refinement, he pulled back her elbows and using one set of rings on the straps, attached them to the pole also.

Every nerve in her body tensed as Flynn ran his finger along the deep crease of her behind, then stroked the red gash of her sex. In one swift movement, his finger slipped in and out of her moist quim, then returned to her buttocks. He fingered the pink, puckered hole of her anus, before pushing, pushing- she screamed as he entered that forbidden entrance, and screamed again as he drove his finger home. Her sphincter muscles clenched tightly, agonizingly around his probing digit.

And then it wasn't his finger anymore that violated her behind- it was something hard and unyielding.

"Didn't he tell you? He wants your arse plugged!"

She heard him walk across to the bedside cabinet. When he returned, he placed the bowl of porridge on the floor by her head.

"Eat it all up, there's a good dog!" he laughed cruelly.

Struggling to reach the bowl, tears of humiliation again poured down her cheeks.

"I've never seen you look as beautiful as you do now" he told her. "Theo's right- there's something about humiliation that becomes you." He took a riding crop from the rack and gave her one sharp whack across the shoulders that sent pain slicing through her. "Remember, everything you go through is for Theo's pleasure. So it follows that the greater your suffering, the greater his enjoyment."

"But he's not even here!" she snivelled pathetically.

"That's what makes it all the more glorious- that you endure it all in his name."

With that, Flynn replaced the crop and left the room, leaving the drapes still drawn, and only the light from a small lamp to give illumination so that she wouldn't know if it was morning or afternoon, and could have no idea of the passing of time.

Left alone to drown in her misery for what seemed an age, her bitter tears made a wet patch on the carpet. It could have been minutes or hours that she was left hog-tied, helpless and sobbing, with her arse plugged and on fire and her bowl of porridge tipped over from her efforts to lap it up.

***

On the seventeenth floor of Paston Communications, eighteen men sat round the long table, with Theo at the head. Gravely, he looked round at the attentive faces of his employees.

"Gentleman, thank you all for coming at such short notice." He paid no attention to the small, Titian haired young woman sitting quietly on a chair in the corner. "I know you'd all much rather be on the golf course this fine Saturday afternoon." His eyes swept over each man in turn. And each man faltered under his steady gaze. "Or with your wives- I know you're all devoted to your families... " Theo let the sentence hang in the air, the threat of what would happen should they disclose to anyone the nature of the meeting implied but not spoken.

"I think you know Flynn Pallister, from the seventh floor," he said by way of an introduction. A murmur of affirmation rumbled around the room as the men acknowledged Flynn, sitting on Theo's right. "As I'm sure you're aware, Flynn has recently been brought across from New York, where he achieved many great things for Zortac. He took up the position of Divisional Manager of the South-eastern Region here at Paston Communications, and has been a great success. Therefore, he's just been promoted, as you yourselves were, to Business Unit Manager, now that all former holders of those positions have been... paid off, shall we say?

"I've called this meeting to spell out my intentions concerning yourselves. As long as you remain loyal employees of Zortac, you'll be looked upon favourably by myself, and indeed, other similar organisations. There will also be great rewards and special perks for those who remain loyal, trustworthy personnel." He waited a moment for the implications of giving him their allegiance to sink in, then added a further threat. "I must stress, however, the importance of secrecy. Anyone who divulges our main interests will, of course, be dealt with severely.

"Now it's time to put my plan into action. As in all walks of life, I believe that women should be submissive to men. And what better place to start than in the office! I want to do away entirely with this absurd idea of equality for women in the workplace, and restore the natural order to the world of business. Let me show you what I mean."

He clicked his fingers and Denise came scurrying across from where she had been sitting in the corner. Pulling out a chair beside him she sat down, holding a notebook and pencil in her hand.

Addressing her in a commanding tone, Theo said "Take a letter", and began dictation, which Denise dutifully took it down in shorthand. And as she did so, Theo reached across and pulled up the hem of her long, flowing skirt, to reveal her shapely, naked legs. With his hand on her knee, he continued with the letter, while Denise scribbled in her pad.

There were grunts of approval from all the men in the room.

"Make the coffee!" he ordered. Denise scuttled off to the adjoining kitchenette. "And don't forget the biscuits!"

The men laughed, heartily applauding their employer's doctrine.

"That, of course, was a very rudimentary demonstration, Gentlemen, but I'm encouraged that you all understand and approve of the principle. Beginning on Monday, I want you to start to put my plans into operation on your own floors. I don't care how you do it, but get rid of any woman in a position of authority, whether it be Regional Manager, Supervisor, or merely some new girl with big ideas about climbing the ladder. There will be no, I repeat no climbing the ladder for women within Paston Communications, just as it's been successfully abolished throughout the Zortac empire.

"I also repeat, Gentlemen, that secrecy is of vital importance- we don't want to create outside interest and bring the authorities down on our heads. Try to be discreet. And remember at all times that you're family men! Don't concern yourself with legal complications, they're not your concern- you're here primarily to make money- money to finance my other... interests, interests in which you are all very interested!"

There was laughter around the table.

Denise came scurrying back, pushing a tea trolley. Hurrying from one to the other, she passed coffee and biscuits around the table. She then returned to her corner, awaiting further instructions. She didn't have to wait long.

Theo clicked his fingers. "Here!"

Obediently, Denise scurried to stand before him.

"Strip."

Without hesitation, her fingers found the small, pearl button that fastened the neck of her white silk, high-necked blouse. Fumbling now under so many watchful eyes, Denise finally opened the front of her blouse. There were gasps from the men when the golden slave collar around her alabaster throat was revealed, and again when the men saw a pair of gold rings through the tips of her rosy pink nipples. Small but well-formed breasts bounced up and down as she pushed down her skirt, to step naked from the pool it made at her feet.

"Any questions, Gentlemen?"

There were several.

"Is she for sale?"

"Do you dress all your women the same?"

"Do we get to fuck her?"

Theo smiled benevolently. "I'll answer your questions in order." He commanded Denise to parade before each of the men. "Feel free to touch her. I regret that, at this time, this particular whore is not for sale, though this may change at some date in the future. If you are interested in a purchase, however, I have a particularly nice piece back at my hotel, by the name of..." he turned to Flynn, "what is that bitch's name?"

"Clitty."

"Ah yes, Clitty. If you ring my secretary, I can arrange a private viewing, though the piece won't actually be on the market for a few weeks yet. Now, to answer your other questions, I prefer to keep most of my sluts naked."

An image flicked into his mind of the new girl back at hotel. How ravishing she had looked through the two-way mirror, deliciously humiliated in the leather and chains, forced to eat like a dog. She had excited him more than any of his other sluts had done for a long time, and he was becoming impatient to take her home with him. But all in good time, there were more important things to consider right now.

"Incidentally," he continued phlegmatically, "I have another particularly nice piece, not with me I'm afraid, who's completely hairless. I removed most of it myself, and she is maintained in the same condition by my loyal servants. It would be sacrilege to clothe her!

"However, it amuses me to have them dressed from time to time, in restrictive basques etc., or some other costume that I've designed for an exhibition."

He watched proudly as the men groped and admired his beautiful possession as she displayed herself in the required manner- head up, eyes down, hands behind head to thrust out her small breasts, and legs wide to give access to her pussy with its red curls frothing around the coral lips. He nodded towards her as he spoke.

"This whore is actually one of my private collection, and as such is just one of the delights you may request to sample should you please me enough to be invited to my private island as my houseguest.

"At the moment, she is actually posing as an employee on the seventh floor, under the watchful eye of Flynn Pallister, who very kindly agreed to keep her locked up in his home while not working. She was brought in to do a specific job, namely to watch and report back to Mr Pallister and myself on the movements, habits and sexploits of one particular female member of staff, who is, as we speak, undergoing special training for her later role-" laughter rippled around the room, "after which she will return to the seventh floor to unwittingly help put my plans into action, with the continued help of this slut."

He gestured towards Denise, and was delighted to see her backside quiver and redden as one of the men slapped her.

"She has a very particular," he continued, "and rather unexpected talent where the females are concerned, and will put it to good use as overseer to the trainee. But to answer your last question, yes, you may fuck her to your heart's content when I leave. Just hand her over to Flynn afterwards, as he has to put her in chains and lock her up for the night."

Theo stood up to go. "I'll say goodbye now, Gentlemen, but please, stay as long as you wish and use the facilities provided." To Flynn, he said, "Return to the hotel when you've put the toys away. I will, of course, expect to see you at my... exhibition tomorrow evening?"

"Of course. I'm looking forward to it."

CHAPTER SEVEN

How long Vivienne had endured the ignominy of her position before relief came, she had no way of knowing. But when it did come, it was in the guise of one of Theo's tall, beefy, suited goons who had arrived at the hotel with them and guarded the door at the restaurant.

"The name's Farrell" he announced, crisply but not unkindly as he drew the plug from her anus. "I wish you could see yourself - you're enough to knock a man's eyes out. Baby, you're real jerk-off material!"

Built like a gorilla, Farrell began to unhook from the pole the chains that held her captive. Then, sliding the pole from her elbows, he unfastened the other end of the chains from the leather cuffs, which he left in place. With a supporting hand under her arm he helped her to her feet. With surprising gentleness for a man of his immense size, he carried her in his arms through to another room.

Dimly lit with the heavy drapes drawn, Vivienne could just make out that the huge bed had a similar brass bedstead to the others. Stripped of all its coverings save one red silk sheet on which Farrell placed her, it seemed somehow intimidating.

"I'm a bit of a connoisseur myself- like the Boss, I have a thing about women who squirm. And your squirming's just what the doctor ordered." He kneaded her breasts as he spoke, flicking his stubby thumbs over her nipples. He leered down at her as they hardened into stiff peaks beneath his touch. Lowering his head he bestowed a trail of kisses in a line from her chin to her abdomen, which had the effect of soothing her.

Slowly, the life force began to return to her tired, aching body. As he continued to excite her nipples, his tongue snaked downward to the point where her thighs joined. He sought out her clitoris and nibbled it gently before his tongue made the return journey up across her abdomen. He licked at the tiny, glistening beads of perspiration between her full breasts, then brought his mouth down over hers.

"I could love you, if you weren't his" he breathed, straightening up. "The Boss won't, not ever. He'll beat you and abuse you, but never love you. I, on the other hand would still beat you but then I'd kiss the pain away. I'd fuck the arse off you, Baby, then shower you with affection. He won't- he'll fuck you into oblivion, then lock you in a cell on his bloody island. I'd keep you all to myself, but he won't- he'll pass you around like a packet of chocolate digestives."

His words plunged a spear of terror through her heart. Yet even as she fought against it, a spasm of excitement thrilled through her. She cursed her own body which fluttered and trilled with delight at the slightest provocation. Here she was, with aching limbs and a sore anus, humiliated, trapped and naked under the scrutiny of a stranger who warned her of yet more terrors to come, and her traitorous body wanted nothing but to yield to him.

She pressed her thighs tightly together, lest he should see the tiny droplets of moisture that were beginning to seep from her quim. As he tweaked her hardened peaks between finger and thumb, she knew the flush of arousal was upon her, making her golden skin glow.

"I've worked for the Boss for years, and never known a girl to colour up as easily as you do, like you're doing now- you bloody well burn with shame. It's pretty as a picture but be careful, Baby, or it might well be your undoing- the Boss might make you eat dirt simply to watch the colour rise."

Forsaking her breasts, Farrell ran his fingers along the cruel, raised ridges that patterned her soft thighs. Despite his words of love, she recognized the look that crept over his face; she'd seen it before. It was the same look that Flynn had, and the same look that transformed Theo's features when he'd laid into her with the whip- it was the look of savage lust.

"I wish I'd been here to see you whipped." There was considerable movement in his trousers as his fingers continued their appraisal of her welts. “Me and Woodly were guarding the door outside. We heard you scream. It was all we could do to stop from coming in to watch. Hopefully we’ll get a chance later. Watch out for Woodly- he’s real mean.”

While one hand continued to stroke her thighs, his other hand unzipped his flies. Then, hooking a finger through the ring of her collar he dragged her to a sitting position.

“Suck me, Baby, like you sucked Theo.”

Vivienne tossed her head like a proud filly, sending her raven hair cascading down her back and exposing her vulnerable throat. Straightening up, she placed one trembling hand on his hip, the other ducked into his underpants. She extracted his thick, hard cock, loving the feel of its iron rigidity as her fingers closed tightly around it.

“I said suck it, not play with it!” His huge hand delivered a swift, sharp slap to her face. When she didn’t cry out, his voice became softly menacing. “Know your problem? You’re a prick-teaser, and the Boss can’t abide that in a babe! So do it, obey me like you obey him, or I’ll tell him you offered me money to help you escape- he’d just have to punish you.” Again he slapped her. “Eat cock!”

Leaning towards him, Vivienne lowered her head. In no doubt that he would carry out his threat, such was his desire to see her beaten, she took the bulbous head of his cock between her lips.

She guessed that Theo had given strict orders that neither Farrell nor his colleague Woodly were to touch her. In fact, Theo had stated clearly that the two guards were to do nothing more than release her after a couple of hours, then restrain her again per his instructions.

She couldn’t know that Theo fully expected his guards to take liberties.

Vivienne swirled her tongue over the crown of Farrell’s cock, lapping at the salty pre-come. Reaching for his scrotum, she weighed his balls in her palm, manipulating them gently. An upsurge of wantonness made her catch her breath as her soft lips closed over the hot flesh of his shaft, pulling it into her eager mouth.

Farrell grabbed the back of her head to bring her closer, forcing her to take the full length, deep, deeper. Now, with the tip of her nose nestling against his pubic hair and her saliva easing the lingering up and down motions, she sucked for all she was worth, breathing in his heady, manly scent.

Bringing as much pressure to bear as she was able to with her lips, Vivienne's excitement increased. Their mutual needs became stronger, their movements more urgent. Farrell's hips thrusted forward and her head bobbed rapidly up and down as his slick cock slid in and out. His splayed fingers gripped her hair as, with devastatingly deep, final thrusts, he shot his scalding come against the back of her throat.

As she gulped it down, all thoughts of her shameful predicament were lost; nothing existed except the turgid flesh that defiled her throat so gloriously.

***

By degrees, Vivienne became aware of the sound of people moving about in the next room, where Theo was inviting people to "take a seat, make yourself comfortable. We won't be disturbed."

Her curiosity aroused, Vivienne strained her ears to listen to the fragments of the low toned tete-a-tete that was taking place on the other side of the connecting door. She could just make out from the whispers that there were several men present. The thumping of her own heartbeat reverberated in her ears, almost drowning out the whispers from the next room. Not that it mattered; she knew instinctively it was herself that Theo and his friends were discussing. If it weren't for her knowing that Theo owned the hotel, she would think that the hotel management had finally got wind of the depravities that were taking place in their upmarket establishment and were demanding that he leave the premises at once.

Trying to convince herself that none of this was really happening, she put all her efforts into arching her back to try and relieve the ache from lying in the same position for so long. At least she was able to move her legs. She repositioned herself as comfortably as she could.

The voices grew louder and the strident voice of a woman rang out above the others.

"I have to admit that even I didn't recognise her potential as a submissive slut."

Icy horror gripped Vivienne as it dawned on her that it was a voice she recognized, though she couldn't put a name to it just yet..

"I knew something of her reputation........"

Blood curdled in Vivienne's veins. She knew that voice- it was as familiar to her as the voices of the people she worked with. She drew in a sharp breath as realization dawned, exclaiming aloud to the empty room, "Bloody hell! It's Roxanne!"

Roxanne Bellingham was the thirty-something blond who lived in the flat above Vivienne's. Surely she couldn't have anything to do with this weird set-up of Theo's, except why else would she be here? More to the point, did she know that Vivienne was here?

The two women had only met once socially, when a mutual friend had invited them both to a party about a year ago. They hadn't hit it off at all and rivalry set in. Vivienne had been wearing a red lycra mini dress while Roxanne had worn tight leather trousers and a black T-shirt. While Vivienne, men flocking around her, had held court in one corner of the room, Roxanne had done the same in the other.

And judging by the number of feet Vivienne frequently heard on the stairs as they made their way to Roxanne's flat, it seemed that she, like Vivienne herself, had a sexual boldness and a penchant for taking lovers. She had been making a play for Nathan recently.

How dare she call Vivienne a slut! But perhaps it was true, perhaps she really was a slut. When one took into account the eagerness with which she had sucked Farrell's cock and her behaviour under the table, perhaps the name was well deserved. Something was definitely happening to her; even the memory of Theo's cruelty caused a fiery tingle that started in her loins and spread throughout her body.

Theo's unmistakable accent filtered through to her.

"I'd like to welcome those of you who've arrived early. I'm glad so many of you gentlemen could make it. The others will be arriving later. As you know, mine is a quality organization, devoted to domination and other little delicacies. Forgive me for dealing with disciplinary matters first. However, the remainder of the weekend will proceed as planned.

"I promise you all a real treat, but bear in mind that the exhibition tomorrow will be her first time, so try to go gently- at least to start with. She will, of course, be used to the full. But remember, this isn't a common whorehouse."

Back in the bedroom, Vivienne knew a moment's relief, only to have her spirits dashed as Theo continued. And although he spoke in a tone smooth as melted chocolate, his words froze her to the bone.

"This is a serious allegation, Farrell. Rest assured that she'll be punished."

"Bastard!" Vivienne was unable to help the sob that escaped from deep inside. In spite of her giving Farrell a blow job, he'd obviously gone running to Theo with some cock and bull story with the sole intent of seeing her beaten. Wasn't there anyone she could trust?

In the adjoining room, Theo's face was merely a mask of credulity. He wasn't a fool and knew very well that his guards took liberties with the girls behind his back. What man wouldn't if given the chance? The mere fact that they had access to the girls was probably what kept his men loyal, probably the primary factor that dissuaded them from seeking employment elsewhere, as well as maintaining strict confidentiality.

It was of no consequence that men like Farrell and Woodly occasionally concocted such fictions. The thought of his girls undergoing indignities, perhaps even beatings during his absences not only gratified his lust but also gave him a sense of omnipotence that made him enjoy the girls' lithe young bodies all the more. After all, the overriding consideration in all of this was that his girls' pain was his pleasure, and it pleased him greatly to think of their suffering even while he was away.

"I want to maintain absolute discipline at all times-" Theo said, "and this is where you come in, Woodly, Farrell, Pallister. She's no good to me if she isn't obedient. It's important that we- all of us- keep strict control of her movements. I expect your full co-operation. While any misdemeanours on her part should be reported to me at once, I give you my permission to take matters in to your own hands, providing of course, that I'm not around to administer discipline myself. She's having trouble with the silence rule. This must be corrected. You'll also instil in her that it's forbidden to look any man, particularly myself, in the face. If she's ever to be a first-class submissive, she needs to have humility beaten in and inquisitiveness thrashed out."

Back in the other room, Vivienne experienced a curious feeling of elation at that.

"She asks too many questions," Theo went on, "wants to know all the whys and wherefores. While I don't want her turned into a mindless, wanton Bimbo who'll open her legs for anyone on the outside, what I do want is a complete package of sexual servitude at the end of it; someone who'll take whatever's meted out to her without question or complaint. I want it drummed into her that first and foremost, her duty is to me.

"She'll need watching at work, too. She can't be allowed to go to any more conferences and such like; we don't want her mixing with outsiders. You'll have to do something about that, Pallister."

"Absofuckinglutely. You can count on my full cooperation."

The colour drained from Vivienne's face. Whatever was to become of her? Panic gripped her- she had to escape. She tugged frantically against her bonds, but they held fast. Terrified of the unknown degradations that lay ahead, she tried to manouevre her hands into a position whereby her fingers could pick at the knot that secured her hands to the bed, but she was unable to even reach it; there was no escape. However, if she had been staggered before, she was thrown into chaotic confusion when Roxanne spoke again. "Are you guys for real? Do you honestly think that you can turn Viv-"

"Quiet!" Theo cut her off angrily. "I don't often allow outsiders in at all! You're privileged to be here and I must insist that you abide by my rules. I'd be grateful, Roxanne, if you refrain from referring to her by name, even if you happen to find yourself alone with her, which is unlikely. Here she's to remain anonymous- a name gives a girl an unnecessary air of importance. I insist that all my girls learn the true meaning of their subservience and that they are of little consequence in the scheme of things. Besides, some people don't like to know the names of those they fuck- I rarely call them anything, even in private.

"In this case however, it suits my purpose that this particular bag of nothing should return to work. But even then, as far as possible, she's to remain nameless- you'll see to that, Flynn. Incidentally, have you any idea what happened to her boyfriend? No? There's been a change of plan regarding him. Find him!"

Vivienne shuddered with dread. Whatever could they want with Nathan? If he was in some kind of danger, she would never forgive herself.

"Do you really believe you can turn her into some kind of sex slave in just one weekend?" Roxanne asked.

"Fucking right I can", Theo assured her. "I guarantee that she'll be a pleasure to watch and a joy to use. By the time I've finished with her, she'll open her legs when ordered and only shit when told to."

"Can I see her?" There wasn't a hint of concern for Vivienne's welfare in Roxanne's voice, only a disconcerting note of arousal.

"I'll have her prepared," Theo promised. "Now, if you're all ready, coffee's being served downstairs in the main lounge. I have to go over a few details with our friendly waiter..."

Theo's words trailed off as somewhere a door closed. The voices had gone.

***

Vivienne must have dozed off. When she awoke, there was a bowl of fruit and a pot of coffee on the bedside cabinet. She was about to curse Theo for his cruelty in leaving it within her sight while she was still secured to the bed when she realized she had been unfastened. Well one hand, anyway- the cuff on the other wrist had been replaced by the green cord and attached like a dog's lead to the bedstead, allowing her enough movement to sit up and reach the meal.

Freedom was in her grasp! She didn't have to remain tied to the bed at all. Someone had been careless; all she had to do was untie the cord from her wrist and she would be free. Of course, Farrell was probably guarding the door with his colleague Woodly, but surely it was worth a try. After all, she wasn't subjugated yet whatever Theo may think. She still had all her sexual wiles and was sure the guards would let her pass if she offered them a few favours. Wasn't that the way she'd always got on in the world?

She had just started to work on the knot when it struck her that this was no error of judgement at all, but a carefully laid plan. Someone wanted her to escape! Who, Farrell? He'd told her all the things he would do to her if she were his - but if that were the case why had he double-crossed her by lying to Theo? Was his desire to see her punished that great? Or was it was to gain Theo's trust so that precautions would be lax, maybe this was Farrell's way of snatching her for himself.

She picked at the knot with her long, Strawberry Breeze fingernails, which was proving more difficult than she had imagined. On the other hand, maybe Clitty, or even Roxanne had taken pity on her. Except last time Vivienne had seen Clitty, she was being carried half-conscious from the room. Though Roxanne and Vivienne were neighbours they seldom saw each other. When they did, it was usually a cranky "hello" as they passed on the stairs. The very idea that Roxanne would help her was ludicrous.

But if it wasn't Roxanne or Clitty, then who was it?

It was always possible, even probable, that Theo himself had set it up as a test, one he wanted her to fail. That would give him the perfect opportunity to punish her. But, she argued, he didn't really need an excuse. Hadn't he told her "your pain is my pleasure"?

Thinking better of it, Vivienne gave up on the idea. No way would she give Theo the satisfaction of seeing her fail. She would do everything within her power to avoid another beating, whoever administered it.

Giving up the idea of escape for the meantime, she settled herself as comfortably as possible given that the cord bit into her flesh, and drank her coffee. How could she ever have imagined that she was capable of enjoying an active sex life without paying the price? But what a price- she was a prisoner, with heaven knew what kind of humiliations still lying in store.

She bit into a ripe plum. It was time to face the truth - she had to endure it. Anyway, it wouldn't be forever. When the weekend games were over she would go back to work- she'd heard Theo say she would. The whole thing would be forgotten and she could get on with her life, a life without Theo.

And a life without Nathan, she reminded herself. Now, because of her, he could be in danger. She wished she could turn the clock back to before their last row.

"Serves you right," Vivienne said aloud, wishing that she'd tried harder to make things work between them. They had been happy once. "But it wasn't enough, was it?" She poured another coffee. "You'd wanted more- and look where it's got you. Beaten and humiliated by a...a..."

Her whispered words died on her lips as a thrill of something akin to arousal spiralled upward from her exposed quim. The acknowledgment of her present condition, along with the thought of being possessed by a man as powerful as the Greek Connoisseur, made her juices rise.

She settled herself back against the bars on the bed and closed her eyes, wondering how long she had slept. Theo had said something about having her prepared, whatever that meant, but that had been ages ago.

As time wore on, the fruit bowl became depleted and the coffee pot emptied, she thought over everything Theo had told her, plus everything she had overheard. Whilst at first she hadn't fully understood the implications she now had a much clearer picture.

Yet that didn't change the way she felt. Something within her had changed; she wasn't the same woman she had been. If she was brutally honest with herself, she actually wanted- no, she corrected herself- in some peculiar way she needed Theo. She needed the kiss of the lash.

The thought struck her like a thunderbolt, leaving her trembling, her mind as well as her emotions in turmoil.

***

How long had it been since Theo had come to her? Had he tired of her so soon? Suddenly she saw herself as a once-prized concubine who has fallen from favour. Vivienne felt his absence almost as keenly as a bereavement. Anxious for his return, she moved to the edge of the bed. With one arm outstretched by the tautness of the cord, she sat with her elbow on her knee and her head resting in the palm of her hand.

Confused, her emotions crowded in. Desperately unhappy, it became too much to bear. She wept silently for her perceived loss of status, her tears spilling down her face and shaking her overwrought body with bitter anguish.

The connecting door opened and her heart missed a beat. Eagerly, she turned her head. But her spirits plummeted still further as Clitty and not Theo entered the room, carrying a bowl of delicately scented water and a fluffy white towel.

Vivienne's eyes fell on the purple welts that covered the younger girl's body, which had the effect of driving the madness from Vivienne's mind. Whatever had she been thinking of? She simply had to escape!

"Untie me, Clitty. I must make it out of here."

"How far do you think you'd get?"

Placing the bowl and towel on the bedside cabinet, Clitty took a short length of green cord from a drawer. She worked quickly, and Vivienne soon found herself lying on her back with her wrists bound together above her head, once again attached to the bedstead.

Anger flared in Vivienne's belly as her capricious nature tried to cope with the situation.

"How the hell can I escape when you waltz in here and tie me up again?"

"I'm to bathe you for inspection."

In that instant, Vivienne knew that Clitty's loyalty to Theo was unquestionable, as was her obedience. If she'd expected any help from Clitty, then she was out of luck; whatever Theo had in store for her, Clitty's compliance would be complete.

Vivienne gave a deep sigh that shook her body, and a wave of shame swept over her. Pressing her thighs tightly together, she arranged herself on the bed as comfortably as her secured wrists would allow. Realizing nothing was required of her save her presence, she tried to regulate her breathing as Clitty settled herself on the bed beside her.

"I heard people talking," she began as Clitty proceeded to bathe her overheated body. "What've they got planned for me, Clitty? Are they taking me away from here?"

"Why do you think that?"

"Theo said something about an exhibition. He took me to look at some paintings before, and I wondered-"

Clitty's giggle was a tinkling sound. "No, nothing like that. Don't wriggle so much, lie still. How can I prepare you if you struggle?" Clitty wiped the sponge over Vivienne's face, where beads of sweat had mingled with fruit juices, tears and mascara, leaving a muddy trail.

The tepid water felt refreshing on her skin. Clitty gently sponged Vivienne's outstretched arms, paying particular attention to the hollows of her underarms, then her firm, rounded breasts. Vivienne coloured up with shame as her dark brown nipples hardened in response.

Clitty's serene gaze met Vivienne's.

"Tell me truthfully, Clitty. Are you happy?"

"Yes. It's a great privilege to be one of Theo's girls, and a greater honour still to have Theo train you himself, so that you can learn how best to serve him. I envy you."

"Skip all the honour and serve shit-"

"I shouldn't even be talking to you." Clitty put the sponge in the bowl. "We're not supposed to speak at all unless asked a direct question. To break the silence rule is one of the worst offences."

Clitty began to stroke Vivienne's breasts with a soft, feathery touch, and unable to stop her, Vivienne's initial shock was tempered by a relaxing warmth. She didn't protest when Clitty took each nipple and rolled them exquisitely between finger and thumb. Powerless to fight the sweet sensations that rippled through her, Vivienne moaned softly and parted her lips.

Tendrils of pure pleasure uncoiled from deep within her. She'd never been touched so intimately by a woman before, and her brain demanded that she tell Clitty to go to hell while her senses revelled in the new sensations. Her eyes closed as Clitty, still gently working her nipples, bent her head, and covered Vivienne's lips with her own.

Clitty's pink, snaking tongue explored Vivienne's mouth. It wasn't the shy, tentative kiss of a young woman on a first date, but the hard, passionate kiss of a lover. Mouth to mouth, tongue to tongue, Vivienne relaxed and melted into the sweetness of the moment, tasting fruits on Clitty's breath.

Slowly, Clitty withdrew. "Don't make a sound," she released Vivienne's nipples, "or we'll both be punished."

Vivienne's arid throat became even drier and her eyes flicked open. There was something lascivious about the way Clitty smiled as she straightened up, dipping the sponge into the water. She held it about two feet above Vivienne's body then squeezed.

"Ooo!" Vivienne squealed as the shock of the water took her breath away, hitting her skin like a myriad tiny, icy lances.

"Shh! Do you want to be punished?" Clitty's smile was like that of a juvenile who's got one over on a parent, and for a moment Vivienne found herself wondering if Clitty would enjoy Vivienne's writhing under the lash as much as Vivienne had enjoyed watching Clitty.

"Ooohhhh!" Once again the water, like shards of fractured glass, robbed Vivienne of her breath. Her face contorted with the delightful agony as new, erotic sensations flooded through her. Flushed with shame, or arousal, she fought to hold back her squeals as the water stung her clitoris, then trickled down between her thighs.

Ultra-sensitive, her clitoris pounded with a hot, erotic rhythm that lit the blue touch paper.

"Oooohhhhhhhh!" Incapable of protest as the water rained down with pin-point accuracy, Vivienne's young body writhed with need. If her hands were free she could have relieved herself. Shocked, she realized that it was only the other day that she'd brought herself off for the first time.

"Raise your legs, Vivienne."

Without a word of dissent, she did as she was bidden.

"No, higher."

Vivienne raised them, stretching them upward.

"Good. Bend your knees and cross your ankles, so that I can see your pussy." Clitty dipped her sponge in the water, then raised it mischievously.

Vivienne trembled with sweet humiliation as Clitty, using her free hand, prised open the hot folds of Vivienne's pulsating quim. Biting into her lower lip, Vivienne braced herself.

Again she squealed as, like tiny arrows, the water stung Vivienne's tender flesh. The water trickled downward, finding its way into the very heart of her sex, bombarding her reddened flesh. She closed her eyes tightly and held her breath, praying yet at the same time dreading that Clitty's sweet torture would come to an end.

Her body tensed. Every muscle within her contracted. There was nothing she could do. Silence rule or not, Vivienne shrieked as she came, wantonly and gloriously.

Clitty smiled like a satisfied cat by the fireside, patting Vivienne's heated body with the soft towel. Then she walked to the head of the bed and took some cosmetics from the drawer. She applied mascara and kohl to Vivienne's eyes, then using a brush designed for the purpose she applied ruby coloured lipstick to her lips.

Unfastening Vivienne's aching limbs from the bedstead, Clitty said "Sit up."

Vivienne sat with her back pressed against the brass bedstead, her bound hands in her lap.

"Go to the bathroom and relieve yourself."

Vivienne raised her wrists. "Untie me, then."

"I can't. You'll have to manage as best you can."

As Clitty turned and crossed the room, Vivienne picked up the clank clank of metal. There was something black hanging down between Clitty's pale thighs.

***

Sitting on the edge of the toilet seat with her legs apart, Vivienne made a move to close them as the bathroom door flew open.

"No, don't get up." Theo stood blocking the doorway. "Stay exactly as you are."

He stepped into the bathroom and closed the door behind him. Crossing the room to stand in front of her, he looked down at her with the kind of look employed by the best poker players. He kicked her ankles apart.

Mortified to be exposed so lewdly, Vivienne positioned her tethered hands between her thighs to obscure her thatch of black hair from Theo's predatory eyes.

He snatched up her hands and placed them behind her head, which had the effect of making her succulent breasts jut out. He gave each a perfunctory suck before grabbing handfuls of her raven hair. He yanked it upward, then let it fall over her hands. Still unsatisfied with the effect, he patiently re-arranged it so that it fell haphazardly over her shoulders. Almost reaching her waist, it hung over her golden breasts, making them poke out between the strands in a teasingly appetising way that had Theo reaching for his crotch.

He took a few steps backward.

"If you think you've been humiliated beyond endurance, then you're sadly mistaken and still have much to learn. As I told you before, I take humiliation particularly seriously, and to that end have devised a little floorshow, with you as the star performer. It means that the next few minutes will be something of an ordeal for you, though it will benefit your education. I'd like to say that it's all for your own good, but it would be a Lie - it's entirely for my pleasure. But make no mistake, I will have obedience."

Paralysed by a hellish fascination, made all the more awesome by the need he provoked within her, Vivienne coloured up. Even his threats, and she was in no doubt that they were threats, had her champing at the bit. If only he would let her get off the bloody loo; it was hardly the most erotic of places to be seen. Had he any idea how uncomfortable she was with her hands behind her head?

Theo turned, opened the door, and called out to someone in the next room.

Vivienne fixed her gaze firmly on the floor. The temperature had been pleasantly maintained since her arrival, so the goose bumps that rose on her flesh had little to do with cold and more to do with anxiety. Yet even in this dreadful state, her sex trickled with the sweet fluids of arousal. She desperately wanted to close her legs but didn't dare disobey, and sat as still as if carved from a slab of marble.

Her heart rate quickened when she heard the steps on the tiles; her throat constricted when she heard the sudden, shocked intake of breath; the remnants of her dignity were torn to shreds when she heard the familiar voice...

CHAPTER EIGHT

Why did it have to be Roxanne?

Vivienne felt more vulnerable now than she ever had, surrounded as she was by complementary bottles of sweetly scented bath gels, shampoos and a basket of small soaps. Even the flurry of white towels, hanging on heated racks affixed to the ceramic wall tiles, brought home to her how subjugated she now was.

Tears welled in her eyes as surely as sap welled in her sex. She could have stood it if it had been Flynn that had come to see her in what had always been, until now, a wholly private business. Humiliation swept through her; she was drowning in shame.

Forcing herself to raise her doom-laden eyes to confront the other woman, the sheen from her unshed tears made the unusual green shade seem even more vivid.

Vivienne took in the tailored linen jacket, open to the waist to reveal a white lace bra that contained Roxanne's copiously rounded breasts, and a matching short skirt with a leather belt. Roxanne's short, choppy blond hair shone beneath the electric light, and her pink-glossed lips opened to emit a sigh.

Then the flood broke; unable to hold back any longer, a deluge of tears scalded Vivienne's cheeks, leaving murky rivers of freshly applied eye make-up where Clitty had cleansed.

Roxanne seemed delighted with the new development.

"How wonderfully degraded!" Roxanne's fringe flopped over her eyes as she took a step toward Vivienne. But Theo caught her arm and held her back.

"Don't touch her. Remember, she's nameless. She won't speak unless asked a direct question, nor will she do anything without my express command."

Vivienne was less than certain of her adherence to the rules. She wasn't finding this new condition of servitude easy and was stunned by Theo's confidence in her ability to obey.

Due to the trembling of her limbs, her distress was painfully evident. What was less evident was the trembling inside, and the tingling sensation that flirted over her body. Despite everything, she felt pulsatingly alive.

Roxanne spoke as if Vivienne were no longer present, her pale eyes alight with excitement.

"You mean she'll actually do anything you tell her?"

Theo's affirmation was a slow nod of the head.

Roxanne smiled salaciously. "She looks so wonderfully... slutty."

"What I find so delightful is that the look is completely natural." Theo's eyes overflowed with passion as he drew Roxanne's attention to the terrible welts that profaned Vivienne's thighs. "As you see, the mark of the lash becomes her." Then to Vivienne, Theo said "Stand."

Despite her shame, Vivienne's body ached with the anticipation of what was to follow. Sobbing now, she couldn't help the hot thrill of arousal that shot through her. There was an intense hunger as she had never known before; her wanton pussy was so ravenous for his cock and her taste now for the whip so keen that she briefly considered throwing herself into his arms.

Common sense and lust fought to assert themselves within her. As her golden skin turned a deeper shade of red, Vivienne longed to be anywhere other than here. If only he'd take her to the bedroom and string her up, as he had done with Clitty. She didn't want to return to work, ever, she wanted Theo to take her away to his island...

Her crushing shame made her afraid that she wouldn't be able to live up to Theo's expectations and take flight at any moment.

With her arms still behind her head, Vivienne stood. Her hair tickled her jutting breasts enticingly as she moved, and she felt the insatiable gaze of Theo's dark eyes freewheeling from her erect nipples to her juicing pussy. She thought- hoped- that he would take pity on her achingly stiff nipples and tweak their pain away.

Taking Roxanne with him, Theo backed up to make more room. "Turn around." His tone was brutally hard.

Vivienne turned around so that she stood facing the toilet with her slender back toward them. Her ragged breath caught in her throat; her nerve-endings became electrically charged as Theo spoke in a voice so laced with lustful malice that she could barely understand his thick accent.

"It's been brought to my attention that you offered one of my guards a considerable amount of money in return for your freedom. When he refused, you hit on him, begged him to satisfy your lust. You tried to tempt him further, suggesting that you run away together to some place I would never find you. What do you say, Bitch?"

Outrage emboldened her, and astounded by Farrell's treachery, she swivelled round and looked Theo full in the face. "No! I... I... He's a liar! For your information, he told me what he'd do to me, if I were his, while I sucked him off."

"Condemned by your own mouth. You're a self-centred whore, and it's my duty to punish you. You'll receive twenty lashes, ten now, ten later. It's time you learnt that you have no rights over your body, no rights at all. The days when you fucked for your advancement in the world, or merely for your own amusement are gone. Your body belongs to me; you exist solely for my enjoyment. And the moment you cease to amuse me....."

"I hate you!"

He laughed. "Of course you do, and you'll grow to hate me even more. I'll issue the invitations to take pleasure from your body- you have no say in the matter. The sooner you come to accept that, the better. There's no escape, for you're bound to me by something stronger than any chain- you're bound to me by my will." He wiped his thumb across her mouth, smudging the ruby lipstick across her face. "You'll also grow to love me, but you'll never mean more to me than..." he took a cigar from his breast pocket, lit it, took a drag, then dropped it on the floor and stubbed it out, "this."

" Let me go, or I'll....."

"You'll what? Go running to the Police?" Theo's voice was frighteningly calm." I don't think so.... D.S. Radley of the local Constabulary is enjoying the delights of my other whore at this very moment. Incidently, for breaking the silence rule, you'll receive five more lashes to add to the first ten, making fifteen."

"I'm not scared of you!"

"We'll see." Theo turned and smiled thinly at Roxanne. "I want to borrow your belt."

Vivienne's mouth dropped open. Neither her brave words nor her excitement could match the fear that choked her as she watched Roxanne unfasten the leather belt and hand it over. Vivienne's heart beat frenziedly, shifting into crisis mode as Theo curled one end around his hand. She lifted her terrified eyes to his.

"For raising your eyes to my face, five lashes to be added to the second ten, making thirty in all. Now turn around, Bitch, and keep your eyes on the floor. You'll count each strike."

Thwack! Pain lit her brain with fire as the leather cracked across the small of her back, smashing the air from her lungs.

Robbed of the ability to scream, she whimpered "One."

The next one struck her shoulders, unprotected now by her hair, with such force that she stumbled forward.

"Two"

Pain sliced through her three more times as the leather slapped across her shoulders. She wouldn't give him the satisfaction of making her scream, not now, not ever.

"On your knees, Bitch!" A laugh like a lion's roar escaped from his throat. "Scream, beg for mercy."

Vivienne's mind was reeling. She had vowed never to let herself be beaten again and yet- no, she wouldn't beg. She could hardly believe the abuse he was meting out, nor the warmth that flooded her veins. What was happening to her? A modicum of cruelty and she felt a surge of pleasure alongside the pain. She bit into her lower lip, determined that she wouldn't scream. The belt curled around her waist, landing a terrible blow across her stomach.

"Six."

Theo grabbed her shoulder and drove her down until she was

kneeling, her arms still behind her neck and her hair hanging forward.

"I demand obedience. Beg!"

She wouldn't- couldn't. Instead, she risked a glance over her shoulder.

Roxanne was standing beside Theo, a wide-eyed look of pleasure on her face, shamelessly watching, deriving some kind of perverse pleasure from Vivienne's humiliation. Hardly able to believe her own eyes, Vivienne saw the elder woman hike up her skirt.

Starbursts danced in Vivienne's brain as two further blows struck her, laying pain over pain.

"Eight." She hated having to ask a man for anything - to beg seemed like obscenity itself. Still, if that's what he wanted... "Pl... please, have pity", she whispered half- heartedly.

That seemed to turn Roxanne on even more, and her hand disappeared beneath her raised skirt as she began to frig herself.

"Eyes front and beg!" Theo censured Vivienne sharply.

She would give it her best shot, try to sound more convincing.

"Please, have mercy."

She wasn't positive that it sounded truly convincing but for the first time she was struck by how dirty her naturally husky tones sounded. The heat of shame engulfed her as she felt the tell-tale trickle of liquid down her thigh, and she bit into her lower lip as if that could somehow stop it.

She shrugged her shoulders. If Theo got off on her begging, she may as well give the man something worthwhile. She took a deep breath, then tried again- after all, she told herself, she didn't have to mean it.

"Don't hurt me."

"What's the matter, Whore? You don't scream- won't beg- perhaps the blows aren't hard enough."

Another blow had Vivienne gulping down her self-respect.

"P...Plea...se-" Her voice fractured pitifully as she pleaded for real. "I beg you, have pity on me."

"You forgot to count."

"N..nine."

That seemed to appease him somewhat. Nevertheless, he ignored her and said to Roxanne, "Let me have your panties."

Vivienne didn't dare turn around, but Theo had the white panties in his hand when he came and stood in front of her. He grabbed her arms, still tied at the wrists, and pulled them over her head so that her wrists rested on her belly. Risking an extra strike, she flicked her eyes up to his, but seeing a dark shadow cross his face she was compelled to lower them again.

"Open your mouth."

Growing fear made her comply. Before she had time to realize what was happening Theo stuffed the panties, damp from Roxanne's arousal, into Vivienne's open mouth, making her gag he pushed them farther in. When she tried to spit them out Theo's hand clamped across her mouth. Staring up at him wide-eyed, the pleading in them was totally unfeigned, carrying more sincerity than her words ever could. She'd never felt so vulnerable, so totally possessed. She retched at his cruelty and at the same time exulted in it.

Even so, her fear was so real she could taste it, and her own lust choked her as much as Roxanne's panties.

"Bound, gagged, wet and willing." His voice rasped with an intensity of passion that was almost tangible. He ran his lust-sodden eyes over Vivienne's burning body as he looked down on her. "You are willing, aren't you?"

Vivienne moaned incoherently into the makeshift gag. Despite her crushing anguish, she hoped he'd understood her assent, while in truth she realized that her assent had gone out of the window the moment Theo had entered her life.

All she could think about was how dominated she was and how dirty that made her feel. From the corner of her eye she saw Roxanne's hand working her own cunt furiously, while Vivienne's own sex was burning with a terrible hunger that was driving her insane with the need to come.

"There'll be time enough for that later." Theo stayed the blond's hand. "Your belt's too long. May I make more holes in it?"

Allowing herself a sigh of relief, Vivienne counted her lucky stars- if he had another use for the belt, then presumably he had finished beating her.

Roxanne must have given her consent, because a moment later Theo took his knife from his pocket and made several extra holes. Then he was standing behind Vivienne, his legs either side of hers. He fitted the belt across her mouth to hold the panties in, then fastened it at the back of her head with the excess length hanging down her back.

"Go to the bedroom, Roxanne, and select an instrument of your choice." When she'd gone, Theo took a couple of steps backward. He stood for several moments, savouring the spectacle of the poor, defenceless girl. "A crude, but highly effective gag that won't come loose. I'll teach you to defy me! You'll want to scream this time, I promise you. But you've been silenced so effectively that I could flay the skin from your bones, and no one would hear either your howls of protest or squeals of delight."

Roxanne returned almost immediately.

Theo came and stood at one side of Vivienne's hot and tethered body, "You'll have a better view over here, Roxanne," and waited until Roxanne had taken up a position on Vivienne's other side before addressing Vivienne again. "Rest your arms on the floor and stick your arse in the air."

Vivienne heard the swish! as Theo tested the whippy cane in the air, but outrage and terror put a brake on her desire to turn and look as he used his foot to push her head to the floor. Her right cheek was flat against the floor tiles, and with a satisfied grunt, he took up the familiar pose with his foot on her neck.

Trying to close her mind off from the sopping wetness of her pussy, Vivienne forced herself to listen to the conversation that continued above her head.

"So what do you think of your slutty friend now, Roxanne? I find it hard to believe that you live in the flat above her yet failed to realize what a horny bitch-"

"I knew she was horny," Roxanne said on a laugh "but I didn't recognise that her real calling was as a submissive. And she's never been a friend, though I can't say the same about her boyfriend. While she was shagging the guys at work, her Nathan was sharing my bed.

He's quite a good fuck, actually."

Vivienne felt herself drowning in their laughter. Rage and anger fought for supremacy within her.

"Pallister's looking into his whereabouts at this very moment. In the meantime, I have this other-"Theo stooped downward "little matter to attend to."

A line of fire raised a welt across Vivienne's bottom. Another, then another, making her tender flesh quiver in a way that brought grunts of approval from Roxanne. With pin-point accuracy, Theo brought the cane down along the crease of Vivienne's buttocks, announcing casually "I seem to have lost count."

Laughter echoed around the confines of the small room as Vivienne screamed silently into her gag. Her face was awash with tears. Helpless, she couldn't do anything but endure the lashes that came in quick succession across her shoulders, back and rounded globes of her buttocks. Fireworks exploded in her head as each strike raised angry welts.

Still the blows kept on coming, until she thought she would die. And all the while, she had to fight to stop herself from coming.

At last the agony stopped.

Without preamble, Theo's finger shot up inside Vivienne's hot sex and her muscles clenched around it like a vice. He gave a laugh that sounded like a dog barking.

"What did I tell you? Her cunt's positively dripping. She's fucking drenched."

He began to agitate her insides, working her into a frenzy. His thumb sought out the hardened bud of her clitoris. Fronds of white hot arousal had her moaning into the gag as her own thrusts drove his finger deeper.

"See how her body gyrates? She's totally helpless to stop it."

To Vivienne's shame, it was true. The lower part of her body was in total control as she ground down on his finger. Her moans grew louder as the pressure on her neck from his foot increased.

Vivienne's muscles tensed. She prayed as she fought a desperate battle to hold back that Roxanne would have the decency to leave the room before she finally climaxed. But Roxanne stood her ground.

Vivienne's muscles went into spasm. She screwed up her eyes as, silenced by the cruel gag, she came gloriously, tremors racking her body. Then, as her climax finally subsided, her legs collapsed beneath her. She lay in a heap on the floor.

Theo removed his finger. Straightening up, he removed his foot from her neck.

"See how sweet she tastes, Roxanne."

Vivienne numbed as she heard Roxanne sucking enthusiastically at Theo's finger, and felt jealousy nudging alongside her shame.

Theo kicked her in the ribs.

"Arse in the air again!"

When she had complied with his wishes, he came round behind her and stood between her open thighs. Bending down, he put a hand on each buttock and spread her rounded cheeks apart.

"I think a larger plug next time."

Vivienne felt a coldness penetrate through her body, and realized it was the chill of fear, not the floor tiles.

"Get up, Bitch. Turn around and back up towards the toilet. Straighten up and sit back on your heels." Theo waited until Vivienne was in the required position, then came and stood beside her.

He grabbed her wrists roughly and looped her arms behind her head again so that her breasts jutted out as provocatively as before. He thrust his hand in his pocket, pulled out another length of cord and walked round behind her. Trembling, she felt the new cord bite into her flesh as he fastened it tightly around her ankle. Jerking it upward, he looped it around the cord at her wrists and then, turning her collar so that the ring was at the back he passed the cord through. He yanked it downward, so that she was obliged to bend her back as he threaded the cord through the knot at her wrists, then attached the loose end to her other ankle. It felt as if her back were about to break.

Protesting at the agonizingly uncomfortable position in which she now found herself, she moaned into the gag.

Theo smiled thinly. Standing a couple of feet in front of her, he reached across and took Roxanne by the arm. Flicking his eyes in Vivienne's direction he instructed "Keep your eyes open and watch." Then, as gently as a lover, he pulled Roxanne towards him, encircling her in his arms.

Vivienne's features crumpled as Theo drew Roxanne into a tight embrace. His lips covered those of the blond, and Vivienne's stomach lurched as Theo's beautiful, strong fingers entwined themselves in Roxanne's hair. He slid the jacket from her shoulders, then his hand slipped behind to undo her bra. That joined the jacket on the floor as Roxanne's rounded breasts with their erect, pink nipples, were exposed.

Vivienne's heart was breaking. She had no choice but to watch as his other hand slid down the blond's back and up her skirt, while Roxanne's hands reached for his fly.

It was as if a knife twisted in Vivienne's stomach. Dying inside, she momentarily closed her eyes tightly, sobbing as the other woman took out Theo's engorged prick. When she opened them again it was to find that Theo had leaned Roxanne backward over the vanity unit. Standing between her long, shapely legs, he was fucking her so vigorously that their joint cries of climax were soon echoing around the room.

While their fucking actually lasted little more than a few minutes it left Vivienne shaken to the bone, and numb with jealously. She hated Roxanne more now than she ever had. Through narrowed eyes she watched as Theo withdrew and wiped his cock clean on one of the fluffy white towels.

After Roxanne had cleaned herself, she swanned off through the door, calling back almost as an afterthought, "What about her?"

"She'll have the rest of her beating later."

"You lost count- she must have had the whole thirty by now."

"Nevertheless, she'll have another fifteen." Theo kissed Vivienne on the lips before following Roxanne out of the bathroom.

The door closed behind him with a soft thud, leaving Vivienne feeling wretched. Still bound wrists to ankles, she sobbed piteously into the gag fashioned from Roxanne's damp panties and leather belt.

***

Farrell wasn't alone when he came to fetch her.

"Here, Woodly, you'll need this."

He tossed a wicked-looking knife across to the second man, who caught it deftly by the ivory-coloured handle.

Of the same build as Farrell, Woodly had the sort of face that looked as if he'd walked into a wall, and put Vivienne in mind of a rather mean bulldog she had known as a child.

Farrell came round behind her. He removed the belt and panties then tossed them across the room. Standing with his heavy hands on her shoulders, he made her wince as his fingers traced the lines of the terrible lashes, searing her flesh anew.

"There's some cream to help them heal somewhere in here. You'll have to look around." His soft tone could have been mistaken for kindness, but Vivienne was learning fast and was quick to notice the catch in his throat as he continued "Then, when they're all nice and healed he'll have you beaten all over again, twice as hard."

He sauntered across to the doorway, blew her a kiss, then left her still cruelly bound and at the mercy of Woodly.

"You're wanted downstairs, but we've got a bit of time to kill." Woodly leaned closer. "What shall we do? This, perhaps?"

He came round behind her.

Her whole body relaxed as he used the knife to cut the cord that bit into her wrists. Then he cut the length that had been looped through her collar ring, enabling her to straighten up. She spent a few seconds rubbing her wrists and wondered if the marks of the cord would ever disappear, then buried her face in her hands.

But the relief was short lived as, instead of releasing her other bonds, he merely adjusted them. Retying her wrists, he grabbed her hair again and yanked her backward, further than before and curving her back painfully. Without allowing her to fully lie back he tied her wrists to her ankles.

To keep her in the uncomfortable, back-breaking, half-lying, half-kneeling position, he opened a cabinet in the vanity unit and took out what appeared to be, and indeed was, a kind of metal tripod designed especially for the purpose. Opening it up, he positioned the three legs over her ankles and placed her neck in the velvet lined, Ushaped neck rest.

With her back taut as an archer's bow, she felt as if it were breaking in two. And it was all she could do to stop herself from crying out.

He walked around and in front of her. Bending down, with his face inches from her own he looked down at her. Taking a packet of cigarettes from his pocket, he pushed one up and drew it from the packet with his lips. At the same moment as he lit up and took a drag, he kicked her knees apart, exposing the inviting folds of her quim.

She spluttered as he blew smoke into her face.

"Quiet!" He took the cigarette from between his lips and held the glowing tip close to her cheek. "Any more noise and I'll give you something to make a noise about."

With a sideways glance towards the cigarette, she swallowed hard. She watched as he put it back between his thick lips, wondering if she really would leave this place in one piece.

Suddenly, without the luxuries of either lubrication or warning, Woodly shoved the handle of the knife up her gaping sex. Roughly, he thrust it in and out, in and out, before turning his attention, nasty and in no way erotic, to her breasts. He slapped their undersides several times in quick succession, grinning down at her as they bounced around, the force of his hand thumping one against the other.

How was it, she wondered, that the brutal malevolence of Theo could turn her pussy into a juicing machine and set her insides on fire while this brute just left her scared and cold.

Leaving the knife in place, Woodly stood over her. He unzipped his fly and thrust his thick cock deep in her throat, making her gag as the combined scents of urine, sweat and tobacco smoke assailed her nostrils.

"I've heard you give a pretty good blow job - I hope for your sake that I heard right."

Pumping her throat for all he was worth, with the cigarette dangling from the corner of his mouth, he looked down into her tear-stained face. His lips curved into an ugly grimace.

With her head held backward in the neck rest, there was nothing she could do but yield to his loathsome brutality as he pounded into her. Almost choking as she struggled to breathe and suck at the same time, she knew that whatever Theo had planned for her, nothing could be worse than this.

Suddenly, with a whoop of delight Woodly exploded in her mouth. It seemed as if gallons of scalding come hit the back of her throat. As she gagged and spluttered wretchedly, she accidentally scratched her teeth along the length of his cock as he withdrew. Gasping for air she spat out as much of his come as she was able and choked on the rest.

"Next time you'll swallow it!"

He took the cigarette butt from between his lips. For a moment she thought he would burn her, but to her relief he tossed the cigarette down the toilet. Then, breathing his tobacco-breath over her, he brought his lips down over hers. As she again struggled for air, she heard the door open as Farrell returned.

"I'll teach you to bite me!" Breaking away from her, Woodly brought his face level with her breasts. Taking one of her nipples between his teeth, he bit down hard.

"Aaarghhh!" Vivienne screamed. And then screamed again as he bit into her other nipple.

Quick as a flash, he withdrew the knife's handle from her quim and positioned the blade against her thigh. "Guess what? You've just broken the silence rule again!" Farrell said nothing, but looked on with some amusement. He dropped what appeared to be a bundle of chains on the floor.

Woodly pulled the blade away, walked behind her, removed the tripod and cut through the cord. Once she was free, Farrell handed her a glass of some kind of pink liquid which he ordered her to drink. Then he told her to relieve herself while he and Farrell watched.

Colouring up, she felt she would die of shame as she squatted over the toilet.

"Shower" Woodly said. "We'll stay here and watch, just to make sure you don't slip."

Both men laughed as she closed the door of the shower cubicle.

Alone at last, she looked down at her once unblemished golden body. Now there were purple weals across her thighs and across her belly, to say nothing of those she couldn't see that patterned her back.

"I don't think you understand," Farrell said as he opened the cubicle door, "when we say watch, that's exactly what we mean. Now hurry up, or you'll be late for your appointment downstairs."

CHAPTER NINE

Back in Paston Wick, a woman opened the door a crack to Flynn's knock.

"I'm looking for Nathan. Is he here?"

"Who wants him?"

Flynn rested his hand against the door and pushed it open. "Is he here or not?"

Dressed up to the nines and obviously about to go out on the town, the dark- haired woman stood her ground.

"I said 'who wants him?'"

Flynn pushed his way inside the suburban house.

"I'll have this place torn apart if I have to." He indicated a man sitting in a car parked outside. "I suggest you tell Nathan he's got a visitor. It would be to his advantage to hear what I have to say. Shall we go through?" His hand gesture took in the hallway. "You lead the way."

She opened a door on the left. "Nathan-"

Flynn pushed past her. Nathan, downing his third whisky, got to his feet as Flynn closed the door, leaving the woman in the hall.

"We meet at last, Nathan. We've spoken on the phone, and as we've so much in common I thought I'd call by to tell you some news about that little trollop you-"

"Vivienne?" Surprise, followed at once by anger and recognition, crossed Nathan's features. "Then you must be Pallister. If you want her, you can have her. As you say, she's a trollop, and I wash my hands of her. As you see..." the sweep of his hand took in the entire room, along with a wedding photograph on the mantelpiece, "my ex-wife and I are giving it another go."

"Highly commendable I'm sure, but I don't think you understand. While it's true that I know where Vivienne is, it isn't I who have her."

"Someone's kidnapped her?" Concern crossed Nathan's face.

"Not exactly."

"Is it ransom you want?"

"May I sit down? A drink, perhaps?"

Nathan crossed to the drinks cabinet and poured Flynn a large scotch. "Where is she? What do you want? Come to the point or get out."

Flynn waited until they were both seated. He took a swig form his glass and cast a glance around the room.

"Nice place you've got here. It would be a shame if it were to be messed up."

"Meaning?"

Flynn laughed softly. "I would have thought that you'd understand my meaning perfectly. However, perhaps I can clarity the situation. The fewer people who know of our meeting, the better. I wasn't aware you'd been married and have had no time to check out your ex-wife. If she should say anything-"

"Say your piece and get out!"

"Oh, I intend to. But after what I have to say, I think you'll probably be coming with me."

***

It was bad enough that Vivienne's wrists were attached by means of the leather straps to the ring of her collar. But to have her ankles manacled made walking almost impossible. With Farrell coming along behind her and Woodly dragging her along by a chain lead that was also fastened to her collar, Vivienne made her way as best she could along the red carpeted corridor.

She was beginning to feel lightheaded. Whatever the drink Farrell had given her was, it didn't seem to agree with her at all.

Ignoring the lift, the two men took her down the service stairs.

Naked and barefoot, she shivered as they descended the steep stairwell. When they at last reached the first floor they took her down another carpeted hallway, lined on either side by guests' rooms. She would die from shame if someone were to leave their room and see her.

At last they came to the main staircase, with its red-roped banisters on either side, that swept downward to the elegant reception area through which Theo had led her on her arrival.

The manacles around her ankles made descending difficult. It was made more difficult still by the effects of the drink, which seemed to have affected her co-ordination. More than once she lost her footing and stumbled, only to be roughly hauled upright by Farrell. Woodly, however, made no allowances and dragged her along regardless.

Having been moved from one heavily draped room to another and kept in near darkness since her arrival, Vivienne had lost all conception of time. She could have been in the hotel for days. Only the empty feeling in her stomach gave her an indication that it had been hours since she'd had any real food. That must be it; she was being taken back to the dining room.

God! She would have to endure the humiliation of a crowded room all over again.

Momentarily relieved that there was no one in the sumptuous reception area to witness her shameful entrance, she was suddenly struck with horror as a door opened and the hotel staff crowded into the small opening. Kitchen staff, porters, waiters- they were all there, some giggling, some whispering, but all looking her up and down as if she were a prize winning exhibit at a county fair.

She felt woozy, and it suddenly dawned on her that they must have given her some sort of drug.

The guards didn't stop at the dining room but led her straight past and down a another corridor. Having gone some distance, they came to a door with a brass plaque that announced they had arrived at the hotel's famed theatre. Many a new playwright, struggling actor and even the occasional opera singer had had their careers launched at this particular, rather exclusive theatre. It was one of the many attractions of the up- market hotel- a hotel the likes of which people like Vivienne seldom saw the interiors of.

The door opened and Vivienne was flung inside. Stumbling awkwardly, she fell forward and found herself alone at the back of the pitch black room, sprawled inelegantly on the floor.

The door closed behind her and in the same moment a bright spotlight lit up the stage. And there in the centre of the beam, surrounded by darkness, sat Clitty.

***

Sitting in the middle seat of the middle row, Theo knew he couldn't be seen. He'd been sitting here in the dark for about twenty minutes, eagerly awaiting what promised to be an exceptional show.

And if everything went according to plan regarding Flynn's current assignment, he would soon have a new recruit, too. There was something inordinately satisfying about manipulating situations and the lives they contained within them.

He checked his watch. Things were running late- no doubt his guards had something to do with it. His thin lips curved into a smile.

In his hand he held his latest acquisition. Acquired for him at auction that very afternoon, it had cost him a quarter of a million pounds. His fingers glided over it lovingly. He'd lusted over this particular piece, an Art Deco figurine of gilded bronze and ivory, for years. About fourteen inches in height, it depicted a bare-breasted woman wearing arm bands and a tight fitting long skirt. It was an exceptional piece...

He turned his head as the door opened. He heard the rattling of chains and the thud! as the slut hit the floor.

This girl was turning out to have real entertainment value, he thought as he heard her struggle to her feet. So much so that he had decided to indulge himself with a private show before exhibiting her publicly.

He congratulated himself on his progress so far. It was a pity that he'd had to have her drugged but after her defiance earlier, he'd been left with little choice. At least this way he could count on her obedience, for tonight he was in no mood to discipline her- tonight he had something else in mind.

The girl's progress was slow, the manacles impeding her movements to a satisfying extent. Already his prick was stirring.

***

With her head full of cotton wool, Vivienne made her way slowly towards the front of the auditorium. She leaned her elbows against the side of the stage and looked up. Black curtains hung across the back and sides of the stage. The wings were in darkness.

Clitty was perched on an upright, wooden block, like an alabaster statue on a bronze plinth. About five feet in height, it had four steps cut into the side on Vivienne's left. Leaning slightly forward, Clitty rested her dainty feet on the second step. This forced her pale legs upward so that her knees were on a level with her pink-tipped breasts.

Vivienne thought she looked magnificent. Her ivory skin looked stark against the black background, and was further emphasised by a black girdle, the same as the one they had both worn the first night in all except one feature- this one had an array of curling black feathers of about three feet long attached to the back. Arranged flamboyantly, they resembled the tail of some exotic bird. A bird of paradise, Vivienne thought with a giggle.

Clitty's black gloves reached to her elbow and stressed the elegance of her arms, just as the paleness of her neck was emphasised by the black slave collar. And with her tawny hair piled on top of her head, she put Vivienne in mind of a painting, a portrait she had seen somewhere.

Keeping her eyes straight ahead, Clitty whispered "You're to come up here."

In her present stupor, it never occurred to Vivienne to protest. Slowly she made her way up the steps at the end of the stage.

Clitty opened her arms wide in greeting.

The sight of the enchanting Clitty sitting demurely before her drove all other thoughts from Vivienne's mind. She was aware only of the frisson of electricity that warmed her insides.

"Come, Vivienne." Clitty beckoned her towards the wooden plinth, and Vivienne soon found herself with her toes pressed against the bottom step. "Now we'll make love."

Through the mist, Vivienne heard her own husky voice. "Look, about before-" she fought to make her mind work, unaware that every word she said was picked up by strategically placed microphones, "it should never have happened. You've made a mistake. I'm not a-"

"Neither am I. Nevertheless, we're here together, alone, so we'll make love."

Leaning closer, Vivienne let out an indignant snort. "Don't be so bloody stupid!"

Without further ado, Clitty also leaned further forward, so that barely a breeze could pass between their heads. Grasping Vivienne's right breast tightly in her upturned palm, Clitty kneaded it gently. With her free hand, she clutched at Vivienne's tethered hands. Then she straightened up, hauling Vivienne up the steps until Vivienne found herself kneeling between Clitty's pale thighs.

Clitty took Vivienne's dark, already painfully erect nipple between finger and thumb, twirling and flicking with an expert touch. When Vivienne responded with little moans of pleasure, Clitty drew Vivienne's other breast level with her mouth. Flicking her long, pink tongue over the hard morsel of brown flesh, Clitty continued to work the first with tiny, circular movements that drove Vivienne to distraction.

Clitty whispered raggedly against the swell of Vivienne's breast.

"Listen to me. Follow my lead and do as I say. You don't want any more beatings, do you? Be warned, there's a special room on the island- you don't ever want to end up there!"

"Why not?" Vivienne hissed back.

"Sh! I've already said too much."

When she'd finished speaking, Clitty took the whole nipple into the warmth of her mouth and devoured it lasciviously.

Almost overcome by the sheer pleasure of the exhilarating charges that shot through her, Vivienne moaned softly. Engulfed in a billowing tide of erotic euphoria, her breathing became more rapid.

But somewhere in the back of her mind there was a miscellany of emotions fighting to make themselves known. She wanted to escape from the debauchery she'd misguidedly let herself be drawn into, yet found Clitty's touch too delectable.

Her head tilted backward and she closed her eyes, her moans increasing as Clitty's skilled fingers and mouth did their work.

Clitty drew her lips away. and let her hand drop to her side.

"Open your eyes, Vivienne." Clitty's voice rang out through the auditorium. "I want to show you something."

With her head still reeling, Vivienne slowly drew back her eyelids. Following the direction of Clitty's gaze, she saw that while pleasuring Vivienne with one hand, the fingers of Clitty's free hand had been frantically stimulating her own clitoris. Her finger was still inserted deep between the lips of her glistening sex.

Vivienne suddenly froze with utter revulsion. She shrank back, hardly able to believe what she was seeing. Clitty wore a ring of the same black metal as her collar, passed through one of her deep pink, swollen labia lips.

Vivienne's mouth opened to admit a cry but no sound came out as she stared in abject horror. It wasn't so much that she was pierced, it was the size of the ring that stunned her. Even through the drug-induced haze she recognized that Clitty's was no ordinary ring, it was much, much bigger. Over an inch in diameter, it was about the thickness of a ring one finds in a loose-leaf binder. Hanging from it were a couple of links, and hanging from the last one was a small key.

And not only that. There was a second chain that was affixed to the top of the wooden block, making it impossible for Clitty to move without doing herself an injury.

"Is...is that the key to your c...collar?"

"No, I told you, mine has a special locking mechanism. Like the ring, it can only be cut off." Remembering her master's orders, Clitty spoke clearly, leaving out nothing.

"The key is a symbol to remind me of my condition as a slave, and can't be removed. The Master didn't only wanted me pierced for practical reasons, such as restraint, but wanted my condition to be obvious to everyone. Even when I walk the chains clang. Not only that, but he wanted it to be so heavy that I couldn't ever grow used to wearing it."

"Why?" Even as she asked Vivienne knew the answer.

"Because he demands suffering, mental and physical from his slaves. It's what pleases him."

Ashen faced, Vivienne stared at the ring. This couldn't be happening; the whole slavery-thing was getting beyond a joke. She was having some kind of weird dream, a mind-blowing hallucination. She would wake up in a moment and be back in her flat, preparing to meet Flynn and his Greek associate. They were about to close a deal, and they needed her...

Unseen by Vivienne, Clitty flicked her eyes towards the darkness, trying to make out where her master sat. As if receiving an invisible signal, she wound her fingers in Vivienne's long, raven hair.

"I need a man to go down on me, but since there isn't one around, you'll have to do." Clitty's voice took on a mesmeric, chanting tone while her words were almost poetic. "Taste my sweet juices, dip your tongue into the honeyed warmth of my pussy."

Even in her confused state Vivienne hesitated. What if someone were to see them? She would die with shame if anyone were to catch her in the act. She had never done anything like this before, and wouldn't want people to think that she liked women that way.

Clitty said mendaciously "Don't be afraid. No one will ever know, only you and I. It'll be our secret." She pressed Vivienne's face hard against her glistening sex. "Taste me, drink my sap."

Despite everything, Vivienne's insides were aflame. All remnants of inhibitions drained away as, in the rapture of the moment she complied. Her hands, still tethered to her collar, groped at the top step as she buried her head deeper between Clitty's pale thighs and, flicking her tongue over Clitty's dew-covered nether lips, she lapped Clitty's luscious liquids.

Then, becoming bolder, she thrust her tongue deep into the warm depths. The metal of the cruel ring and heavy links pressed hard against her cheek while Clitty's fragranced fleece tickled her.

And the eidetic picture that built up in her mind thrilled her. What a wonderful sight they must make, she naked and shackled, with her face buried in the dripping cunt of another woman. What would an on-looker think if they should happen to come upon them? The thought generated such a sizzling hot thrill that she sucked even harder.

She felt the beginnings of Clitty's orgasm as the muscles tightened around her tongue. Clitty's hands gripped the back of Vivienne's head -there would be no escaping the violence of her convulsions. Then powerful spasms suddenly ripped through the younger woman.

As Clitty screamed out in wild abandon, Vivienne's body also tensed. She heard her own moans as her orgasm built up.

But Vivienne was allowed no such luxury. Strange, black-gloved hands gripped her legs; others grabbed her round the waist. Dressed entirely in black with masks covering their faces, her abductors carried her to another part of the stage. Lying her down on her back, one pair of hands removed her wrists from her collar. Then the chain linking her wrists together was removed, leaving the wrists straps in place, and the same was done to her ankles.

Before she could scramble to her feet, she heard the terrible clanking of heavy chains. In terror she realized that one was being attached to each ankle strap and others to her wrists. Then there was the sound of machinery above her and she felt herself being raised off the floor, pulling her arms and legs upward. She let out a shriek as her legs were opened wide, as were her arms, until she was in a sort of X.

Her own weight caused the skin across her back to tighten. She cried out as a fire raged across her back as her welts were stretched. Every part of her throbbed with pain.

Her arms and legs were pulled taut and her head hung downward as she was hoisted higher. Feeling faint as the blood rushed to her head she thought she would black out at any moment.

With a jolt that sent shock waves crashing through her, the machinery locked in place. But it wasn't over yet- without warning she was swung back across the stage.

Glancing down, she saw that she was only a few feet above the floor. When she stopped moving, two arms grabbed her legs and guided her towards the goal.

It was only then that she began to understand what was happening.

Clitty's hands guided Vivienne's legs until she was able to rest one on each shoulder. Then, inch by inch, Vivienne was moved towards the other woman. At last she came to a stop, with her crotch pressed snugly against Clitty's soft lips.

Clitty's tongue probed deep inside Vivienne's quim. Dying with shame, and desire, she shuddered as the tip of Clitty's tongue sought out her hardened clitoris. After only a short interval of bliss, her body tensed. She caught her breath. She moaned. She was going to come-

At the very last moment, the machinery started and she was lifted free. Sobbing now with frustration and fear she could do nothing but let her head hang down, her wonderful hair like a curtain. With taut arms and legs she was raised even higher, elevated to a position that, if the theatre lights were on, she could have seen the entire auditorium.

As suddenly as the spotlight had been turned on, the stage was now plunged into darkness. The machinery stopped. And the chink chink of chains and various scuffling sounds many feet below her suggested that Clitty was being released.

"Don't leave me! Please!" Vivienne wailed at the top of her voice, but no help came. "Please! I beg you! Have pity!"

Surely they hadn't forgotten her?

At last, everything was quiet and she was alone in the darkness, suspended from the rafters.

The last thing she was aware of before slipping into unconsciousness was a loud groan that seemed to come from the middle of the theatre. It sounded just as if someone were shooting their load...

CHAPTER TEN

Vivienne awoke from her stupor. Exhaustion and the drug had ensured that she had slept soundly for hours. Whether it was day or night she couldn't tell, for she was still in darkness. No longer suspended, she was lying on something hard and, racked with pain she groaned loudly. Immediately she was dazzled by a spotlight, and realized that she was still on the stage.

She blinked rapidly, her nerves juddering, and tried to shield her eyes. Stricken with terror, she found shc could move her arms barely more than an inch. Dread churned in the pit of her belly and travelled to her sand-papered throat. Pain laid siege to her arms, and a dreadful ache in her armpits made her acutely aware of muscles she never knew she had. Struggling vainly to shift position to try and relieve the discomfort, the alarm bells only really began to clang at full pelt when a jangling sound assailed her ears.

As her eyes slowly became accustomed to the brightness of the beam, she saw that a full length mirror had been set up beside her. Dredging up every last shred of courage, she turned her head. With the spotlight projecting its harsh brilliance upon her, she saw her prone body in naked explicitness, and a high-pitched squeal erupted from her parched throat.

With her body marked by bruises and welts, she was lying on a raised wooden platform. Placed centre stage, facing the dark auditorium, the mirror blocked her view of the wings to her left. The reflection threw back the image of a wooden cabinet placed alongside her right shoulder. Glancing now to her right, she saw she was completely alone on the stage.

By means of short a chain attached to the leather straps at her ankles and wrists, her arms and legs were stretched out tautly, held in place by chains affixed to each corner. There was another strap under her breasts that held her flat to the platform, and another one still across the top of her breasts, imprisoning the golden twin globes.

Jerking against the chains wildly she kicked her feet in a frantic attempt to somehow raise herself. But it was impossible.

With her arms stretched almost to the limit of physical endurance and her legs open wide, the deep cleft between her thighs would be visible to anyone in the audience.

Audience? Panic gripped her as she listened for sounds- anything at all to ascertain whether or not she was being used in some kind of perverted sex show. Was this the exhibition she'd heard Theo speak of? Were he and his friends that twisted?

Feeling like a trussed-up turkey waiting to be devoured, Vivienne bit into her bottom lip and whimpered. Picked up by the microphones, it was boosted many times.

A tiny sound that came from the blackness of the orchestra pit caught her attention. Holding her breath she listened, as anxiously as a dog listens for the sound of his returning master, but heard nothing save the beating of her own erratic heart.

Suddenly, a terrifying form, like the spectre of evil from some horror movie detached itself from the protection of the pitch-dark shadows. Intimidating and mysterious, the figure was clad in a black silk, balaclava-type mask, with a small zipper where his mouth should be, and an ankle-length, black silk cloak that fastened at the neck sheathing his nakedness.

Slowly, he advanced towards her.

Terror-stricken, knowing she was helpless to defend herself against any outrage he cared to perpetrate, Vivienne sucked in her breath. The resulting tightening of her belly and swell of her breasts brought a muffled growl of approval from the apparition.

The blood froze in her veins, and inexplicably, juice began to leak from her gaping sex.

Her nerves were brittle as a fine decanter deposited into a bottle bank, and her voice broke into as many pieces when she tried to speak.

'Wh...who are you? W...w...what do y..you want?'

She realized it was an absurd question, but then the whole situation had an absurd quality about it. And, as with the best theatre, it was breathtakingly gripping.

He stepped forward to stand in the light. She turned her head to watch as with cold precision he set a goblet of blood-red wine on the cabinet. Some corner of her brain that was still functioning normally registered the fact that a figurine stood beside it.

Unzipping his mouth, he leaned across her exposed body.

Trembling, she felt his hot breath as he homed in on her neck, like a blood-lusting vampire inexorably drawn to the pale flesh of an exposed throat. In little doubt that she would be found drained of blood with two tiny punctures in her neck, every particle of her being tensed with the expectation of the abominations that she feared were only seconds away.

His long, snaking tongue flicked a tingling trail from her earlobe to her collarbone, then back again, with the tenderness of a cat washing its kitten. The silence was almost mystical as he continued down between her breasts, leaving a wake of saliva that left an after-sensation of coldness as it dried.

He placed his hands on her succulent breasts, as yet unblemished by the lash. His fingers feathered over her golden spheres, caressing and stroking, kneading and massaging her slowly into a state of utter relaxation. And, gripped by the dizzying effects of his seduction, Vivienne relished his soft exploitation of her cruelly exposed and chained body as if it were the last act of gentleness she would ever know.

For even as he ignited a response of something vital inside her, giving her life a clarity as she'd never known before, he threatened to take it away. In her heart she knew that, like the vampire, her hooded lover only feigned affection, and was in little doubt that his heart was as cold as the grave.

He seemed suddenly to change his mind, and with lightning speed forsook her breasts and clamped his hand over her mouth. Petrified, she stared at him wide-eyed and sank her teeth into his flesh.

She must have bitten him harder than she thought because he snatched his hand away with a cry, and a threat that left her in no doubt that the sensitivity was over.

"You'll pay for that. Now it's your turn to scream." His voice, distorted by some kind of mechanism in his mouth, sounded like one of those electronically synthesized voices, cold and impersonal, un-recognizable as human.

He bent down to remove something from inside the cabinet. When he straightened up, Vivienne shook with terror. She had a strong desire to scream but with his threat still echoing in her mind she fought against giving him that satisfaction. Besides which, when she opened her mouth to give full reign to her fear, the sound wouldn't come out and choked in her throat. At first glance, what appeared to be ordinary nipple clamps were in fact far more sinister. Vivienne saw that the clamps were joined by a flex.

Teasing each nipple in turn until it stood hard as a bullet, he applied some kind of gel to each before he clamped each nipple. Then she saw the flex had a plastic-covered wire coming from it, which he attached to what appeared to be a box with dials and knobs on it.

Realization sliced through her at the same time as the pain- the current leapt through her tortured flesh and her scream, picked up by the microphones, filled the theatre with the anguished cries of a torture chamber.

He turned off the current. Hardly able to believe what he'd done to her, she stared up at the cruel eyes that pierced her through the slits of his mask.

"Bastard!"

His hand gripped the controls and again the current was turned on. Her body leapt and quivered. If it weren't for the straps that held her down she felt sure that her body would have been thrown clear of the platform.

"What kind of madman are-"

The current cut her off and her screams rang out.

"Unpleasant as it may be, as it's designed to be-" like a predator marking its prey, he kept his hungry eyes fixed on her as he spoke, "it will do you no harm as long as you co-operate. But don't let that give you a false sense of security. With this little box of tricks, I have the power of life and death."

The slight disturbance of her trembling body made her chains clink, which in turn had the strange effect of driving her wild with mad desires. How could she possibly be enjoying this torture, she asked herself. And his electronic tones didn't do a thing to lessen those desires; indeed they sustained them.

" For hours I've watched you as you've lain spread-eagled, naked and shackled. Your mouth-watering tits, heaving with each breath, had me panting to abuse them. Your cunt, flushed with arousal, feverish, red and parted, made me ache to ravish you in your enforced helplessness. I've been driven crazy with the longing to see my seed spattered over your defenceless body. You've no idea what you do to me."

With the opening of his cloak forced open by his rampant cock, Vivienne was in little doubt as to what she did to him, the same as she was in no doubt that his masked features were distorted with wild lust. On the other hand, her own emotions were less easy to define.

His hand reached for the controls again. This time the current was reduced and flowed through her, making her quiver and twitch as all kinds of new feelings, not all of them unpleasant, began to assail her in ways she could never have imagined.

If it had to be endured, she told herself defiantly, then she could at least try to blot it out, close her mind to the madly erotic images that her mind conjured up. But, gripped by a paroxysm of wonderful quivers and shudders as he removed the clamps and gently fondled her breasts, Vivienne was helpless to ward off the fire that raged in her belly or stem the heated wetness that gushed from her pussy.

Without even a thin veneer of sophistication, he thrust his long, probing finger deep into her wide open sex. Withdrawing it again almost immediately, he held it up for her to see how it glistened with her juices. He ran his tongue up its length, put it in his mouth and sucked it, before re-fastening the zipper.

Speaking through the zippered mask, his electronic voice was nevertheless laced with the intensity of lust.

"You taste delicious. I've never met a woman that juices as freely as you do. And how delectable you are with fear in those extraordinarily green eyes- a gastronomic delight in leather and chains. I've never seen a slit so ripe for ravishing. I'm going to fuck you so hard that it'll rip you in two, like a peach cleaved by a sabre."

As she lay helpless her senses were awash with conflicting intensity of feelings. Spirals of something bordering on need tingled from her tight breasts to her quim. Fire spread throughout her insides, while every fibre of her being told her she should be afraid. Menace was everywhere, pervading the very air she breathed.

But as her masked lover appeared to know only too well, the keenness of her arousal was dramatically heightened by her discomfort and fear, creating within her a breathtaking need for him to fill her burning, empty sex.

His finger, agitated and anxious, prowled through the dense black filaments that curled at the apex of her thighs, giving them a sharp tug that brought tears glittering to her terror-stricken eyes. She wanted this dark, gothic figure as she had never wanted anyone before; she needed him.

She was also scared stiff.

His fingers explored her saturated pussy, alternating aggression with tenderness until she thought she would die from the sheer ecstasy of his touch. Yanking at her chains, she tossed her head from side to side, as pressure on her clitoris sent her into delirium. The pleasure was too painful as he rubbed it briskly, working her clitoris remorselessly until she cried out, barely able to stand the thrill of it.

"So, you like to be frigged by strangers? Is it the fear, the chains, or the unknown identity of your seducer that gets you so steamed-up?"

How long she was forced to endure the deliciously tormenting attentions of his skilled digits she couldn't tell, nor how many times he took her to the crest of a wave only to bring her down again. His cruelty soon had her begging to come. Her muscles clenched around his finger and her body jerked against her chains, as again and again she neared climax. But even as she hovered on the brink of ecstatic turmoil, he withdrew his glistening finger with a brisk movement that left her gasping.

"No-" he said sternly, "not yet."

As he climbed on top of her his cloak billowed around him, again putting her in mind of a vampire lusting for blood. Without further ado, his iron hard shaft impaled her, and her whole body stiffened in sweet apprehension as she anticipated the savagery of his frenzied lust.

She wasn't disappointed. While he sat astride her with his cock thrusting ferociously in and out, he squeezed her imprisoned breasts roughly in his huge hands. He flicked her tortured, ultra-tender nipples with his thumbs, and the pain that assaulted them was almost too much to bear- almost, but not quite.

"What's the matter?" His chuckle told her that he knew exactly what the matter was. "Painful, are they? Believe me, Slut, they haven't tasted pain yet."

He pulled back the zip that covered his lips and spat out the small device that had distorted his voice. Lowering his silk-hooded head to her breast, he grazed the hard morsel of flesh with the jagged teeth of the zip as he took her nipple in his mouth. Again, he chuckled as she flinched. His teeth closed around it and, with a tigerish growl, he bit down.

Clenching and unclenching her fists, her howls filled the theatre. Yet before they had subsided she was drowning in the erotic sensations that rippled through her as he twirled each rigid, dark nipple between finger and thumb, turning the core of her being to liquid sensuality. He quickened his thrusts, and his cock seemed to take on a life of its own, plunging to the deepest depths of her being.

Flames of desire licked the walls of her womb. And she welcomed each powerful thrust of this sadistic profligate as if it were the last she would ever know, bucking and writhing beneath his thrilling caress.

"If you climax now I'll see you get a thrashing."

Something told her that it wasn't an idle threat; that this cruel, brutal, sensual stranger, with eyes that devoured her through the holes in his mask, would like nothing more than to see her punished. A frisson of alarm ran through her. She whimpered and writhed, trying to hold back the climax that she so desperately longed for. The leather that bound her breasts seemed to tighten, almost restricting her breathing.

"You're the horniest bitch I've had in a long time- such a crazed wanton that, even as you lie shackled with your tits bound for pleasure and your nipples charged with electricity, you relish the unknown prick that rapes you."

His words rasped derision, humiliating her with every breath as he thrust his cock even harder, seemingly turned on by the scorn that he heaped upon her.

"You're completely in my power. Dominated and abused, even that can't put the lid on your lust. You're nothing but a filthy whore that's going to get what's coming to her."

He bunched her hair on one side and yanked hard. But her scream brought no pity to his heart; he merely laughed and tugged harder before opening his hand and letting her hair drop back over her face.

"Your hot little cunt's as wet as fucking Niagara- you like the rough stuff, don't you? Then it's good that you slept so well- there'll be precious little sleep for you from now on."

With a flourish, he pulled his mask off over his head and tossed it into the blackness.

"Theo!"

His name was torn from her throat as his dark, lust-filled eyes locked on to hers, and she wondered why she hadn't guessed. But even his accent, always thicker as he grew more aroused, had been disguised. Or had she been so wrapped up in terror that she hadn't thought it through?

"No, you won't call me by name anymore. You'll call me Master! I'm truly your master, and you my slave. And as such it's my right to do what I please with that golden body of yours. I might never fuck you again- or I might fuck you five times a day every day for the next year. Who knows?"

His black hair, disarranged by the quick removal of the mask, gave him a wildly dangerous look; the stray lock was lost amongst the disorder that flopped over his forehead, and his stubble was no longer designer- for once, he really was in need of a shave. Yet somehow his dishevelled appearance, made even more lascivious by the cloak that was still fastened at his neck, made him look even more villainous than usual.

Sure her ordeal was over, she gave a sigh as some of the tension drained away.

"You're not getting off that likely, Bitch, I haven't finished with you yet." He shadowed the line of her slightly parted lips with the tip of his finger. Of their own accord her traitorous lips automatically closed around it.

Sliding his finger rhythmically in and out, he demanded "Suck it, let it slither in and out as if it were my stiff dick which screwed that tight cunt. Take it in, let it violate your throat as if it were my cock violating your crack." He laughed as a look of loathing registered in her eyes. "What's the matter? Does my language offend you? It's something you'll have to become accustomed to, if you're to please me in the way I intend."

She felt dirty, abused, yet even as her snaking tongue curled around his finger, she was aware of the wetness of her crotch. She could taste the saltiness of his perspiring flesh and began to suck enthusiastically as his long digit continued to fuck her mouth. She closed her eyes and moaned.

He withdrew his finger. As he climbed off her and edged his way round the platform, she was struck by the pure magnificence of his body. Her eyes strayed down his torso to his erect phallus, thick and long as it stood straight as a ramrod from the dense black bush at its base. Delighting in its magnificence, she feasted her eyes greedily- except, fine as it was, she was growing tired of merely looking at it- she wanted to feel it inside her wet, quivering cunt again. She gasped involuntarily.

Theo turned from her to take something from the cabinet beside the bed. When he swung round again, she saw it was the figurine. It was exquisite, and probably worth a great deal of money. He clasped it tightly in his huge hand and, making no sound, he sank down on top of her.

He positioned himself with his arse facing her, his open thighs either side of her head so that his tight balls filled her vision. Then, without word or warning, he rammed his rock-hard phallus in her mouth.

Gagging as he pumped his organ ferociously up and down, forcing her to take its full length down her throat, she tried to scream out, but his cock silenced her very effectively. Hardly able to breathe with his weight crushing the life out of her, her eyes bulged with the prolonged effort of keeping herself from choking. Notwithstanding the distress that gripped her, a feeling of elation began to creep insidiously through her; she relished the debauched ferocity of it all.

Beads of sweat ran down his back. She felt his dexterous fingers exploring her folds of burning flesh. Suddenly, something cold and hard entered her, brusquely pushing, pushing, pushing deep into the yielding warmth. What the hell was it that plundered her so deliciously - the figurine!

Despite the pain that ripped through her, her cunt seemed to suck it in, hungrily lusting for its cold rigidity; her muscles clenched rapturously around it. Her breasts tightened as the inflexible object, like some great bloodless prick, sent her kaleidoscopic emotions into overdrive. She couldn't tell whether her moans, stifled by his engorged cock, were from pain or pleasure. Either way, her body exulted in the new sensations with which she was bombarded as the ivory figurine slid in and out of her as if it were a second cock that profaned her.

In a delirium of rapturous pain she flicked her eyes to the side and caught sight of herself in the full length mirror. Stunned by the reflection of herself bound with leather and chains to the wooden platform, she was unable to tear her eyes away. She watched enthralled as Theo sat astride her with his cock in her mouth and his hands gripping the figurine that he fucked her with so expertly.

Every muscle in her body constricted and shudders shook her body as she viewed the scene, abandoning her very being to subservient bliss.

Suddenly, Theo tore his cock from her mouth and turned around, leaving the figurine in place. Sitting astride her waist, his body convulsed with hard, jerking movements as he neared his own orgasm. Oaths, and howls of pleasure were ripped from deep in his throat as he threw back his head. Holding his huge shaft in his hand he spurted his scalding, creamy fluid over her naked, harshly bound breasts, and face.

Denied her own fulfilment yet again, Vivienne cried out in bitter anguish.

"Theo! Help me! I must come!"

He ran his hands through his wild hair. Now, as he sat astride her, cold arrogance replaced his dark expression of lust. Almost as if he were oblivious to her presence, as if the woman whom he had just ravished were of no consequence to him, he leaned forward, stretched across her sweating, trembling body and reached for the wine goblet.

"Master! You'll call me Master, or have another ten lashes added to the fifteen outstanding."

Vivienne's mouth was parched, her throat sore, and her body cried out for sweet release. As he lifted the goblet to his own lips and sipped the blood-red liquid, she turned her pleading eyes to meet his. Thirsty, and almost dying with the need to come, she began to sob.

"Master, please- I beg you - give me release - and wine."

With an almost imperceptible twitch of his lips, he leaned forward, raised the goblet, and poured the contents slowly over her face. Desperately trying to evade the steady stream, she thrashed her head from side to side, causing the wine to trickle down her cheeks, in her hair, over her forehead, into her mouth-

"Bastard! I hate you!"

"No, you don't. You worship me as a Greek god, a god who holds your life in the palm of his hand." Theo flashed her an indifferent smile, then replaced the empty goblet. Using his thumb, he wiped tears from her eyes, before brushing her unkempt, raven hair from her hot, wine-spattered forehead.

With the cloak still fastened at his neck, he eased himself off her sweat-covered body and swung his legs over the side of the platform. Standing level with her head, his eyes raked over her, and his look told her that he liked what he saw. Leaving her still chained with her breasts tightly bound, the figurine still rammed up inside her, his come trickling over her heaving body and the red wine mingling with her tears to stain her face, he gave a slight nod of his head.

She stared back. With her resentment came the return of the aches to her limbs. Unbelievably frustrated, she felt cheated, abused- yet at the same time she became aware of a sneaking feeling of happiness that had no right to be there. No, she shook her head, it couldn't be; but there was no denying it, she was happy.

She kept her tear-drained eyes focussed on his, and recognised at once a trace of compassion that she felt sure he didn't want her to see.

"Keep your eyes fixed on my prick while I talk to you."

Obediently, she turned her eyes to the phallus that dangled tired and spent between his legs. By now she knew better than to disobey, for the time being at least. Perhaps later, when she had regained her freedom, had recovered herself and had tired of Theo and his little games, she would tell him straight what she thought about obedience. Vivienne was well aware that in the long term she could never be a subordinate to any man; it wasn't in her nature.

But now all she wanted was to come, and drink.

"You'll never know freedom again. Nor will you ever orgasm again without my permission. And now that you've had a taste of what humiliations and cruelties lie ahead, along with the pleasures, there's another rule that you must obey. From now on, as your Master, I demand gratitude. You'll thank me, my associates or attendants every time you're mistreated."

"You've brought me here against my will, had me whipped, chained, drugged and now you expect me to thank you for it? Come on! Even you can't be that sadistic."

Theo's callous laugh pealed around the auditorium.

"You have no idea what I'm capable of! Say it, tell me what I want to hear, or..." he indicated the transformer on the top of the cabinet.

"Thank you", she mumbled.

Crack! A line of fire blazed across her thighs as he brought the hitherto unseen cane crashing down over her tender flesh.

Swish! Crack!

Swish! Crack!

It was enough to make her see reason.

"Thank you Master, for taking your pleasure with this humble slave. I live only to serve you. My pain is your pleasure. Do with me what you wish, I'm yours. Do to me whatever you want, and I shall be grateful."

God! Had she really said that?

"Very prettily put." His lips twisted into the semblance of a smile that she was becoming to know so well. He took one last look at her bound and chained body that glistened with sweat, with his come that had dried on her wine-stained face, then turned on his heel and headed for the wings.

Her mind was reeling as her own, hoarsely spoken words echoed relentlessly around her brain. Once again, a battle raged within her. Defiance won. Before she could stop them the words, amplified many times, tumbled out.

"I'll hate you for the rest of my life!"

Her muscles relaxed and the figurine was expelled from her body.

CHAPTER ELEVEN

Exhaustion and the extreme discomfort of her position ensured that the next hours merged into a blurred state which was neither sleep nor wakefulness. At some point, desperate to relieve herself, Vivienne lost control of her body's natural rhythms and functions. Even in her isolation, she burned with shame as the watery stream was ejected.

Her humiliation was heightened when Woodly came for her.

"What's this, my pretty little whore?" He stooped down to inspect the damage. "You haven't only busted the bloody Connoisseur's mega-dosh piece of Bric-a-brac but you've added insult to injury by peeing over it!" He came round the platform. With his posture full of menace, he showed her the figurine with its head detached from its body, and dripping with Vivienne's waste. "We'll have to see what he wants done about it."

Working quickly, he detached her bonds and had her stand beside the platform. She groaned in agony as her bruised body protested at her every movement.

He fastened her hands behind her back, manacled her feet and clipped a lead to her slave collar. Lastly and most alarmingly, he threw what seemed to be, and indeed was, a black velvet sack over her head and shoulders. With no slits for her to see through, she trembled with terror as she stumbled along behind him. Completely disoriented, she was unable to work out where he was taking her.

They came to a halt. "On your knees!" Woodly pushed her down roughly. Without being told to, she spread her thighs as wide as her position would allow.

When Woodly removed the sack, to her horror she found herself kneeling before Theo, and a dark skinned Arab dressed in white robes. Sitting opposite each other, the two men were discussing business over a late breakfast in the magnificent dining room, where the mid-morning sun streamed in through the floor to ceiling windows.

Theo's eyes locked on to the close-clustering black curls around her quim. She cursed her own demanding body as the lips of her exposed pussy began to redden and swell under his licentious examination.

Theo set down his knife and fork and his lip curled contemptuously.

She felt dirty and abused as the hook-nosed Arab ran his eyes over her, smiling appreciatively as her full breasts rose and fell. Naked and bound before a stranger, never had she known such shame and her golden skin turned scarlet from her neck to her hairline.

What must she look like, she wondered, with her ordinarily sleek, long black hair matted and unwashed, with red wine, dried semen and tears staining her usual good- looks? Flynn had once told her that she looked exotic, but now she felt like one of those beggar-women she'd seen huddled in doorways. And she smelt little better. What good was she to anyone now? More miserable than she'd ever been in her life, she wanted to die of shame.

Her worst fears were confirmed when Theo addressed Woodly tersely.

"I left orders that Prince Saad and I were not to be disturbed. Why have you brought this filthy heap of nothing to me? Didn't I tell you that she was to be taken away and flogged? She still has fifteen strokes owing."

Trembling with fear, Vivienne listened in amazement as the conversation took place above her.

"I had no idea," the Prince told Theo, "that Western men knew the true value of a woman."

"There are a few of us who have been enlightened, though Western lawmakers are sadly misguided. You understand that I must ask for your word in maintaining silence on the matter."

"But of course. In my own small kingdom, the laws allow a man to have several wives. If a man's wealthy enough to keep a harem, then he may do so. I've brought five of my wives with me, though sadly I've had to leave my concubines at home."

"Then I extend my hospitality." Theo gestured towards the kneeling girl. "Feel free to examine her as we talk. Once I've dealt with this problem, perhaps you'd like to try out a nice little redhead? My associate has her under lock and key even as we speak, but I could have her delivered to your suite by this afternoon."

Shocked and appalled by Theo's words, Vivienne bristled as Prince Saad leant forward. His hands closed around her tantalizing breasts. He gave them a spiteful squeeze then reached for her nipples, still throbbing and sore from the electricity with which they had been so cruelly ravaged. To her shame, they stiffened brazenly under his touch.

The Arab smiled, then trailed his finger downward, over her soft belly to the cleft between her legs. His fingers combed her black curls, then she felt one bony finger slide up inside her. Despite her deep shame, she felt her body respond to his touch as her muscles closed around it.

"This one tempts me." He pulled his finger, coated with the sweet essence of her arousal, out of her. Straightening up in his seat, he never took his eyes from the trembling girl as he spoke. "I trust she scrubs up well?"

"For sure. She's being exhibited for the first time this evening. You'll be attending, of course? I'm afraid she'll be out of service until then."

So that was it! He wasn't taking her to an exhibition, she herself was the exhibition. Woodly gave a vicious kick to her bottom.

"Tell him what you've done."

Quaking now with panic, she couldn't believe either her own subservient act as she bowed her head to the floor, or the words that fell from her quivering lips.

"Forgive me, Master. I've broken your valued possession, and defiled it with my waste."

"She pissed on it!" Woodly added, producing the broken figurine..

Theo's body stiffened with rage but his voice was frighteningly calm.

"Look at me, girl."

Raising her tragic eyes, she saw the cruelty in his.

"For years I've waited patiently for this treasure to come to auction. Have you any idea how much it hurts me to see it broken and contaminated?"

Theo clasped the two pieces, one in each hand, and cursed her in Greek. The foreign words rained down on her as, barely able to contain his rage his face contorted with the effort. He speared her with an icy gaze.

"I don't believe in cheap things. You can always find cheap things, but it's harder to find true quality. And quality like this is supposed to survive. Unlike you, this kind of beauty can't ever be replaced. You've insulted me, and for that you'll be punished severely."

For a moment he looked thoughtful, then there was a quick flicker of something else that crossed his face. Vivienne thought for a moment it was pity. A spark of hope lit up her face with a nervous smile.

"You can't seduce me with your smile. Don't mistake me for one of those fucking, lovesick puppies that's hot for your favours. My judgement won't be affected by your seduction, so wipe that leer off your face!"

Theo said something to Woodly in Greek, then in English added "See that she's fed and watered. Have her cleaned up. She has fifteen lashes outstanding- " he turned to Prince Saad. "I'd be honoured if you'd carry out her sentence, in the same way that you'd punish one of your own women. Her punishment for this latest crime will, however, be a private matter."

"My dear friend, I'd be delighted! You have the necessary equipment?"

Theo nodded. "Shall we say... two hours from now?"

"An hour and a half." The Prince leered at Vivienne in an ugly way that filled her with loathing. Surely Theo wouldn't turn her over to this stranger?

"Woodly. Take this quivering nobody out of my sight."

Woodly threw the sack over her again, hauled her to her feet and dragged her away.

***

When they reached the room with the two beds he tore off the stifling sack. Although the heavy drapes were still drawn across the windows, there was enough light from several, strategically placed candles for Vivienne to see that Clitty was asleep on the second bed.

For a moment, she stood rooted to the spot, horrified. Clitty was anchored to the foot of the bed by means of a chain attached to the black ring that pierced her fleshy labia. As if that wasn't enough, there was also a chain linked through her black slave collar to which her hands were fastened, securing her to the ring above the bed. Thus movement was prevented; she couldn't even turn over in her sleep.

Woodly dumped Vivienne on the spare bed.

"You stink!" He freed her ankles, leaving the leather straps in place. Then he fastened her wrists to her collar, which he secured to the ring above the bed by a chain. Thus she was able to enjoy a measure of movement, if somewhat restricted.

The room was dimly lit with a soft, amber glow that gaveit a warm, intimate atmosphere. But Woodly immediately set out to change that. He drew back the drapes that usually hid the various whips, crops and rings set in the wall, then switched on harsh wall lights angled above the drapes to illuminate the equipment as a reminder that this was far from being the honeymoon suite.

She saw that as well as the canes and whips, there was also a selection of chains of varying lengths and durability on a shelf, along with a coil of rope and other bits and pieces that she couldn't identify from her position on the bed.

Woodly came and stood beside her. Taking an ultra-tender nipple in each hand, he twisted them sadistically. Vivienne bit into her lower lip, refusing to cry out.

"I'm real pissed off that I don't get a chance to thrash you."

Woodly unzipped his trousers and let them drop to the floor. He pulled off his underpants, then climbed up onto the bed. Stretching out on top of her, his weight drove the air from her lungs.

"Look at you!" His breath stank of cigarettes. "You're nothing but a messy, beat- up, filthy whore- but a man's got to take his pleasure where he can find it." Without preliminaries, he rammed his cock inside her. "At least I get to poke you before the Prince does."

She shuddered with loathing as his shaft pistoned in and out. Grunting like an animal he spewed filthy names over her as his excitement grew. Like a man possessed, he drove his cock home.

She thought she'd vomit when he grabbed her breasts.

Yet despite her revulsion, warmth flooded her loins as her body began to buck and writhe beneath him. Helpless, she couldn't stop the sheer exhilaration she felt at being used so basely.

Suddenly, with a holler of triumph, he exploded inside her, filling her with his hot sperm.

He kissed her mouth savagely, almost choking her with the cigarette fumes. Then he pulled out of her. He leant across her and unfastened her wrists, leaving the straps in place. Then, leaving her on the bed with semen dripping from her and puddling on the bed, he strutted across the room. On reaching the door, he stopped and drew her attention to something that had a sheet covering it that was propped up against the wall.

"I nearly forgot," with a bow he removed the sheet, "this came for you."

"Oh my God! Andromeda Waiting."

The more she looked at the painting, the more she came to see the likeness between herself and the subject, and the more her heart froze. This was more than a painting - this was her life.

***

Time passed quickly. The waiter brought her a bowl of muesli, and a pot of coffee to wash it down. He didn't speak to her but eyed her dishevelled appearance with disdain. When he returned later to remove the dirty dishes he didn't even glance in her direction.

Not long afterwards, a middle aged woman wearing the uniform of the hotel's housekeeping staff came in. Without speaking, she unclipped the chain from the wall ring and fastened Vivienne's hands behind her back. Hauling the poor girl to her feet, the woman led her through to the bathroom. Opening the shower cubicle, the woman looped one end of the lead over the shower hose and clipped it back on itself. Then she switched on the power jet.

Vivienne screamed out as thc torrent of freezing water drenched her, making her teeth chatter with the cold.

The woman ignored her and disappeared back into the bedroom, leaving Vivienne to endure the agony alone. After what seemed an age, she returned and switched off the water. The housekeeper unfastened the lead and briskly rubbed Vivienne down with the towel. Afterwards she dried and brushed Vivienne's luxuriant hair, then took her back to the bedroom and made her sit on the bed. Using cosmetics she found in the bedside cabinet, the woman made-up Vivienne's face.

Having completed her task, she had Vivienne take up her former position sitting on the bed. She clipped the lead to the ring again, leaving Vivienne's hands still fastened behind her back. Then, still without a word being spoken, she left the room.

Vivienne glanced across to where Clitty slept soundly, amazed that Clitty could sleep at all when she'd been tethered so cruelly.

Vivienne studied her elegant prison. There were two doors leading off the room, one of which led to the bathroom, and was set at the end of the equipment wall adjoining the windows. The other was set in the wall opposite the windows, beside a mirror that took up a large proportion of the wall, and led down a short passage to further rooms. Preferring not to dwell too long on the array of instruments, she amused herself by checking out the series of small paintings that hung on the wall behind her. Each depicted a fat man that reminded Vivienne of an illustration she'd seen once of Charles Dickens' Mr. Pickwick; in one picture the man was taking a voluptuous woman from behind. Another depicted him with a bare-bottomed woman across his knees, with her voluminous skirts around her waist. He was spanking her backside with a fat hand. Another showed him with a woman wearing a riding habit. Still with her hat on, she was leaning across a desk with her skirt around her waist and her drawers around her ankles. He was standing beside her and laying into her with a riding crop.

Vivienne felt eyes upon her, and turned her head.

Theo stood, Metaxas in hand, at the end of the bed. Looking devastatingly sexy with his designer stubble and curled stray lock of hair tumbling across his forehead, he was dressed entirely in black.

"Enjoy the luxury while you can- it won't always be like this."

She listened in wide-eyed horror as he told her something of his plans. There were no specifics, no mention of the time-scale involved. It was merely a list of events. It was as Woodly had said, Theo preferred to keep her in ignorance.

"Soon I'll return to my island. In due course, I'll send for you. There you'll live in a cell. You'll be beaten every day, and tortured to orgasm if it pleases me. As one whore among many, I may choose to fuck you, or maybe leave you to rot."

Coming to stand beside her, he looped one finger through the ring of her collar and brought her face on a level with his crotch.

"To tell the truth, I'm fucking disappointed in you. I'd hoped that you'd have learnt your place by now, to obey without question or complaint. You should also have learnt respect for my property."

Anger at the unfairness of it all made her rash.

"It was your bloody fault!" she blurted out, waking Clitty who raised her eyes skyward at Vivienne's folly. "You shouldn't have left me with that thing stuck up me. If you hadn't left me like that for hours-"

"Silence!" The blow that struck her cheek lifted a patch of fire. "You're the slave, I'm the master. It's for me to decide what's best, and for you to take what's meted out to you. It seems we have a long way to go yet." He took a sip from his glass before continuing coldly. "To displease me is a sure way to end up on the garbage heap of life."

His marauding gaze followed the beads of moisture that trickled down between the deep cleft between her breasts. His hand alighted on her left, juicy globe. He pulled and twisted the nipple until she cried out.

"Later, you'll be punished for your earlier misdemeanour. But first, the Prince will administer your remaining strokes of the lash, as if you were one of his own. You'll therefore undergo the humiliation of a public flogging."

Her voice, barely a whisper, begged for mercy.

"N..no.. please. That's barbaric!"

"So I believe. He won't mark you too severely- my guests have parted with a considerable amount of cash for that privilege."

She could hardly believe it was true. But one look into his cruel eyes told her all she needed to know- he relished the prospect of her pain and humiliation.

Stepping backward, Theo removed his finger from the ring and pushed her away. Cool indifference descended upon him, as if her feelings were of no interest to him. For the time being at least, she'd ceased to amuse him.

But the real absurdity was that she felt the loss as keenly as when he'd slapped her. She strained on her leash to reach him, her eyes pleading forgiveness. He could take her as brutally as he wished and she would be pleased to serve him. Suddenly, nothing existed but an agonizing fear of him tiring of her and setting her free.

"Guards!"

Woodly and Farrell appeared instantly.

***

Following Theo's instructions to the letter Farrell selected a fearsome looking whip, several feet in length, from the selection. Vivienne watched as he coiled it into a manageable size. Using a clip he attached it to his belt so that only the end was visible beneath his smart, grey, suit jacket.

Next he found a chain with a crocodile clip at one end. He opened its jaws, holding it close to her eyes so that she could see just how spiteful it was. With a sadistic grin, he snapped it closed around the soft flesh of her labia. The agony as it bit into her tender flesh gave birth to the shrillest scream she had ever emitted.

Whimpering with pain, she could hardly stand still as Woodly checked the fit of the leather cuffs at her wrists and ankles, and that earned her a sharp slap on her bruised bottom.

Farrell attached her wrists to the ring at the front of her collar. She was made to stand and wait directly in front of the mirror. With her back straight, she confronted her reflection.

She'd always been aware of her beauty, and now the sight that greeted her eyes filled her with a certain pride. She tossed her head defiantly. She may be nothing more than an abused sex slave to Theo, but inside she was still Vivienne Trevayne.

Even the chain that chinked annoyingly with even the slightest movement as it dangled between her legs seemed strangely erotic, making her shiver as the end brushed against her ankles. Standing with her legs apart so as not to rub her thighs together and therefore exacerbate the pain, her golden breasts bobbed temptingly as she moved her weight from one foot to the other. Her raven hair cascaded over her narrow shoulders to her waist, while her hands bound to the golden collar at her throat put her in mind of a virgin about to be led away to her fate.

She stole a nervous glance at Andromeda tied to the rock.

***

In the secret room behind the two-way mirror, sitting with his feet up before him and crossed at the ankles, Theo watched the proceedings with sadistic delight. This weekend was turning into one of his most successful yet. He was sure his invited guests, among their number an army colonel, a pop star and a bishop, would find it most rewarding, especially the colonel, who had a special fondness for treating girls as boys.

Theo had arranged this function months ago, his original intention being to exhibit Clitty. But on seeing Vivienne for the first time, from his Merc when she had arrived at work after her liaison with Flynn, Theo had known he'd found a new star. Contrary to what he'd told her, she was everything he'd hoped she would be, and more besides.

He always enjoyed the spectacle of a public flogging, so much so that he made it a regular occurrence on his island. And this one had the added attraction of having the girl's ex-boyfriend present. Flynn had done a good job in tracking him down.

While Theo knew that his guests would undoubtedly appreciate the opportunity to observe the flogging, he didn't want this evening's entertainment spoilt by their having already witnessed the raven haired beauty being beaten. Luckily, most of his guests would be having lunch in the dining room, entertained by the bouzouki players he'd had flown in for the weekend.

Of course, the hotel was still open to the public this weekend, so there was the possibility of the arrival of unexpected patrons. However, he had his own way of dealing with those kinds of problems should they arise. He'd always found that most people have a price.

He leaned forward as the girl came so close to the mirror that he could almost touch her. What a perfect treasure she was! He touched the glass, tracing her provocative curves with his finger.

She was made to be fucked, like a whore in the night. Trussed up and presented to a lusting world, she would revel in her captivity, though she didn't know it yet. She was a true submissive, though as yet the knowledge evaded her. It was up to him to open the door. He could see her now, in his mind's eye, tethered at his feet against the backdrop of the Aegean. Or tied between two marble pillars and flogged by one of his hooded guards. Ah, the possibilities were endless.

But that was in the future. What of now?

He watched as she tried to ease the pain from the crocodile clip by keeping her long, shapely legs apart. He smiled lasciviously, knowing her efforts to be largely ineffectual. If the pain were that easy to deal with he would have found something more efficient. He couldn't have his girls getting the better of him, especially one like this one!

How Theo loved to see that exquisite face contorted in agony. High cheek-boned and sultry, it showed all the rapture of a nun in prayer, a quality the bishop would find most agreeable.

Soon Theo would watch the tears flow as her ravishing body

trembled and jerked prettily under the lash. A public flogging was just the thing to prepare her for her greatest hour. Tonight she would give more pleasure that she'd ever dreamed possible.

With her sensual, golden body stripped naked and striped by the lash, she was a powerful picture of everything carnal. Her hair fell provocatively around her shoulders, and both her yawning cunt and generous mouth were open to violation. Her backside... ah yes, her backside... her hole must be stretched if it were ever to take his considerable girth without damaging her.

"And what of your nipples?" he whispered hoarsely to the mirror. "Yours are no delicate, blushing rosebuds, my sweetest whore. No, yours are the colour of mahogany, hard as stone, begging to be pinched."

He heard the golden-skinned slut scream out as Woodly walked up behind her and yanked on the chain. He took her over to where Clitty stood, her hands fastened behind her back. With Vivienne's back toward Clitty, he pulled the chain backward between her thighs and, using a special clip, linked it to the black ring that pierced Clitty's pinkened flesh. Once the two girls were linked together, Woodly attached another chain to the front of the crocodile clip like a lead.

Theo knew that the pain suffered by both girls would be intense as one guard pulled on the lead at the front, while the girl following behind would have to jog along to keep up. Clitty would be the cause of her friend's added pain by pulling in the opposite direction- not to mention her own agony as the lead girl pulled on Clitty's labia ring!

***

Walking behind, Woodly chivvied Clitty along with well-aimed strikes on her bottom using a cane. In front, Farrell gave intermittent yanks on the chain that was attached to the vicious crocodile clip. It was all Vivienne could do from crying out. But the worst moment came when Clitty stumbled. The resulting jerk on Vivienne's labia as the clip bit in had her shrieking again at the top of her voice.

Following the same route as they had taken with Vivienne before, the men led the two girls down the back stairs until they reached the first floor. Then they were led down the main staircase. But this time there was a sizeable group of people gathered in reception.

Floundering in shame, Vivienne turned a deep shade of red as the group turned their eyes towards the little procession. Then, like the parting of the red sea, they moved aside to let the parade pass.

To her horror, Vivienne saw that there was quite a crowd gathered, that included several of the hotel staff. And Roxanne.

A group of women dressed in black garments that covered them from head to toe, apart from an aperture for their eyes, were huddled together. Vivienne guessed these were the wives of Prince Saad.

The Prince stood beside Theo. At a given signal, they joined the head of the procession. The doorman, dressed in his smart, dark green uniform, opened the door and stood aside. He looked the two women over with unbridled lust as they passed.

Once outside, Farrell turned to face her. He unfastened the lead from the crocodile clip and clipped it onto her collar. Roughly brushing her legs apart, he removed the crocodile clip and let it fall.

Behind her, Woodly gathered up the clip and chain, which he detached from Clitty's ring and attached to her collar instead. With her hands still fastened behind her back and out of Vivienne's range of vision, a man led Clitty away.

Vivienne could hardly believe the scene that greeted her eyes as she stood with her hands still fastened to her collar. There, in the centre of the gravel forecourt, was a contraption that filled her with horror. Made of wood that had been painted an ominous black, it looked like a latter day, more refined version of the old stocks on the village green at nearby Aldberston, and had more than a passing resemblance to an instrument of torture.

Slowly, Farrell led her down the steps and out onto the large expanse of gravel in front of the hotel.

CHAPTER TWELVE

Theo took up a commanding position on the steps. When he had the attention of everyone present, he addressed the assembled crowd. As his voice rang out in the stillness of a summer's day, broken only by the sounds of birds and distant traffic, Vivienne noticed that his accent was once again thick with his lust.

"I believe that women should be subservient to men. Every woman should know her place, and man should be master in his own home."

He paused as loud guffaws broke out, along with clapping and cheering. Comments from the women present, if indeed any comments were made, were drowned out.

"I'm an uncompromising master and demand four things above all else from my women. These are pleasure, beauty, pain, and obedience in all things. The greatest of these is obedience. Any failure to comply is always dealt with severely. This girl stands before you as an example.

"Her repeated disobedience earned her a sentence of thirty lashes, fifteen of which she's already received and fifteen still outstanding. It's to this end that I hand over this difficult, unruly, trouble-making whore to my honoured and trusted friend to administer the beating."

Shaken by his words, Vivienne shivered with dread. She ran her eyes over the sea of expectant faces. Surely someone would come to her aid? There were women in the crowd, ordinary hotel staff, Roxanne- surely someone would object to his outdated, macho display of sadistic discipline? This was a new millennium- things like this just didn't happen anymore.

Vivienne searched the women's faces for signs of revulsion, but saw only a curious blend of fear and fascination in their eyes.

"Her penalty will be pain and humiliation." Theo continued. "May it serve as a warning to those among you who crave a master of their own."

Vivienne was staggered to see him look directly at one of the waitresses, who bowed her head in acknowledgment, while Theo's final words turned her blood to ice.

"Take her away and let the proceedings commence."

The gravel hurt her bare feet terribly as Vivienne was led towards the cruel- looking apparatus. Quaking with terror, she bit into her lower lip. It was only when she tasted her own blood that she realized quite how hard she'd been biting.

There were four sturdy uprights at each corner of the apparatus, each one three inches square and five feet high. There was a platform at waist height, which could be raised or lowered according to preference. At one end there were rings attached near the top of the posts, with further rings placed at intervals down them. At the opposite end were two adjustable crossbeams, both several inches deep with a half moon shape cut from the centre of each. These, she realized with horror, formed the aperture for her head.

Woodly raised her onto the platform and had her kneel. He tethered wide leather straps around her legs just above her knees, and using chains, attached them to the rings a few inches above the platform. Her legs were spread wide, displaying her deep red slit shamefully.

He detached her hands from her collar and let them fall to her sides. But her relief was short lived. It felt as if he were wrenching her arms from their sockets as he yanked them outward and twisted them. He used other chains to attach her own wrist cuffs to the rings at the top of the posts.

Meantime, Farrell adjusted the crossbeams. He positioned the lower one level with the platform and, grabbing the end of her lead, he pulled her forward. She felt as if she were putting her head on the block as he arranged her with her neck resting in the cleft. He detached the lead, then turned her head so that she was facing her sadistic audience.

With a whispered "I wouldn't let anyone else flog you if you were mine" he lowered the second beam until the contraption fitted snugly around her neck, holding her head in place.

Now she was secured with her arse in the air, proffering the tender flesh of her inner thighs lusciously. The curved line of her back sloped downward to her head, her raven hair tumbled almost to the ground, and her breasts dangled ponderously. Theo licked his lips appreciatively- it was a scrumptiously aesthetic pose of utter humiliation.

Prince Saad handed Farrell a strip of rough cloth and ordered Farrell to gag her. When he was satisfied with the result, he motioned Farrell to hand over the whip.

A whorl of terror spiralled from Vivienne's stomach to her throat as she saw Farrell place it across the Prince's unturned palms.

Prince Saad waited until the two guards had withdrawn to an acceptable distance, then positioned himself behind her. She heard the whip whistle through the air and the Crack! as he tested it. He took a few steps sideways and repeated the process.

Vivienne tensed.

Whizz! Crack!

Fire ripped across her bottom as the whip struck.

Whizz! Crack!

A blaze of fire was laid over the first, instantly lifting a cruel, red line.

Whizz! Crack!

She jerked against her bonds as white light exploded in her brain. Once again, the expert hand of the Prince had laid a line exactly over the other two.

Whizz! Crack!

Whizz! Crack!

Ten more to go. Vivienne sobbed into her gag. In her line of vision, the Prince's wives put their heads together and whispered. Clitty had been made to kneel at the front and watch, and flinched with every lash. No stranger to the whip, Clitty knew first hand what suffering her friend must endure to please their master. Behind Clitty, holding her lead and bending slightly to fondle her pale breasts, stood a man.

Suddenly, stricken with shame and confusion, Vivienne realized who the man was- Nathan!

The pain caught her unprepared and exploded across her lower thighs as three more savage strokes fell in rapid succession, raising red lines across her tender, quivering flesh. Instinct made her jerk against her chains, earning her a severe strike across the soft skin of her inner thighs.

She screamed into the gag, tears spilling from her eyes like rain off a roof. Her golden body glistened with sweat.

Swish! Whack!

Her inner thighs quivered under the lash. Pain flooded her mind and body, to mix with the heat that suffused her loins, causing something curiously close to pleasure.

Swish! Whack!

Tiny beads of moisture leaked from her swollen slit and trailed down her inner thigh. Please God, don't let the Prince see!

The Prince saw.

Whizz! Crack!

Agony blazed across the sensitive flesh of her sex.

Only four more to go. She reddened with shame as she felt an orgasm building. No, she mustn't- not here!

The agony that assailed her body was beyond anything she'd known before- so was the peace. She felt deliriously happy as pleasure overcame pain.

Whizz! Crack!

Her muscles tensed- the strike had brought her right to the edge. She mustn't come. Please God, don't let her come in front of Nathan- she would die of shame.

Too late! The biggest orgasm of her life ripped through her, sending her into blessed oblivion as the final blows struck.

***

When she regained consciousness, Vivienne thought at first that she was lying in a darkened room.

As her senses returned, so too did the pain. Alone in her misery, she winced at the sensations that bombarded her already tortured body, and tried to make sense of her present situation.

With a jolt it hit her- she was wearing a blindfold. A tight band covered her face from eyebrows to the flare of her nose, leaving her nostrils free. She lowered her eyes to try and see beneath the blindfold, but it was fitted too securely to allow even a glimmer of light.

There was no way she could see her surroundings.

She was lying on her back on a hard surface. The way her legs dangled over each side suggested she was lying on a wooden bench. But it wasn't until she tried to raise her legs that she realized her ankles were somehow secured to the floor.

A series of loud sobs shook her frame. After the pain and humiliation of the flogging, she couldn't believe that anyone was sadistic enough to bring her here to undergo further degradations. Hadn't she suffered enough?

Her hands were joined at the wrists and her arms were stretched out tautly at an angle over her head, secured by some means that prevented her from lowering them.

To make matters worse, the uncomfortable, full feeling in her back passage told her that once again her arse had been plugged. Her breathing grew more agitated as she wriggled about to try to attain some degree of comfort. But instead of dislodging the thing, it seemed to have the effect of driving the plug further in. It felt worse than before, and she realized with horror that this was a larger plug than last time.

Not only that, but she had a dildo rammed up inside her sex. Putting all her efforts into ejecting it, she bore down. Gritting her teeth and pushing with all her might, she tried again. But it stayed fast.

Briefly she felt the graze of stubble across her face. Instantly recognizing Theo, part of her dared to hope that he'd come to release her, while another part of her knew he'd come to add torment to her misery.

She breathed his name as his lips covered hers. A snaking tongue explored the warm recess of her mouth, entangling with her own. Hands closed over her breasts, and her nipples responded by blossoming into instant hardness. Her clitoris throbbed hot between her legs. An insidious shiver of delight passed through her as fingers pinched and twirled her nipples. Her sinews melted as the pressure increased, hurting her, yet sending messages of elation to all her nerve-endings. A sweet warmth flared in her belly and in some crazy, incomprehensible way she knew that she loved him.

He abandoned her mouth at the same moment as his hands forsook her breasts.

"Please, Theo-"

"Shut up and listen. Your flagrant disobedience is beginning to piss me off. I intend that you be reminded of each rule in a way that you'll never forget. You won't speak again unless invited to do so, except to thank those who chastise you- which you consistently fail to do! Thank me now for having you flogged and for using you as an instrument of pleasure. Thank me as your master - don't ever presume that I'm your Greek lover - before I gag you to ensure your adherence to the silence rule."

"M...M...Master, your hu...humble s...slave thanks you f...for the cruelties which...have been heaped upon her, and..." her naturally husky tones broke in beguiling subservience that brought a twisted smile of satisfaction to Theo's lips, "h...h...hopes that she can continue to... to bring you pleasure."

It was almost with regret that he lifted her head and fitted the ball gag. But he wasn't done yet.

"Also, and perhaps most importantly, you'll never climax again without permission. Your disregard for this particular rule was witnessed by many, and charming as it was, it can't go unpunished."

Vivienne drew in a horrified breath as she listened for him to pass sentence.

"For this you'll receive five lashes across your sex lips, to be held in abeyance since you have a heavy night ahead of you. But rest assured, you will receive them in due course.

"Finally, I instructed that you were to be punished for breaking and defiling my possession. It so happens I want your tight little arsehole stretched, so I have had a plug inserted, two sizes larger than the last. Also, as you've already discovered, you have a dildo in your cunt. And, to make sure that this time what goes up stays there, you're wearing a harness," he slipped his finger under the various straps to illustrate the point, "that will keep both the dildo and plug in place. Removal of the harness is impossible since your hands have been immobilized and your arms fixed to a pulley system in the ceiling."

He fastened another strap around her waist, which had the uncomfortable effect of flattening her to the bench and holding her fast. Now all her movements, save for moving her head, were restricted. There was a low whirring sound. Rigid with terror, she realized that her arms were being stretched upward even as the bench seemed to move beneath her, stretching her body painfully.

Tears flowed beneath the blindfold as her cries were stifled by the cruel gag.

"I call it the 'rack' for rather obvious reasons. While it inflicts no real harm, it does inflict a great deal of discomfort. Incidentally, you've been brought down to a kind of dungeon. I've had it built next to the cellar, as an exact replica of the one I have on my island. If you weren't wearing the blindfold, you would be able to appreciate the refinements. But no matter, you'll experience the joys of the real one soon enough.

"But in the meantime, as you won't be wanted for a few hours yet, I suggest you get some sleep. You've an exceptionally busy night ahead of you." He gave a laugh that chilled her marrow. "I doubt you'll make it in to work tomorrow after all."

She listened as his footsteps receded across the room. There was a click as a light switch was thrown, followed by a thud as a heavy door closed. The key that turned in the lock seemed absurd and unnecessary, given the nature of her confinement.

Unless, she reasoned, it was to keep someone out rather than to keep her in.

For the first time she began to have some real idea of the full horrors of what she'd got herself into. Her life would never return to the way it was. Everything Theo had said was true - she was his property to do with as he pleased, and her pain was indeed his pleasure.

Somewhere in the kernel of her being, a feeling of happiness at having a purpose in life began to take hold, even as terror made her quake at the prospect.

***

In Vivienne's dark world, time was meaningless; it could have been hours, or merely minutes, that she waited. With most of her senses denied, her hearing seemed more acute. She heard the two sets of footsteps in the corridor long before she heard the key in the lock.

The hinges creaked as the door was flung open. Footsteps passed through, then the door closed.

"The poor, unfortunate wretch is in here?"

She heard the shocked gasp as the flick of the light switch revealed the full extent of her tortured, ravished condition.

"Release her now."

Vivienne didn't recognize the sandpapered tones, but she did recognize those of the voice that answered- Woodly.

"What's in it for me?"

"Your reward is in-" there was a pause followed by a rustling sound, then a grunt of acknowledgment from Woodly before the voice continued "heaven. It's a good thing you're doing here, my son."

A glimmer of hope, like a pinprick of light in the dark, suddenly illuminated her dark world- Woodly was accepting money in return for her freedom!

It only took a few minutes for Woodly to lower her arms and release her ankles. He unfastened the straps at her waist and pulled her to her feet. But fatigue momentarily paralysed her limbs and it was some time before she was able to stand unaided.

Woodly unbuckled the harness and removed it with the dildo and plug still attached.

But to her surprise, he grabbed her wrists and crossing them behind her back, secured her hands together before she had time to remove the gag and blindfold.

Frightened and disoriented, she didn't dare move an inch from where she stood for fear of crashing into something and falling in an embarrassing heap on the floor. She felt her body swaying.

With her hands crossed and her wrists bound tightly, the back of her hands rested against her buttocks. She used her long nails to relieve an itch between them, easing the endeavour by moving her arms up and down. She ran her nails from top to bottom of the deep crack that separated her rounded, sore cheeks.

"Very nice," it was the stranger's voice, "very nice indeed." Then to Woodly, he said "Leave us. I must try to save the wretched soul of this pathetic creature."

The stranger's warm breath grazed the back of her neck as he stood behind her. Immediately, she felt the colour rising to her face and snatched her hand away.

Woodly snorted. "I'll be outside. Just knock when she's saved."

The heavy door closed and the key turned in the lock, and she was alone with the stranger. Just what kind of 'salvation' had he in mind, she wondered as panic gripped her.

She didn't have to wait long to find out.

"Don't let me stop you. Continue." His voice carried the weight of authority as he arranged her hands back in position. "I want to see you finger-fuck your arse."

No! She couldn't do such a thing! She screwed up her eyes beneath her blindfold as if that would help her blot out the godawful thought of it. But instead, she saw in her head a vivid picture of herself with her finger stuck up her back passage. Immediately, darts of electricity struck her nerve-endings.

When she didn't immediately comply with his wishes, he snarled "Get on with it, Whore!"

She breathed a protest against the ball gag, then pushed her long fingers deep into the warm, tight crevice between her buttocks. Red with shame, she tried to quell the fission of sexual arousal that ignited deep within her breasts. But it only intensified as it flared downward through her belly and fired her aching quim. She adjusted her stance and projected her belly forward, thus giving easier access to her probing digit. At last her fingernail located her puckered hole.

Deeply ashamed, she tore her hands away, only to have him put them back.

"Do as you're told, and frig your arse. How can I save you if I have no knowledge of your sin? Let's see a bit of real finger-fucking."

This time she obeyed. She thrust her abdomen forward and ran her secured hands down the hot, tight crevice. The tip of her nail scratched as her finger once again located the puckered hole. Circling it tentatively; bit by bit she inserted her finger experimentally.

"Deeper. Faster." His hoarse whisper in her ear coincided with the swishing sound in the air, culminating with the unbelievable sting of bamboo on bare skin; Vivienne screamed silently as pain exploded across her thigh.

"There's more where that came from. Flagellation is the only way to salvation for a whore." His hands crept over her vivid welts. "I see that others have tried before me."

Vivienne heard the next Swish! but there wasn't time to steel herself before the lacerating pain struck the back of her legs.

Prayers for her salvation alternated with obscenities, pouring down on her like acid rain. She wasn't sure which was worse, just as she couldn't tell whether it was her fear or her shame that was greatest. Trembling, she felt the heat of humiliation consume her, and a more intense heat still in those regions where the cane had struck.

"Deeper," he commanded, "or I'll be forced to use the cane again." Spurred on by his increasing fervour, he used it anyway.

As her body jerked under the biting blows, her finger slipped deeper inside. Her muscles clenched tightly round her finger. The intensity of pain and pleasure were in equal parts as her probing digit continued to violate that forbidden passage.

The stranger was breathing heavier now, his rasping groans betraying the vigour with which he began to masturbate. Strangely, the knowledge that he'd been brought to a high state of arousal by the self-defilement of her own body, together with her captive condition, filled her with a strange sense of delight. Her own breathing became more ragged as she began to gyrate her hips, tempting him to violate her other entrance.

"Slut! Whore!" The cane came down across her tethered hands, then he snatched them away.

Then she felt the tip of his cock at her hole. She drew in a terrified breath. This wasn't what she'd meant- wasn't what she wanted!

Feeling filthy, sensual and alive, pain sliced through her as he thrust his prick deep inside her, battering against the walls of her anus. Despite the stretching effect of the plug, it felt as if he were ripping her apart and she screamed into the gag. Tears flowed beneath the blindfold as he rammed his prick in up to the hilt. And, full to the brim with rigid flesh, she relished the passion with which he breached her virginity.

His hoarse tone dropped to an intense whisper as his insults continued. The end of his cane brushed against her sensitive, hardened nipples. Thinking he would strike her there, she tensed. But instead of raising it to bring it crashing down across her breasts, he continued to use it to graze her nipples. Unexpected pulses of fire ricocheted through her. She wanted him to fuck her as she had never been fucked before.

His cry was fierce as, with a convulsive jerk, he discharged his seed deep into her anus. Then he raised the cane.

Swish! Crack!

Fire and light exploded across her senses as he brought it down sharply across the swell of her breasts.

The pain as he pulled out of her was almost as intense as when he went in.

"You're a hopeless case, Whore!" He came and stood beside her. "May God have pity on your soul, for I swear I do not. May you long suffer the torments that lay ahead, for you're beyond even my powers of redemption!"

Swish! Crack!

He struck her breasts with such force that she almost lost her balance. Yet, even as she trembled with fear, she felt the betrayal of her loins. She thrust her abdomen forward.

"Never have I failed so spectacularly in my endeavours to save a soul." He pinched each nipple severely. "If you should ever whisper one word of our battle with Satan, then I shall be forced to take steps."

There was a final Crack! across her breasts that sent her crashing to the ground. Leaving her huddled in an abused and frustrated heap on the floor, he rapped on the door. She heard it creak on its hinges.

"My labours have been long and arduous, but I'm afraid the whore refuses to repent. There's nothing more I can do here."

Woodly laughed a soft, menacing laugh.

"I know, she's a lost cause, thank the lord!"

As the stranger's footsteps receded along the corridor, the door closed. In less than a heartbeat, Woodly had dragged her to her feet.

"It's the rack again for you, my beauty! One word of this to anyone," he said as he helped her back into the harness, "and I'll make your life hell."

As if it isn't already, she thought as he fitted the plug and dildo back in position.

CHAPTER THIRTEEN

Propped up against a wall in the bathroom, with her secured wrists in her lap and the blindfold removed, Vivienne was still wearing the harness with its outrageous attachments. Blinking to get used to the harsh light, she watched one of the housekeeping staff drawing a bath, and smiled in appreciation as the woman added pink bath foam.

She grabbed Vivienne by the wrists. Dragging her over to the bath she helped her out of the harness. The relief when the plug was removed was tempered by pain. On the other hand, the relief that came with the removal of the dildo was more than she could cope with, and her bladder emptied itself copiously.

The woman's contempt was written all over her face.

She stood and watched silently as Vivienne sank down into the comforting bubbles, enjoying the sensations as they clustered and popped over her skin. Perhaps Theo was setting her free after all. No sooner had she thought it than her smile disappeared. No! She could endure anything but that.

***

Two men came for her, clipping a lead to her collar. With her hands still secured in front, one man walked in front and the other behind. Vivienne was led naked, save for the leather straps and her slave collar, through the main hallways of the hotel.

At last they came to the Health and Fitness Centre. Passing through the different treatment areas, where female guests were undergoing varying levels of therapy with equally varying results, Vivienne was taken into a small, white-walled room. With stainless steel appliances and large ceiling lights over a central table, it reminded Vivienne of an operating theatre rather than a beauty parlour.

Her hands were released. She was made to lie on her stomach on a masseur's table, and the end of her lead was attached to a metal bar, six inches from the floor, that ran between the front legs of the table.

Suddenly she became aware of her own insignificance. She felt unimportant, de- humanized, like a lump of meat on the butcher's slab as one of the men's heavy hands pressed down on the hollow of her back while his two fingers shot up inside her quim.

To her further shame, her tired, bruised, double-crossing body responded by flooding her with an erotic warmth. Her pussy was growing moist, and it wasn't long before she heard the sounds of his fingers as they excited her.

She lifted her head when the other man came and stood in front of her. With the bulge in his trousers level with her eyes, it was all she could do to stop herself from giving in to her own desires, to stop herself reaching out to take that tantalizing cock in her mouth. But knowing that Theo needed very little encouragement when it came to punishing her, and would be only too pleased to have these men report back any indiscretions on her part, she resolutely linked her hands behind her head.

He slid his hands between her and the table. Finding her nipples, already hard as walnuts, he began to manipulate them skilfully. Without a word being spoken, the two men doubled their efforts. Soon she was writhing. Moans of pleasure escaped from her lips, turning to moans of protest as she neared the orgasm that was forbidden her.

At the very last moment, just as her legs became locked in spasm, the door opened and a stunning black girl in her mid twenties entered, wearing a high-necked, dazzling white coat that seemed even brighter against her sleek, ebony skin. Immediately, both men pulled away, leaving Vivienne frustrated but strangely relieved as they left the room in silence.

"I'm Destiny, your masseuse."

Did this woman have authority over her too, Vivienne wondered. Not sure what to say, Vivienne said nothing as Destiny ran soothing hands over Vivienne's bruised and whip-streaked back.

"Someone's been busy!" she said as Vivienne flinched beneath her competent fingers. Her voice was soft and reassuring. "Don't worry, you're not the first, and you certainly won't be the last."

"Is that supposed to make me feel better?" Vivienne mumbled churlishly, resting her chin on her arms.

Destiny began to rub soothing lotions into Vivienne's skin, massaging away the aches and pains.

"There's no real harm done, they seldom mark too severely, otherwise the wounds don't heal fast enough and they're unable to do it again. Most of them get turned on by a striped body but like to have a clean canvas to work on."

She went on to explain that there were some people who refused to touch a girl unless each stroke was clearly defined, and that some masters had their slaves whipped every day. Vivienne shivered in horror as she recalled Theo saying something of that nature concerning herself.

Destiny turned Vivienne's collar so that the ring was at the back, and had her turn over so that she could work on her front. Then, to Vivienne's shock, Destiny began to unbutton the front of the pure white coat.

"Let me show you something."

She slid the coat over her shoulders and let it drop to the floor. Vivienne was stunned to see that the girl was completely naked underneath. With heavy breasts and the narrowest waist Vivienne had ever seen, the long-legged girl was quite lovely. As graceful as a jungle cat, she slowly spun round so that Vivienne could see her back.

Covered in ridges and scars, in some places the skin was broken. And it wasn't just her back. Thighs, legs, stomach, breasts. Vivienne gasped in horror as Destiny twirled for her. She ran her eyes over Destiny's lithe body and shuddered- and not just from fear. A thrill of arousal coiled in her loins as she noted a golden ring passed through her labia, where her wiry black hair tangled protectively.

"The Master likes to keep me marked." Destiny ran her index finger under her own collar, solid gold like Vivienne's.

Destiny explained "The Connoisseur bought me at an auction a couple of years ago. Several girls were put up that day. It was the happiest day of my life when he made the highest bid of the afternoon for me.

"We were displayed in the hotel grounds. I'd heard about his island and longed to be part of his collection. But always the businessman, he decided to keep me here, so that the Health and Fitness Centre could make use of my talents. I'm not paid a salary, of course, but everything I need is provided - a slave doesn't need much."

As she continued with the massage, her breasts swinging freely as she worked, she told Vivienne that Theo was recognized as one of the harshest masters around, even when absent.

"When he's out of the country, I'm left in the custody of one of his employees, who just happens to be a member of the hotel staff. That means I don't miss out on the beatings.

"There's only a handful of girls that he has beaten every day. But he gets tremendous pleasure just knowing that one of his slaves is being beaten in his absence, at a set time every day - in my case every evening, at 6.30 precisely, directly before my custodian goes about his other duties. Afterwards, I'm tied down until the next evening, unless I'm needed in here.

"I get to see and meet all kinds of people - the rich, the famous, and slaves who belong to other masters. Sometimes I'm even allowed to make love to someone's slave, though unfortunately I'm not allowed to touch you other than in a professional way. But it's a different story for my custodian. As one of the Master's most loyal employees, he gets to use some of the Master's girls from time to time; he's dying to use you!"

"Who's your custodian, Farrell or Woodly?"

"No, they're guards from the island and go with the Master. I'm left with one of the waiters."

"And I bet I know which one." Now it all made sense. Vivienne closed her eyes as a re-run of the waiter ramming his cock up Clitty's behind, the same waiter who had been so 'helpful' that first evening, played like a video tape in her mind. No wonder he'd told her that he was an "interested party."

It was all so bizarre she couldn't believe it.

Destiny remained totally professional. Vivienne couldn't fault her as she massaged her distress away, though she was slightly curious to know what making love with this gorgeous black girl would be like.

"If you're going to the island, there's someone you should look out for", Destiny warned. "I don't know what her name is, but you can't mistake her- she's got long red hair. Be careful, she's not what she seems. She's a slave like us, but she's got a vicious streak. I've heard whispers that she's been brought over to England for a while, to do some special job."

That made Vivienne think briefly about Denise, the irritating little redhead at work with the saccharin voice; a real goody-two-shoes with as much backbone as a blancmange. She probably had the sexual appetite of a glacier, Vivienne thought dismissively.

"What about Clitty?" Vivienne asked, remembering that she'd last seen her being touched up by Nathan.

"Word has it that she's flavour of the month, the current favourite", Destiny told her, and as such Clitty's treatment would be even harsher. "Competition among the girls is strong. Everyone wants to be Number One, even if it's only temporary! I've heard that Clitty's days are numbered - she's going to be sold."

"Why?"

Destiny giggled as her fingers swirled over Vivienne's temples. "There's a new kid on the block."

When Destiny had finished the massage, she announced that Vivienne was to be depilated. Vivienne wasn't unduly worried, since she thought it would save her doing her underarms and legs when she went home.

"The Master wants it done," Destiny's hand cupped Vivienne's black-fleeced mons, "here."

"No! I hate to see my pussy shaved."

"You don't understand," Destiny said as she applied a dab of mousse "he wants to do it himself."

"With this!" Theo stood in the doorway, brandishing the wicked-looking penknife he'd shown Vivienne in the Merc.

"Tie her down" he instructed coldly, narrowing his eyes. His mouth curved into the semblance of a smile. "I'd hate her to struggle and knock my hand."

Destiny worked quickly. Vivienne's arms were stretched out tautly above her head, the wrist straps joined together and rope threaded through the rings. Destiny tied the end to the metal bar to which the collar's chain was already fastened. Another rope was passed over her belly and beneath the table. Destiny wrapped it round and round, until four strands of rope flattened Vivienne to the table and held her securely.

"Spread her wide."

Destiny came round the table and passed the rope through each ring of the ankle straps. Theo smiled as the exquisitely boned, ebony-skinned girl complied with his wishes, tying the ends of the rope to the legs of the table.

"To make it more interesting," he dipped his hand into his jacket pocket and produced a pair of handcuffs, "we'll have you participate in the proceedings."

Vivienne watched open-mouthed as Theo yanked Destiny's slender arms behind her back and cuffed her wrists, making her breasts jut out invitingly. She was shocked to see Destiny's nipples harden as he used surgical tape to gag and blindfold the black girl. Next, he lifted Destiny onto the table.

"Kneel!"

He positioned Destiny with her legs either side of Vivienne's head and facing towards her legs, blocking Vivienne's view down her body.

"Sit on her face!"

Spreading her knees, Destiny slowly lowered herself over Vivienne's open mouth.

"And you," he smacked the undersides of Vivienne's breasts, smiling as a red patch appeared on her golden skin, "lick her out! I want something to watch while I work."

Vivienne's tongue pushed open the tumescent folds of Destiny's labia, tasting the bitter-sweet fluids of Destiny's arousal. Her own sex throbbed in reply. She felt the gold ring against the side of her nose, and the wiry curls tickled deliciously. Even with Destiny's weight covering her face making it almost impossible to breathe, she relished the debauchery of it all.

Flinching as the cruel blade struck cold against her burning skin, she tried to call out her distress as Theo began to scrape away her black curls. Her abdomen jumped as the blade nicked her painfully.

Juice and Vivienne's own saliva mixed to smear her face with the essence of desire as Destiny writhed. Sucking and lapping, she held herself rigid, frightened to come.

Destiny tensed, nearing her peak.

"I'll tell you when you can come!" Theo said sharply.

Vivienne heard him cross the room, and sighed with relief that the ordeal was over, then tensed again when she heard the clatter as he made further preparations. Her heart pounded in terror.

Her nipples were painfully erect. Her quim was beginning to leak its own juice.

She heard his footsteps as he crossed back towards the table. Redoubling her efforts, she sucked and licked for all she was worth.

"You may both climax..... "

Vivienne screamed out as blinding light filled her head and agonizing pain seared her belly.

"Now!"

Both girls convulsed violently as they came, with the smell of burning flesh filling their nostrils.

***

Only when Theo was satisfied that Vivienne's golden body was smooth as satin and that the brand was clearly defined, did he lift Destiny from Vivienne's face. Still blindfolded and gagged, he sent her scurrying to the corner where he instructed her to stay until someone came for her.

"This evening I'll beat you myself," he informed her dispassionately, "at 6.30 sharp." Addressing Vivienne, he said "You'll be returned to your room, where someone will prepare you."

He released her from the table. He checked that her collar was still positioned with the ring at the back, then clipped the wrists straps together behind her back.

"You'll be given others to wear. They'll match your collar- and be permanent."

Using the chain, he yanked them upwards between her shoulder blades, making her groan with discomfort.

She kept her eyes submissively lowered as he attached the chain to her collar.

"Haven't you forgotten something, Slut?"

"Th..thank you, Master."

Theo stood beside her in the middle of the white room. His stubble grazed her sensitive skin as he kissed her neck. The fingers of one hand worked her clitoris with tiny movements that caused her to moan softly, while the other pinched her nipple so spitefully that she had to bite her lip to stop herself from crying out.

"You'll be given instructions later which you'll obey without question or complaint, or earn the punishment of instant dismissal. I see from your eyes that you no longer want the freedom you craved at the beginning."

His voice became low and menacing, flowing thickly, like honey from a spoon. And Vivienne knew that this was when he was most dangerous.

"Do everything I demand and you'll please me greatly. Behave well, do as you're told, entertain my guests and you'll be rewarded- I'll keep my word and have you delivered to my island. Otherwise, you'll be forwarded to a faraway backwater where it always rains, where you'll begin your life over in obscurity. Do I make myself clear?"

Keeping her eyes lowered to the floor, Vivienne nodded mutely.

"Whatever else happens tonight, you will climax- for my guests' pleasure, not your own. Afterwards, orgasms will be denied you for the foreseeable future. Incidentally-" his free hand explored the swell of her breasts, where the cruel stripes had faded to leave purplish discolouration, "I gave strict instructions that your breasts were to be left unblemished, until I found time to deal with them myself. Clearly someone had other ideas. For this you'll be punished."

She knew he meant what he said, and opened her mouth to protest at the unfairness of it all. Luckily for her, no sound came out.

Theo headed for the door. Turning to look at her, his eyes were full of passion and his accent thick with arousal.

"You're only the third to wear my mark. Carry it with pride."

***

Sitting in the secret room, Theo rested his feet on Destiny. Still gagged and blindfolded, with her hands still handcuffed behind her back, she knelt on the floor with her forehead touching the carpet.

Neglecting the graceful, ebony-skinned girl as he sipped his metaxas, he concentrated instead on the sight on the other side of the two-way mirror. He fixed his eyes on his mark, burned into the soft flesh of Vivienne's belly.

It was quite an intricate design for a brand; a butterfly with a pin through the centre, which summed her up perfectly- she was indeed a captured butterfly. It would take a few days to heal properly, but sadly he hadn't the time, nor the inclination, to let her rest. The exhibition must go ahead as planned.

He glanced at his watch: 6.28. He reached for the whippy cane on the table just as Vivienne approached the mirror. Hauling Destiny to her feet, he made her stretch out across his knees, presenting him with a pair of rounded, savagely striped, black velvet buttocks.

6.29: He raised the cane as Vivienne studied her own reflection, almost as if she were looking Theo straight in the eye. As the hairdresser stepped up behind her to affix a mask, Theo brought the cane down on the girl's quivering flesh- 6.30 precisely.

Unaware of what was happening a few feet away on the other side of the mirror, Vivienne studied the reflection that bore little resemblance to herself, even though her shining, waist length hair had been left to hang loose.

To hide her identity, she wore a mask that been moulded and

painted to resemble a Siamese cat. Fitting snugly over her scalp, it covered the top half of her head, hiding her eyes and nose but leaving the flare of her nostrils clear, and her moist, ruby lips assessable. With slits for the eyes, before being fitted it had been demonstrated to her that the eyelids could be closed, thus doing away with the need for a blindfold when the necessity arose. Her toenails and long fingernails had been painted the same ruby colour as her lips. Attached to her slave collar by special, decorative clips was a weighty piece of jewellery, a necklace that was worth a small fortune. Studded with huge rubies, it fitted snugly around her golden, elegant neck. Row upon row of the exquisite jewels were fashioned in such a way that the whole formed a kind of gorget that draped from her neck downward and outward, effectively covering her upper chest. Almost touching her armpits, it left her luscious full breasts free to bounce enticingly. Then it tapered away again to end with one enormous ruby that dangled in the deep cleft between her mahogany-tipped globes.

Around her waist she wore a heavy, golden linked chain. Two further chains were attached to the front above each hip and secured at the end to make a V, the point of which extended to her pussy; her branded soft belly and nude sex were in effect framed by gold chains.

A chain of smaller links was attached to the bottom of the V, forming a G-string that threaded between her labia lips, and had the effect of rubbing the delicate membranes when she moved. Passing up the deep crack of her buttocks and scraping against the puckered hole of her back passage, it was secured to the heavy golden links round her waist.

Fastened at the back, the device could only be removed by means of a golden key that unlocked a tiny golden padlock- the same key that unlocked her slave collar, still attached to Theo's watch chain.

Finally, round her wrists and ankles she wore tight-fitting gold bands with rings attached that matched her slave collar. These had special locking devices that made removal impossible, except with a hacksaw. Her wrists were secured behind her back by a short, gold-coloured chain. Another, longer chain was fastened to her ankles, which once again made walking difficult.

She looked one last time at the terrible, still painful brand. She'd been given painkillers, though they had done little to deaden the agony. But she bore it bravely, proudly, gratefully. Destiny had told her that Theo always treated his favourites more cruelly than anyone else. And, since she'd been made to suffer so much in so short a time- a weekend that seemed much longer- then it followed that she, Vivienne, was his current favourite.

Behind the mask, she smiled as the hairdresser lowered the mask's eyelids, and she was led blindly to the next phase of her terrible, wonderful degradation.

CHAPTER FOURTEEN

Vivienne was taken to the sitting room to stand for inspection.

In her dark world behind the mask, her sense of hearing seemed more acute; she recognized at once the cultured tones of Flynn Pallister.

"Leave us."

Vivienne's flighty nature got the better of her. In an echo of her former self, she tossed her head so that her glorious raven hair fell about her golden shoulders. Fastening her hands behind her back had ensured that her breasts, accentuated rather than devalued by the extravagant jewels, were temptingly assessable. Aware of the effect on Flynn, she drew back her shoulders to project them further.

Shifting her weight from one leg to the other, she swayed her hips provocatively.

"Girl! Come here." There wasn't a hint of tenderness about his barked order.

Slightly miffed that he no longer called her by name, she took a few steps forward until his cygnet-ringed hand on her belly stayed her. As his skin made contact with her own, she couldn't help the flare of warmth in her belly.

Her nervousness robbed her of her senses.

"You know you want me, Flynn- you always have. Why don't you take me now?"

Smack! She screamed shrilly, hardly able to believe the pain as his spiteful hand struck the raw brand.

"Shut up, whore."

It still came as a shock to Vivienne to realize that the whore in question was herself. Whatever she'd done, or whatever had been done to her, she would never think of herself in that way.

But on reflection, perhaps that was exactly what she had become. The man in the dungeon had seemed to think so. Or maybe men simply got off on thinking of her in that way. It seemed to her that they were aroused by their own outrageous behaviour as much as the violation of her body.

In a way she didn't fully comprehend, she got off on it too.

Flynn's fingers swirled over the livid brand, at the same time sliding an insidious finger beneath the chain V. He gave it a sharp tug.

The effect was electric; a deliciously tormenting sensation set her clitoris tingling as the chain rubbed against her hardening bud.

"You've still got one hell of a problem with the Silence Rule. You'll have to have it thrashed out of you. And I'm just the man to do it."

She saw herself as she had been, thrust up against the wall in his room, beaten for the first time in her life. Then she'd hated him- now she realized that he'd awakened something deep and carnal within her, so that now the merest hint of pain made her ache with need.

If she were to have that time again, she would change nothing, except that, in her mental picture, it was no longer Flynn that flogged her with his belt- it was Theo.

Theo, the Connoisseur... her one true master. She knew now that the true purpose of her life was to be Theo's subjugated slave. She wanted nothing more from life than to worship him, and make him proud of her.

Flynn's urbane tones again became shadowed by the coarseness of his words.

"I can smell your excitement- you're all fired-up and ready to go. You're so hot you're fucking sizzling. I made a mistake in selling you to the big man; I should have kept you myself and fucked the arse off you. I'd have had my own office toy to play with, my own bundle of hot pussy to gag and cane. I'd have kept you in chains, pierced your cunt and shagged you senseless over the photocopier. You'd have liked that, wouldn't you?"

Not sure if she was supposed to answer him or not, she stayed silent and stood with her head submissively bowed.

Trembling now, even the air seemed to hum with the dark dangers that surrounded her.

She swivelled round at the sound of the door opening.

Recognizing the blended scents of metaxas, olives and that uniquely animal scent that only Theo exuded, before she had time to consider the wisdom of her actions, she threw herself to the floor in supplication, to lie prone at his feet.

"Master, I'm frightened."

If the eyes of her mask had been open, she would have seen the fire that burned within Theo's eyes, glittering with savage hunger. To have a beautiful girl, particularly this girl, submit herself with such abandon at his feet ignited a feverish impatience to dominate that he could scare contain.

"It's time you learned that fear," she felt his harsh, heavily-booted foot on the back of her neck, "heightens the senses like a blindfold does. This time...."

"This time?"

"Quiet! One more outburst and you'll be confined to the dungeon indefinitely. You already have five lashes across your delicious cunt outstanding. Perhaps I'll double it!

"Tonight there'll be no special draught to dull your senses; I want you fully conscious throughout. Pain and humiliation- you'll learn to embrace both with equal fervour. Everything that's been done and will be done in the future, is for my amusement. It's not my intention that you be harmed, but tonight's exhibition is special, and for the gratification of my guests." He removed his foot. "Guards! Fetch the pole."

Someone grabbed the chains that shackled her ankles and wrists and threaded a long, metal pole through them. With a guard at each end, they lifted the pole.

Vivienne's arms were dragged upward behind her; it felt as if they were being wrenched from their sockets. Her legs were pulled back as she was lifted off the floor. It wouldn't have been so bad if she were bound the conventional way with her belly uppermost, but like this the pain was almost unbearable.

Slung between the two guards, with her back forming a perfect arc and her breasts hanging ponderously, they hoisted the pole to shoulder height. Her head hung downward, with her waist length hair covering her face and touching the floor. Despite Theo's cruelty and virulent words, she knew that her love for him was more real than anything that had gone before. She would do whatever it took to make him happy- to make him fall in love with her.

"Guards, take the whore to the roof garden."

***

While the beauty of the extensive hotel grounds were well-known, boasting gardens at the rear that included a lake, a folly, and several strutting peacocks, the roof garden was completely unknown to the public. Concealed behind the hotel's high walled parapet, the flourishing roof garden, complete with a pump-operated stream and fountain, was quite invisible from the ground.

No one would ever dream that such an abundance of vegetation and garden statues, illuminated by strategically placed lights, existed above them, nor guess the reason for so many chairs having been set out in a semi-circle.

And they would never guess the true purpose of the strange stone structures, each one standing about six foot in height. Scholars, however, would recognize them at once as letters from the Greek alphabet- Alpha, Lamda and Omega , , .

Exclamations of delight from the assembled crowd greeted her as Vivienne's naked, bejewelled body was carried into the night. Breathing in the cool air, fragranced with honeysuckle and night scented stock, she found it welcoming on her hot skin.

The guards set her face down on the cold flagstones, removed the pole, then hauled her to her feet. With her ankles and wrists still chained, she was marched across to one of the stone structures. At one end of the semi-circle, it resembled the Greek letter Omega, an almost complete circle standing upright with rings set into the stone at intervals all the way round.

Someone removed her ankle chain and roughly kicked her legs apart; someone else grabbed her wrists. Yanking them up between her shoulder blades, he fastened them to a long chain that dangled from the top of the curve before shortening it so that she was forced to stand on tiptoe.

Her legs were spread wider, then her ankles were secured by chains to the feet of the structure. As if that weren't bad enough, chains were attached either side of her narrow waist, by means of the links of her belt, and secured to the widest part of the structure.

She didn't have to be able to see to know that she was displayed for a completely male audience, though how many men she couldn't even hazard a guess. It was with a strange sense of pride that she listened to their roars of approval as her body, bearing its cruel brand, was revealed to them.

She knew too that, due to the pose in which she now found herself, her nude, gaping red slit, effectively cut in two by the chain, was clearly visible. There was something wildly exciting about being displayed so publicly, she decided.

Under the night sky, a dozen or so men were seated in each of the three rows, some as naked as herself while others, like Theo himself, remained fully clothed. One of the men worked his cock with enthusiasm. While all the men feasted their greedy eyes on her lewdly illuminated, lithe, youthful body, one among them fondled a crop as fervently as if it were his shaft.

Vivienne drew in a breath as familiar stubble grazed her cheek.

"I've had many beautiful girls beaten." It was Theo's voice, and her heart leapt with joy. "I've fucked and abused more than I can count. But you-"

She felt his raw breath on her neck, and shivered with delight. She drew in a sharp breath as his teeth bit into her flesh.

"You're something special."

Like a panacea, Theo's whispered voice was soothing and sweet. But while his heavily accented words of affection took her by surprise, she was no fool. These were not words of romantic love, merely words of ownership and lust.

Standing beside her, Theo's hand cupped her breast and kneaded it roughly. His other hand slipped beneath her hair and caressed the back of her neck.

Straining against her bonds to rub her cheek against him, she felt a dizzying sense of liberation. Whatever happened now was beyond her control; she felt absolved from any wrongdoing and was therefore permitted, even encouraged, to enjoy whatever wicked perversions were heaped upon her without blame. Within her slavery she'd found a new, exciting freedom.

Theo's hands fell away. After a moment's silence, he addressed the audience.

"Gentlemen, welcome to this exhibition, a presentation of submission. While some of you will be attending for the first time, for others it is something of a regular event. You'll find this, my latest acquisition, fascinating, agreeable and extremely accommodating!"

Laughter filled the night air.

Visibly trembling, either from cold or fear, or something more pagan, Vivienne inhaled deeply, listening to her master's voice as he continued dispassionately.

"Who she is, or how she comes to be here is of no importance."

Theo gave the chain between her labia lips a sharp tug, relaxed it, then pulled again. Abrasively, it rubbed against her most sensitive regions, blindingly sweet as it was terrible. Several times he repeated the process, agitating the chain faster and quicker, driving her crazy with desire.

Soon her cunt was ablaze and her clitoris throbbing wildly. Her muscles tightened. Behind the mask, Vivienne screwed up her eyes in an effort to stop herself coming instantly.

"Reach for the moon-" he told her as, fast and furious, he continued to excite her with the chain, "climax as you've never done before." Then in a loud, masterful voice he commanded "Come, Whore, come."

Oblivious to everything save the rigidity of her limbs locked in spasm, she screamed as the first violent wave hit. Only her restraints prevented her knees from crumpling beneath her.

Floating in a bubble of joy, she was only half aware of Theo unlocking the small padlock at the back of the belt. He removed the chain from between her swollen pussy lips, then unclipped the chains that formed the V from the golden-linked belt, which he left in place. Other hands unfastened the chain that had held her arms in the agonizing position for so long, then unfastened her wrists.

Instead of being released, her arms were raised above her shoulders and her wrists were fastened to the metal rings further up the structure. Now she formed a perfect X inside the circle with her waist still attached to the widest point.

Theo announced "Let the entertainment begin" and right on cue, another woman appeared.

Dressed in black leather, she was only about five feet in height, but the thigh high boots with five inch spiked heels made her appear taller. With an abundance of flowing red hair, her gold slave collar marked her out as another of Theo's possessions. Her alabaster breasts were small but shapely. The gold rings that pierced her hard, rosy nipples had the men ogling her delightedly, commenting excitedly on the frothy red curls that adorned her sex.

Elbow length gloves gave her a certain elegance while the mask, like the mask of Zorro, leant her an aura of menace, as did the curled black whip in her small hand.

She took up a wide-legged stance beside Vivienne and uncurled the whip.

Had she been able to see, Vivienne wouldn't have believed that the woman she thought of as prim and girlie could have looked so intimidating- never have believed that Denise could wield a whip so expertly.

"Aarghh!"

Chained, and forced to take the lash solely for the entertainment of a bunch of perverted men, Vivienne smiled. Drowning in erotic submission, she welcomed the pain.

"Aarghhh!"

As the second scream of many filled the still night air, several shapely young girls appeared, carrying drinks trays. Each girl wore a specially designed white tuxedo. With long sleeves and three buttons at the front, the jackets were cut with deep, square necklines that ended below the bust, so that the girls' breasts were barely contained and bounced as they walked. Leaving the midriff bare, the sides tapered away to points that grazed their thighs, while the back of the jacket was split up to the waist.

Each girl also wore crotchless white knickers, a white bow tie and high, spike- heeled, white sandals.

While the whipping continued, the girls moved unperturbed among the audience, bending prettily so that Theo's guests could take full advantage of their proffered breasts and quims.

***

At last, the whipping stopped. Confined to her upper thighs, the strokes had been as agonizing as any that had gone before, and left red stripes of flame across Vivienne's golden skin. The click click of retreating stilettos had stopped, and the chatter and chinking of champagne glasses died away.

Once again, stubble grazed her cheek.

Rough hands unfastened her chains, and she was led away from the structure. The wrist bands were joined together behind her back. The heavy necklace and the chain around her waist were left in place.

Sharp fingers dug into her bare shoulders. Someone spun her around, round and round, until she was dizzy.

She heard Theo's voice, "Do with her as you will, but don't damage the goods, she was rather expensive" followed by scraping sounds as chairs were pushed back across the flagstones.

Almost at once, strange hands fell upon her where she stood, seizing her breasts. A wet mouth closed over hers, then trailed saliva down her chin and neck as it sought out her breasts.

Two calloused hands seized her under the arms, while sharp fingers grasped her ankles. She was carried a short distance, then laid on the cold, hard flagstones. Her hands, still secured behind her back, dug uncomfortably into the small of her back. At first, she tried to pull herself upright, but the man with the calloused hands held her down firmly for his companion.

Still gripping her ankles like a vice, the fingers pushed her feet towards her, scraping her soles on the hard slabs and raising her knees. The man flexed her legs, opening her dewy cunt, and whispered chillingly.

"Before the night's out, you'll be fucked so hard you'll be split in two."

It was Flynn!

Flynn released her ankles and heaved his heavy body over hers and shoved a dirty, smelly wad of cloth in her mouth.

"Gagged for my pleasure!" With no preamble, his demanding cock entered her with sweet brutality. "All the jewels in the world-" he said, fondling the ruby that hung between her juicy globes, while she hovered on a cloud of pure bliss, "can't disguise the fact that you're nothing but a fuck-crazy, dirty whore."

Grinding his crotch against hers as she arched to meet him, he gasped between the powerfully frenetic thrusting of his iron prick. All the while his refined tones loquaciously acquainted his accomplice with the delights of her body.

"The mask suits the slut- she's a real hell-cat. Her hot cunt's practically foaming. Her tits-"

Vivienne closed her mind to the filth that continued to rain down on her, concentrating instead on the calloused hands that kneaded her breasts roughly. A rope was produced and wrapped around each breast, binding it tightly. Even as tears sprang to her eyes warmth flooded through her. What was happening to her? A little cruelty and she was engulfed in joyous delirium.

Flynn continued to plunge in and out, while the other man crossed the flagstones and tied the ends of the rope to the wide crossbeam between the uprights of the structure behind, parting her breasts and tugging them towards her shoulders. As the rope bit into her soft, malleable flesh, he came and squatted over her, his knees either side of her head.

"Let's see how you like having your face fucked", he said, ripping Flynn's disgusting rag from her mouth and ramming his cock in its place.

***

Theo watched as Flynn and D.S. Radley profaned his latest treasure with an enthusiasm he'd rarely witnessed.

The man seated on Theo's right leaned closer.

"A most unusual brand. Freshly applied?"

"Today. I saw little point in waiting."

"Her pain must be considerable."

"Having one's flesh seared," Theo's lips twitched at the corners, "is always painful. She'll be in agony."

"How does she feel about it?"

"How she feels about it is of no consequence. I wanted it done, so it was done. A slave, Lord Stewkley-Smythe, has no say in the matter, though this particular slave seems to thrive on pain."

"Whoever marked her breasts enhanced their beauty considerably."

Theo fixed his eyes on her brutally striped globes, cruelly dragged apart and tethered. He knew the identity of the man who had marked her, but he wouldn't tell the girl that, just as he would never tell her the identities of those who violated and ill-treated her tonight.

"I intend to keep her marked", he told his companion. "She'll be beaten every day."

"What of the delightful redhead?" Lord Stewkley-Smythe shrugged his shoulders and raised his hands in a questioning gesture. "I wonder... how much would a piece like that fetch?"

"I need her to perform a specific task. While I'm away, she's to keep an eye, so to speak, on the other whore and administer the daily beatings. As you've seen, she's remarkably talented in that department. However, if she should come to the market in a week or two - somewhere in the region of..." Theo named a figure.

Lord Stewkley-Smythe nodded. The two men shook hands.

Theo turned his attention back to the entertainment, where Flynn and D.S. Radley were laying siege to Vivienne's soft, yielding body. The rise and fall of her tortured breasts as the rope bit in was almost more than Theo could stand. Usually content to sit back and watch, tonight he had a throbbing need to join in. It was all he could do to keep a rein on his lust as he watched Vivienne in the throes of a riotous orgasm.

In a simultaneous outburst of bestial rage, both men who raped her climaxed, saturating Vivienne's warm, fleshy cunt and succulent mouth with their hot, milky fluids.

Mad with desire, Theo signalled to the two men to withdraw.

Theo stood over the quivering girl, admiring the way her sweat glistened on her golden body. Sperm dribbled from the sides of her mouth and leaked from her cunt, where it mixed with her own juices to dribble down her legs. With the jewelled gorget sparkling in the moonlight and her golden chains and bands glinting, she seemed all the more ravished amidst the finery. His heart was bursting with pride.

***

Lingering somewhere between delicious afterglow and erotic humiliation, Vivienne trembled as stubble grazed her skin, recognizing Theo at once. Stiffening in apprehension, she waited for his exquisite cruelty to begin, rejoicing in the knowledge that once again, he was claiming what was his. Feeling wholly owned, she would accept his gift of pain as a benediction. She would make him proud.

"Arrghhh!"

Sudden pain blazed through her nipple as Theo sank his teeth into the hard morsel. He bit her again, unhooking the necklace from the slave band as he did so and beckoning a guard to take it away.

At last he drew back. Leaving her breasts imprisoned, he gestured for more rope to be brought. Tying it to her ankle bands, he raised her legs and, flinging them wide, tied the ends to two statues that stood several feet apart, one of Athena and the other Aphrodite.

Now, lying on her back with her hands still secured behind her, her breasts brutally separated, her ankles at waist height and her legs held wide open, she afforded the onlookers a perfect view of her glistening quim.

Even without him speaking and sight denied her by the mask,

she knew he'd called for a whip. Made of several strands of plaited leather, the end consisted of many strands of soft leather, each about nine inches long, which he trailed lightly over her body.

She felt a tickling sensation from her toes upward, trembling as the strands stroked the insides of her thighs, knowing that at any moment she would feel the first strike. Then the leather found her sex, open and red, and began insidiously stroking the inner membranes. For what seemed like ages, the strands lingered, igniting the walls of her cunt until the juices once again flowed.

Theo trailed the strands upward across her belly. She screamed out as they touched the raw, newly-scorched imprint that identified her as his.

Then, so gently it was maddening he continued upward. Across her bound breasts, toying with her nipples, before tracing the contours of her chin, over her open lips and nose.

She tensed, knowing he was positioning himself for the first strike.

Swish! Crack!

Pain exploded across her pliable flesh as the whip struck, the leather strands stinging as they curled around her breasts. A torrid warmth spread through her, and the line between pain and pleasure began to grow fuzzy.

Her excitement mounted and she screamed again as fire ravaged her flesh, a direct hit over the first strike.

Swish! Crack!

Swish! Crack!

Fireworks lit up her senses as the fast and furious strikes raised red ribbons of exquisite agony across the back of her thighs, the ends curling round to sting her inner thigh where her skin was softest.

Her cries rose and fell with each carefully aimed blow. Then, fire as she'd never known blazed across the lips of her sex, as Theo carried out his barbarous threat.

One.

The strands flicked across her stiffened bud.

Two, three.

Tears ran down beneath the mask.

Four, five.

Still the blows kept on coming.

Six.

She lost count as her screams turned to wails.

Swish! Crack!

Her shrieks rang out, not just with pain, but with the delicious orgasm that ripped through her, taking her almost to the edge of unconsciousness.

Theo wasn't about to be denied his pleasure of keeping her awake. He snapped his fingers and a guard brought a bucket.

Vivienne was suddenly drenched in icy water.

While she lay motionless, wet and shivering, Theo glanced around. His guests were on the edge of their seats, some pumping their cocks while one man shot a fountain of come into the air.

Theo spotted his new recruit. Knowing that if he were to maintain the newcomer's interest, absorb him fully into the organization and at the same time fulfill Theo's own fondness for manipulating lives, then he must be given a taste of the delights that awaited a loyal employee.

Theo crooked his finger.

With trembling hands, Nathan took the proffered whip. Following Theo's gestures, Nathan stepped back to position himself. After only a moment's hesitation he brought the whip down, savagely flaying the belly of the girl he'd loved.

***

Vivienne could hardly breathe for the pulsating need that caught in her throat as the night wore on. Knowing that somewhere Theo still watched her, she relished the debauchery as a way of proving her submissive devotion. More than that, she wanted to justify her right to claim him as her master.

Heat seared through her veins as anonymous lovers took her one after another, some tenderly, others with wild abandon and cruelty.

For a while, she was able to pick out the refined voice of Flynn, peppered as always with his crude words, along with the sandpaper voice of the man from the dungeon. But as time wore on, voices became irrelevant. Only actions meant anything in her terrifyingly delirious state.

She was flogged and fucked time and time again. Sometimes, they tied her to one of the stone structures, sometimes not. But always her hands remained secured behind her back and the mask kept in place.

She was made to lie on her back, or sometimes her stomach. They had her kneel, or lean over some kind of huge stone slab, which necessitated her standing on tiptoe with her legs splayed open and her belly flattened against the rugged stone. With her head bent downward, her hair fell like a black curtain.

While she writhed in delirious agonies of rapture, she sank further into a haze of euphoria, climaxing again and again. Every time she came close to fainting, she was drenched in cold water. She didn't know, or care, if she was in heaven or hell.

Night stretched into dawn. She had come over her face, her neck, in her hair; everywhere was covered in semen, sweat and saliva.

Someone made her stand. Turning her slave collar so that the ring was at the back, he dragged her wrists up between her shoulder blades. First attaching them to her collar, he then fixed another chain to them which he hooked to one of the stone structures. While he shafted her back passage, someone else rammed their cock up her cunt. She suspected, rightly as it turned out, that it was Theo who chained her, then profaned her anus.

At last, Theo allowed unconsciousness to claim her.

CHAPTER FIFTEEN

Things didn't progress as Vivienne had expected. Firstly, when she awoke it was to find that the heavy drapes at the windows had been pulled back. She squinted as the sun blazed in, flooding the room.

Secondly, she was unchained. Naked, apart from the slave collar, wrist and ankle bands, she was free to move about the room. She was lying on one of the beds; the other was vacant with its bed coverings pulled up.

It was odd how respectable the luxurious room appeared. With the vast array of equipment hidden behind the drapes, no one would ever suspect that sadistic acts of sexual exploitation were routinely administered here.

Something brushed against the insides of her sore, inflamed cunt. Afraid to look along her own body for fear of what she might discover, she brushed her hand over her bruised thigh, smiling softly as her fingers skimmed over the raised ridges of brutalised flesh.

She cried out as a needle-sharp barb caught her finger. She snatched her hand away. God no! Someone must have fitted some dreadful apparatus of torture to her pussy while she slept. Raising her finger for examination, she shrank back at the globule of ruby blood where her skin had been punctured.

Dredging up every ounce of courage, she stole a glance in the mirror.

A blood red rose projected from her ultra-sensitive quim. No empty gesture on Theo's part, she recognized it as a highly significant act, showing the high regard in which he held her

Careful not to catch the thorns on the raw, delicate membranes, she withdrew the stem. Lifting the bloom to her nose and inhaling deeply, she breathed in the sensuous cocktail, the subtle fragrance of the rose that mingled enticingly with her own sweet juices.

Smilingly, she slipped the rose in her hair.

She swung her legs off the bed and stretched her aching limbs. But far from rejoicing, she found her sudden freedom of movement strange, disconcerting- no longer her natural state. It meant that she had control.

The frailty took her by surprise. Every part of her body hurt. Her arms and legs were stiff and sore from her constant restraint and her quim was sore from frequent violation. Both her throat and jaw hurt from having been forced wide to accommodate so many stiff cocks, and the rounded globes of her behind were raw.

There was discomfort, too, in what Flynn had coarsely referred to as "the servant's entrance".

Wincing at the various aches and cramps, Vivienne nevertheless welcomed the pain as if she'd earned some kind of reward.

Staggered, nothing could have prepared her for the erotic image before her when she checked the mirror. Without a trace of conceit now, she viewed the image dispassionately, as perhaps Theo himself would see her.

Her tousled, raven hair, matted with dried sperm and with the rose hooked behind her ear, gave her the sensuality of a feral she-cat as it fell abundantly to her waist. The golden slave collar and bands hinted at an attempt to tame that very wildness. Multi- coloured bruises blossomed and red and purple welts criss-crossed her golden skin. Breasts, belly, thighs- every inch of her front bore the marks of her beatings.

She turned slowly so that she could see her back. Once again, hardly an inch remained unmarked, confirming the severity of her shameful ordeal.

Facing the mirror again, she gently touched the cruel brand. Still livid, the butterfly that had been sadistically burned into her flesh enhanced rather than invalidated her sensuality.

A weekend had come and gone, and she'd been transformed.

Realization suddenly hit her. A weekend - then today was Monday - the game was over!

***

Guards would be posted outside the main door, of course, but there wasn't a sign of anyone else. It was as if no one else had ever been there, as if she'd dreamed it all. Except that her once unblemished body bore evidence to the contrary.

She went through the entire suite like a whirlwind. Apart from one door along the corridor, every room was open to her, though the cupboards, wardrobes and drawers were locked.

As she flitted from one luxurious room to another, her throat went dry with sudden panic as the full implications of being by herself dawned on her. She would have to face up to the debauchery alone.

Curiously, at first she wasn't the least bit concerned about the salacious nature of her ordeal, nor how she would live with the shame. She gave no thought as to how she was going to get home without clothes or transport, nor even how she could erase the marks from her body. What did concern her though, was a sudden sense of incompetence.

Gone was the career-minded, fun loving, sexually dominant woman of a few days ago; in her place stood a submissive sex slave who's only purpose in life was to please her master. Theo had made her his slave, then abandoned her.

"Bastard!" Vivienne yelled the word to the emptiness of the sitting room. She'd given him everything and couldn't face the thought of life without him. She needed a master. She tugged furiously at the collar around her elegant throat, then the matching bands around her wrists and ankles. "Bastard! Bastard!"

Crushed and confused, instinct alone guided her to the computer in the corner. She clicked the mouse. Words flashed up on the screen, replacing the swirling patterns of the screen saver.

Monday: rest day. Clothes provided. Proceed to Dining Room - food provided.

Meet Representative - obey him as you would your Master.

Tuesday: return to work. Daily beatings will begin.

She smiled. How could she ever have doubted him? She should have known that, even in his absence, Theo's power over her would be irrefutable, his ownership stamped into the very fabric of her life as surely as it was stamped into her belly.

***

Having showered and dried her hair, she brushed it vigorously to remove all the tangles it had acquired during the events of last night. She did her make-up, using the cosmetics that had miraculously appeared. After lining her eyes with kohl, she applied thick layers of mascara, then coated her lips with the flame red lipstick. Someone had arranged clothes on her bed. No underwear, she noticed.

The very low cut leather bodice, little more than a front-clasping bra, barely contained her striped breasts as she fastened the two metal studs between them. The matching leather skirt fitted snugly round her waist. The hemline, level with her nude sex, rubbed enticingly against her quim with every step she took.

It took a little time to put on the thigh high boots with spiky heels. Leaving a gap of bare, striped skin between the hem of the skirt and the top of the boot, they laced up the side of the leg, so that bare flesh showed through the gaps. With a wide, studded strap that buckled at the top, another buckled around the ankle.

Wide-eyed, she checked her appearance. Now she really did look like a whore.

Regretfully, she left the suite, and closed the door. Two guards fell into step behind her.

Not in the least appalled that she hadn't escaped from Theo's scandalous demands after all, she was surprised that no one seemed to pay her any attention as she made her way to the dining room, followed by Theo's goons. It made no sense, for not only was she dressed like a hooker but she felt as though she were wearing a sandwich board that declared her as such to the entire world.

The guards positioned themselves inside the dining room, either side of the door. The waiters brought her food and drink without taking her order. It seemed Theo controlled her diet as well as her body.

A man approached her table as she drained her coffee cup. Wearing a kaftan that was thirty decades out of date, his bulk was immense. Over six foot, at first sight he reminded Vivienne of a massive bear. His lengthy, black hair was wild and curly. His moustache and long, woolly black beard all but covered the lower portion of his weathered, olive face. He was frightening, like a wild man who'd been living alone in the woods for too long.

"I'm Steffano." His accent was unmistakeably Greek.

He looked her over from head to toe. Only his penetrating eyes, like tiny beads of glittering jet, registered his approval. His command was simple.

"Come."

The doorman acknowledged her with a nod of his head and a knowing smile as she followed Steffano out through the heavy, studded oak doors of the hotel.

***

Steffano led her across to an old, beat up red ford.

"I'm sorry," he said with no regret at all in his tone, "but your Master insists upon your further degradation. It pleases him to know that while he sits in luxury aboard his private jet back to Greece, your suffering continues." He led her round to the back of the car and opened the boot.

Working quickly, he manacled her hands behind her back, then walked round to the front of the car. Raising the bonnet, he checked the oil, wiped the dipstick on an oily rag, then closed the bonnet again and returned to her side.

She heaved at the noxious fumes as he used the rag to gag her.

Next he manacled her ankles.

He thrust his huge hands, with hair sprouting from his knuckles, into her bodice and withdrew her breasts. Roughly, he worked her nipples into stiff peaks, then held up two wicked-looking devices for her inspection. Identical, they consisted of two rings that could be slipped over the nipple and tightened. Each had fiendish metal spikes of about an inch long placed at intervals all the way round. These, he assured her, though not deadly were sharp enough to puncture the skin.

Once he'd fitted these in place, he produced a camera. She stiffened as the shutter clicked.

"If he's pleased with the result, your Master will have the photograph copied in oils to hang here, in the hotel, or on the wall of his private rooms on the island, or somewhere where his other slaves are obliged to look at it." Steffano grunted as he put the camera back in the boot. "As the Connoisseur's advisor and closest friend, I'll be recommending that he has the photograph reproduced as compliment slips to send to his associates. Incidentally," his little laugh held a trace of malice, "I understand he branded you himself. I hope it wasn't too painful. I would have used anaesthetic. In my capacity as doctor to his girls, it's I that usually perform such operations as he deems necessary. It's I that pierce their bodies, take care of their general health and prescribe birth control."

He placed a hood over her head with the explanation "Your Master requires that your destination remain a mystery." A drawstring at her neck ensured that the hood wouldn't become displaced during the journey.

Panic gripped her as Steffano picked her up and shoved her into the boot of the car. He arranged her in the foetal position, causing the barbaric spikes around her nipples to dig painfully into her flesh.

The boot slammed shut.

***

The Victorian house in which Vivienne found herself was a rather grand, fully staffed property, ostensibly owned by Theo. Here his friends and associates, or in this case his right hand man, could entertain in a more private, congenial atmosphere.

The housekeeper, Mrs. Hall, informed her that Steffano came once a year, when he enjoyed a break from his more usual role on the island. His usual reward for dedicated service was to pick a slave of choice to serve him for the duration of his stay, but this time the girl had been chosen for him; on this trip he was to combine business with pleasure by supervising Vivienne.

Under Steffano's guardianship, Vivienne's life acquired a hitherto unknown uniformity. The day began at 5.30 sharp when she was roused by Mrs. Hall. After showering, she was made to exercise in the basement gym. Only when Steffano was satisfied with the results was she allowed to eat, alone in her room.

Kept naked in the house, when Steffano delivered her to the office she wore the clothes that were laid out on her bed each morning. A white silk, long sleeved, high necked top concealed her collar and wrist bands. Instead of a skirt, she was obliged to wear close fitting, black leather trousers that showed off her tight, rounded arse to perfection, while at the same time having the desired effect of hiding her ankle bands. She was also required to wear strappy black shoes with spiky heels.

While the outfit, enhanced by her waist length hair, flaunted her sexuality, at the same time it made it more difficult for her colleagues to take advantage, as did the meshed metal covering Steffano strapped tightly over her sex each morning. Held in place by narrow leather strips around her hips, with another threaded between her lower lips and up between the cheeks of her buttocks, there was just enough slack to allow normal bodily functions which were difficult but not impossible. Secured by a tiny padlock at the back, hidden beneath the waistband of her trousers and to which Steffano had the key, to the observer it was no more visible than an ordinary thong.

Under the watchful eye of Flynn Pallister, Vivienne's talent for business continued to be an asset to Paston Communications. It seemed that, for the time being at least, Theo was unwilling to send for her.

Her flighty nature of earlier times was strictly controlled, as was her attitude towards the male workforce, now beginning to outnumber the women by more than was politically acceptable. Invariably with lowered eyes, some of the men with whom she'd previously flirted found her newfound quiet servility disconcerting and wondered at the change, while those in the know took full advantage and pushed her around.

Forced to work alongside Denise, the two women never conversed, except when business dictated, though unspoken hostility grew between them.

But events took a dramatic turn each lunch time, when Vivienne received her prescribed daily beating. Flynn oversaw the arrangement as instructed, taking full advantage of his permitted, though somewhat curtailed, privileges. While his abuse of Denise was quite acceptable, his entitlements concerning Vivienne had been unexpectedly reduced- he was only allowed to make use of her back passage.

At 1 pm precisely, Flynn took the two girls down to the basement. Among the boilers for the heating system, water pipes and the various items that were kept in storage, the girls would strip on command, leaving Vivienne's sex encased by the mesh.

Vivienne was made to lie either on her back or her stomach, or lean over some piece of heating apparatus that burned her belly terribly. Then, in the hot, stuffy atmosphere, she was strapped down.

Flynn always provided the ball gag, which he fitted with obvious relish, and got off on verbally abusing her.

Expecting Flynn to administer the beatings, it came as a shock to Vivienne the first time that the diminutive, naked figure of Denise took up her pose. And, while she soon got used to the idea, Vivienne never found out that it had been Denise who'd laid into her so viciously that night at the hotel.

With her Titian hair cascading round her shoulders and her nipple rings glinting, Denise sometimes used a riding crop that Flynn issued her with, or sometimes he gave her a small whip, or an evil looking, whippy cane.

The redhead delighted in her domination over a fellow captive and laid into the tender, golden flesh that was presented to her daily with as much severity as the chosen implement would allow.

For her part, Vivienne writhed in the agony of her ordeal, sobbing helplessly into the gag. Beginning to believe herself forsaken by Theo, she rarely gained any sexual enjoyment; it was purely cruelty that had to be endured.

Afterwards, Flynn would use Denise as he saw fit. Sometimes he'd take the whip to her, though it was obvious to Vivienne that these weren't Denise's only beatings. Her small frame was always covered in purple weals, as was Vivienne's.

In the evenings, Flynn took Denise home with him but handed Vivienne over to Steffano. As on that first day, Steffano always bound and blindfolded her before shutting her in the boot for the journeys to and from work.

Back at the house, Mrs. Hall returned her to her attic room, where she would strip and shower before presenting herself to Steffano in his study. Then he'd remove the mesh from her quim and examine the marks of her beating. He administered cooling ointment to the bruises and lacerations, explaining it was more to aid the healing process so that she could be beaten again than to lessen the pain.

"After all," he reminded her, "your pain is Theo's pleasure. I'd be guilty of gross misconduct if I were to alleviate that pain altogether."

Steffano had a free hand to do with her as he wished after the main meal, again taken alone, provided he continued to send daily bulletins and pictures to Theo via e-mail.

At night, Mrs. Hall took Vivienne back to her room. She wasn't allowed TV, radio, books or even magazines. The only thing she had to look at in the otherwise bare room was Andromeda Waiting, hanging opposite her bed like some beautiful, dreadful glimpse of her own life.

The bed was hard, and Mrs. Hall fixed one end of a chain to her collar and the other to a ring in the wall, before attaching her hands to her collar so that she couldn't play with herself.

At weekends, after her ususal exercise and the fitting of her mesh, Steffano set her to work in the kitchen, or cleaning the house, until 1 pm, when she again presented herself in his study, where he meted out her daily beating. Sometimes he removed the mesh and, with his immense weight crushing her, he pounded into her with his not insignificant prick. Afterwards, he replaced the mesh and sent her back to her duties.

Naked, apart from her slave bands and collar, and with her sex imprisoned by the mesh, she soon got used to being leered at and groped by the servants.

***

Life with Steffano, Theo mused as he settled himself in front of his computer, had been far from pleasant for the English girl over the past weeks. Having regularly received Steffano's pictures of her, Theo could see for himself the results of Steffano's rigorous regime.

Her diet had been healthy, though not necessarily appetizing, her exercise periods had been strictly controlled. Now her waist was even more slender, making her breasts appear bigger and heavier. Her thighs flared even more sensuously, and her once shapely legs appeared longer and were positively erotic in their elegance.

"Steffano was right about her tits, too", Theo mused as he touched his finger to the screen. He stroked the dark, turgid nipples that now had large rings passed through them, as had the fleshy, labia lips that protruded from the thick, black bush that once again adorned her pubis.

Today's picture was particularly horny, showing her sex pulled apart by a chain attached to each labia ring and tautly secured to bolts in the floor.

Theo zoomed in on her gloriously red slit, moist and open for him, and was soon panting with desire for her. In response to his need, his fingers shot up inside the nineteen year old who stood beside him. Paying her no real attention, she was merely another nameless slut to slake his body's demands while he looked at the screen.

Secured to the leg of his desk by means of a chain attached to her slave collar, her arms were affixed to her sides by means of her wrist bands clipped to leather straps around her thighs. He rammed his fingers hard into the girl, then when she screamed out he doused her with metaxas. He poured another with his free hand and lifted it to his lips.

Fleetingly, he wondered if he'd fallen in love with the English girl, but dismissed the idea as absurd.

With his eyes rivetted to the screen, he put down his glass. Never had he been so bewitched by a slave that it was he that endured the torture. He reached for the 'phone. He had to put an end to it and have the slut dispatched to him immediately.

***

One lunch time, as Vivienne lay on her stomach and tied in the favoured X over the top of an old desk beside the boiler, Flynn removed his clothes.

"Things will be different today", he said, grabbing fistfuls of her hair and jerking her head upward. "I won't even gag you. This is the last chance I'll have to screw you- you're to be shipped out to your master! He's sold this other bitch to some Lord." Flynn nodded in the direction of Denise. "He got a good price for her, too. I've offered Theo a fucking fortune to buy you back, but it seems you're not for sale. Still, I've got a new playmate, someone to train up to my own standards."

Vivienne froze as Roxanne appeared from the shadows. Naked, she came and stood beside Flynn, who answered Vivienne's unspoken questions.

"She was so impressed by what she saw she asked me to take her. Seeing as I couldn't have you, then why the fucking hell not? In case you're wondering how she got past security today, she came with a friend of yours, someone who just wanted to say good bye. Bribery's an ugly word, but Security let them both in without any trouble."

CHAPTER SIXTEEN

Vivienne gasped as Woodly emerged naked from the shadows, with a cigarette between his lips.

"What Theo doesn't realize-" Flynn held up a small key for her inspection, "is that everyone's not as trustworthy as Steffano. It was easy to have the key lifted, but like Cinderella it's got to be home by midnight." He laughed bitterly as he proceeded to unlock the padlock. "Steffano won't be back from arranging your travel details until then."

"We'll have to make the most of you", Woodly said threateningly .

Vivienne didn't care what they did to her. All that mattered was that Theo had sent for her at last. Her heart was singing.

Grasping his iron cock, Flynn guided it towards her, forcing open her lips.

"Suck, you filthy, whip-crazed slut!"

Helpless and spreadeagled across the desk, she couldn't do anything but comply. But as she sucked, taking his prick deep into her throat, she realized with shame that she was enjoying herself.

She savoured the feel of the tumescent flesh just as she savoured the feeling of vulnerability that swept over her. She was lost, a victim - albeit a happy, willing one now that Theo had sent for her.

"This is the end of life as you know it, " Flynn said, "you'll spend the rest of your days in a cell, or shackled to a post and flayed, with an open cunt and your arse on fire. He'll make you eat dirt just for the sheer hell of it."

As she lay defenceless and vulnerable, with every opening of her body accessible, his frightening words came to her through a mist of joy. She was going to her master!

"You're not a name. Hell, you're not even a number!" His words were punctuated by his ragged breath as he continued to fuck her mouth. "You're nothing but wet cunt and tortured flesh." Flynn slipped his hands between her body and the desk, feeling for her newly-pierced nipples. She shrieked as he gave them a sharp tug. "You think you know pain? Don't you believe it! He'll hurt you till you beg yourself dry, then he'll hurt you some more. And for what? His fucking amusement." He threw back his head and laughed.

Suddenly, Flynn withdrew. Before she had time to catch her breath, Woodly took his place. She choked as he speared her throat, lunging frenziedly into the wet depths.

"I'm going to fill your mouth with hot milk!" he said, taking the cigarette from his mouth. Spiteful and mean, he held it close to her face.

She heard Flynn walk around the desk.

"You enjoy it all, don't you? Even your arsehole beckons to passing trade- I wonder if your precious master realizes just how much you enjoy a prick up your arse. He thinks your pain is for his pleasure and doesn't know what kind of masochist he's got on his hands. You've got a body that begs for the lash!"

Yes, yes, it was all true! As long as Theo wanted her, she welcomed the humiliation and pain as one welcomes the sun after winter's blizzards. For the first time in weeks, she was alive!

Flynn hoisted himself up onto the desk. With his legs either side of her backside he lowered himself. There was a terrible ripping sensation as he tore her hot flesh with his frenetic pounding, driving his shaft deeper into her backside.

Her cry was stifled by Woodly's cock as the vigorous thrusting in and out of both openings brought tears to her eyes. And not only that. The smell of urine, sweat and cigarettes that seemed ever present from Woodly's prick filled her nostrils, making her gag.

Hot with humiliation and need, pain combined with pleasure so that she could hardly tell the difference; on the edge of delirium, she couldn't tell which was stronger. She felt the inexorable building up of tension in her muscles, and fought to hold back the tide of orgasm that threatened to engulf her. She mustn't come!

With her eyes bulging, she caught a glimpse of Roxanne strapping on a large dildo.

Flynn, still crouched over her, momentarily stopped thrusting.

Vivienne flinched as Roxanne's skilled fingers touched her pussy with light, feathery strokes. Then suddenly, Roxanne drove the dildo fiercely into Vivienne's sex at the same moment as Flynn resumed his brutal fucking of her back passage.

Vivienne moaned as the mixed delights engendered wild sensations that flooded through her body. With a cock in her arse, a dildo up her cunt and a cock in her mouth, she was drowning in erotic bliss.

And all the while, the blistering shame kept her paralysed.

Vivienne grunted, trying to ignore the growing tension as once again, her climax approached. There was an involuntary tightening of her muscles as she fought to keep it at bay, knowing if she were to come now, Flynn and his accomplices would betray her to Theo. She didn't care that it was she who'd be punished and not her abusers, but couldn't bear to think of the displeasure her disobedience would cause her Master. So she closed her eyes tightly and put all her efforts into holding back the tide.

But it wasn't over yet- she'd forgotten about Denise.

Whizz! Crack!

With spot-on accuracy, Denise wielded the whippy cane. Strike after dreadful strike fell across Vivienne's back, causing her to jerk as each blow struck. At last Flynn let out a roar, filling her rectum with scalding liquid. Rocking back and forth, violent after-spasms shook his body.

Woodly, racked by his own climax, yelled like a madman, filling her mouth with hot, salty come that she was forced to swallow.

The dildo was removed; the thrashing stopped. There were moans of pleasure as Roxanne and Denise turned to each other for release.

Then Vivienne's own orgasm hit. Spasms shook her body, sending her into a delirium of howls and shudders, until the familiar darkness of oblivion once again claimed her.

***

Vivienne didn't return to work that afternoon. Instead, she was left in the basement until everyone had gone home. Then two men, accompanied by Flynn, came for her. She was made to stand while Flynn fitted the mesh back in position, then handed over the key.

"Remember, give it back to Mrs. Hall."

So, it was Mrs. Hall who'd sold out!

They drew her arms behind her back, joining her wrists. They fitted a chain to her ankle bands.

"You'll never know how much I love doing this", Flynn laughed as he fitted a ball gag. Then he blindfolded her.

Bundled up in a blanket and hefted up onto one of the men's shoulders, Vivienne was lugged outside like a rolled up carpet. One of the men opened the doors at the back of a white transit van and chucked her inside.

With no thought for her safety, the van was driven like madly into the night, propelling her around the back.

At last, the doors were opened. She recognized Mrs. Hall's voice and knew they'd arrived back at the house.

"Quickly! Get her upstairs. I've got to get her ready before Steffano gets back."

By midnight she was standing in the study, waiting. In accordance with instructions, the mesh had been removed and she'd been fed. Bathed, with her hair washed and brushed, she stood naked and barefoot. Her hands were again fastened behind her back and her ankles chained.

She turned her head as Steffano entered.

"Good", he said. "Soon you'll be aboard the plane, and in Greece within a few hours. But you're not quite ready to travel just yet."

Vivienne gave a nervous laugh. "Well, I can hardly go like this, can I?"

For the first time, Steffano struck her face, sending her crashing to the floor.

He hauled her to her feet and gagged her with wide tape.

" It looks as if Theo will have to gag you for keeps if he expects silence from you."

Dragging her across the room, he drew aside an antique silk screen, revealing a wooden crate in the alcove. He opened the lid.

"Get in."

***

Vivienne counted herself lucky that there were enough gaps between the slats of the crate to allow air in. At least she could breathe.

Through the silent sobs that shook her body, she listened to the men's voices as the crate was loaded aboard the plane.

"Another consignment for Greece?"

"It's another national treasure, destined for the Connoisseur."

"Then we'll take good care of it, Sir."

Frightened in the cold and dark, even the humiliation of being smuggled abroad in a crate, hardly big enough to contain a pig, could dampen her burning need to be with her master. Wretched as she was, the poor girl told herself that she could bear it all if he willed it.

For an age she remained cramped in the stifling crate. In desperate need to relieve herself, she had no choice but to ease the pain in her bladder. Sitting in the wet, the stench of her own urine added to her misery.

What was to become of her? She'd been a fool if she'd ever believed she could make Theo love her, to believe that she was anything more to him than he himself had proclaimed her to be- a nameless piece of nothing. She could be bought and sold, drugged, chained, fucked and beaten, branded and pierced, and shipped off to who knew where without anyone lifting a finger to help her. No one knew she was here, and if they did, no one cared.

It was all true. Life as she knew it was over.

***

The voices around her were Greek.

Nauseated by the rocking motion as they crossed by boat from mainland Greece to Theo's island, it was all she could do to stop herself vomiting.

Dry land at last. As the crate was hoisted ashore, excited male voices crowded in on her as men swarmed around the crate.

One rose above the others. Theo!

A spiral of warmth ignited her belly.

Not understanding his furious words as he instructed the hooded guards to fetch crowbars, Vivienne was sure that he was tearing someone off a strip for the scandalous way she'd been crated up like some animal.

She couldn't have been more wrong.

"Where's the fucking painting? " Theo yelled in Greek. "It was supposed to arrive with her. Spiros, get on to it now; find out what the hell's happened. I don't care if you have to go to Athens yourself and collect it, but get it sorted and make it quick. Take the chopper."

At last the lid of the crate was removed. Momentarily blinded by the bright sunlight, Vivienne was unable to move due to having been crouched in one position for so long.

Several pairs of rough, male hands groped her as they helped her to her feet. Gasps of delight came from the small group of hooded men as her body was revealed to them. Unable to protest because of the tape across her mouth, she shot them an indignant look. But that only made them guffaw loudly.

Standing unsteadily in the strong sunshine and blinking dazedly, she searched the crowd for Theo. Then, with her hands and feet still shackled, she fell joyously into his arms.

Immediately, his fingers sought out the two new rings through her labia, then shot up inside her. He whispered in English against her hair.

"Even dirty and foul smelling you make me want you. But there'll be time enough for that later. Soon you'll be cleaned up and fed, then taken to your cell to sleep," the familiar thickness of lust stoked his accent as his mouth twisted cruelly, "tomorrow's your big day.

"But first, I'll take you on a little tour. It's time you learned about this island paradise that you were so keen to come to."

He produced a metal ring of about two inches in diameter. With four short chains hanging from it, he clipped one to each nipple ring, then attached the other two to her labia rings. Lastly, he attached a lead to the ring.

Giving it a sudden jerk to encourage her to follow him, her pain showed in her eyes, bringing a smile to Theo's lips as her nipples and pussy lips were elongated by the pull on the lead.

The chain between her ankles made walking difficult. She couldn't help the tears that cascaded down her face as Theo half dragged her away from the quay. Stumbling ungainly behind him, the sun baked ground burnt her bare feet. The way was made more difficult still by the stones that slipped and scraped her feet as Theo led her up the hillside.

Vivienne got her first view of what she took to be an ancient temple on the hillside, glistening white against the backdrop of the turquoise Aegean.

But nothing could have prepared her for the sight that met her eyes en route. It took several moments for the full horror to dawn on her.

Beautiful young girls were dotted about like living statues. Chained to posts or large iron rings sunk into the ground to prevent them from moving, each girl, either naked or wearing a flimsy chiton, was lewdly positioned. While some poses could be considered artistic, others verged on the bizarre.

One pretty blond, her curvaceous body bearing the marks of a recent beating, had been arranged in the position known as " the crab", with a tripod placed in the small of her back to support her. Her outstretched arms and legs were chained to the ground. A huge stone phallus that looked as if it had been pilfered from a carved idol was rammed deep into the poor girl's sex.

Theo said, pointing to a doorway set into the temple wall, "That's the way to the cells."

Vivienne could just make out the steep, narrow steps leading downward.

"But today you get to use the VIP entrance."

***

Vivienne found herself standing in the centre of a large, marble expanse that she guessed had once been part of an ancient temple. Now open to the sky, huge marble columns that had once supported a roof were put to more devilish uses.

Everywhere she looked there were naked girls. With gold slave collars and bands, some were slung between two columns and secured by chains sunk into the marble. With arms outstretched, all had recent whip marks across their torsos.

One poor girl was undergoing a flogging by a hooded guard even as Theo spoke. "My guests are brought here on their arrival. But it has other uses too, as an exhibition hall and punishment area. I have a magnificent torture room, the identical twin to the dungeon at the hotel, in the punishment wing. You're familiar with the rack, but there are other delights that you can't even imagine.

"Now and then, you'll spend time in the contemplation room, where you'll be left to dwell on any crimes you've committed. What actually constitutes a crime can vary, though you're familiar with most of the hard and fast rules. I warn you that I won't tolerate any, I repeat any breech of the Silence Rule! " without warning, he ripped off the tape, bringing instant tears to her eyes, "though screaming is permitted."

I bet it is! Vivienne thought with an inward smile, it's what turns you on.

"Today you'll be excused your daily beating - tomorrow you'll receive double, administered by myself. And, to celebrate your arrival, I'll flog you 'til I draw blood."

Her heart leapt into her throat, but before the horror of his words had fully sunk in, he continued.

"You'll take most of your meals in the refectory unless I decide otherwise. Now come -" he tugged sharply at the lead, "you stink!"

Inside, they passed along corridors where magnificent paintings adorned the walls. But there was one passage where living, breathing girls had been arranged to imitate works of art, replacing statues of the gods that had doubtless once graced the top of the plinths.

"Don't even think of going through that door without permission." Theo pointed to a heavy, studded door. "It leads to my private apartments."

They came to a second door, smaller and rather insignificant looking. Shivering with dread, she didn't have to be told to know that she was going underground, and would only surface again when Theo willed it.

Like something from an old movie, the long, musty passages were narrow and dimly lit, with only candles placed in wall sconces to guide their way.

"This" he explained, stopping outside one of the doors, "is the preparation room." Brusquely, he skimmed his stubbled chin across her face and kissed her on the lips. With a warmth in her loins that had no business being there, she knew that everything she could ever want from life was here on this island. She was his obedient slave to command, to do with as he wished. If it made him happy to abuse her, then she was happy to be of use.

Suddenly, he gave a quick, sharp tug on one of her nipple rings that brought a cry to her lips and a smile to his. Then he threw open the door and flung her inside with a "Clean her up" command to the group of elderly women inside. "I don't want her head filled with nonsense - see that she's fed alone tonight. When she's finished with, get a guard to take her to her cell."

***

Nobody spoke to her, and the hours passed in silence.

After they'd bathed her, washed her hair and submitted her to their razors for removal of underarm hair, the women sat her in a corner of the room. She was given wine, and the first appetizing meal she'd had in ages. Then, as if she were forgotten, she was left huddled in the corner for several hours, until one of the hooded guards came for her.

As usual, her wrists were secured behind her back and her feet shackled. The guard slipped a clip through the two rings that hung from her fleshy lower lips and attached a lead. Then, without a word being spoken, he led her away.

They passed many heavy wooden doors that stretched into the distance, each with a small, barred aperture at eye level. A peculiar coldness descended upon her as she realized that these were the cells.

Eventually, they arrived at her own windowless cell.

Twelve feet square with whitewashed walls, the only source of light was a naked bulb hanging from the middle of the ceiling, and the amenities were basic. Adjacent to the door there was a low pallet with one sheet and a velvet cushion that served as a bed, with huge metal rings set into the wall above it. In the corner at the end of the bed there was a small wash basin with a mirror above it and a narrow shelf , which contained essential toiletries and a few cosmetics. There was a shower and toilet, and more rings were set at various heights and intervals along the adjoining wall, opposite the door.

But most striking and somehow intimidating was Andromeda Waiting hanging on the wall opposite the bed.

The guard removed the lead, instructing her to relieve herself. Burning with shame, she lowered herself onto the toilet, knowing that she'd never again have the luxury of privacy. Yet even as the humiliation of it all made her weep, her spirit soared.

Standing beside the bed, she submitted without complaint to the guard's brisk and demanding fingers that thrust hard into her sex.

"It's instant dismissal to have you before tomorrow," he told her "but you should know that guards have certain rights."

He unshackled her ankles and unfastened her hands, only to fasten them to the front of her collar. Then she was made to lie on the bed, where a chain was attached to her collar and secured to a ring in the wall.

"Sleep tight."

The door clanged shut. Two heavy bolts were shot home. Then the light was extinguished.

Alone and cold, she wondered at Theo's cruelty. To tell herself that she wasn't frightened would have been a lie. Yet in her heart she was willing to suffer anything for the fulfilment of Theo's desire.

As she awaited her fate she was aware that both she and Theo, wherever he was at this moment, knew that tomorrow's scheduled pain and humiliation would be nothing more than a sweet panacea that she'd earned. And, that terror in all its glory had become an aphrodisiac to her, the way inflicting pain had become to him.

CHAPTER SEVENTEEN

A guard came for her at first light.

"It's time, Bitch!" He unclipped the chain from the wall but left her hands fastened.

One hand seized her breast while the other delved deep into her. He swung her round so that she was lying across the bed with her legs dangling over the side. Releasing her, he grabbed her by the wrists and pulled her to her feet.

With a command to "Go and pee!" he flung her across the room with such force that she almost lost her balance.

Recognizing that this was a particularly vicious guard, she obeyed without dissent.

Tall and athletic, like all the guards on the island he wore a black leather mask that covered his entire face. But unlike the other guards he was naked, save for a strangely intimidating, black leather harness.

Consisting of a belt, from which a huge bunch of keys and a nasty-looking whip dangled, it buckled around the waist. Two adjustable straps passed down his belly on either side of his scrotum and up over his buttocks, the ends of which were attached to the back to the belt. Two more adjustable straps were attached at the waist, passed up his muscular chest and over his shoulders, down his back where they were joined to the belt. A further strap circled his chest, crossing his pectorals.

Afterwards, he shackled her arms behind her back. Then, as Theo had done the day before, he slipped a clip through her labia rings and hitched it to a lead.

Without another word he dragged her past the cells and through a labyrinth of subterranean passages. Finally, he yanked her through what turned out to be a gap in some rocks and out into the dazzling light of day.

They followed a winding path that led upward along the rugged cliff face, with the full might of the Aegean crashing thirty feet below.

The ledge on which she found herself was about four feet at its widest part. Sadistically, the guard stood her near the edge. Still manacled, Vivienne faced him with her back straight and her head held high.

Her time with Woodly and Farrell had taught her that Theo's guards didn't merely follow orders but liked to add refinements of their own. In this case she received a sharp slap across her breasts, followed by another across her thigh.

But she felt no thrill, no rush of sexual excitement, just pain. He wasn't a lascivious lover or sadistic, whip-wielding master, he was just a brute.

Clutching his now erect cock that dribbled salty liquid rom the tiny hole in the centre of its purple head, he taunted her.

"Feast your insolent green eyes on my magnificent dick. Look at it, Whore. You may be the Greek's favourite, but you're still a slut! I bet you wish your hands were free to wank me - it's been a long time since you were allowed to take the initiative!" He laughed. "Don't you just long for a good fuck? Look at it! Imagine it thrusting inside your sopping cunt. Imagine how good it would feel."

Vivienne did indeed imagine, and soon found herself desperate for a cock. But not just any cock. Theo's cock! A thrill of arousal shuddered through her at the thought and she thrust her abdomen forward. She closed her eyes and watched the scene that played across the insides of her eyelids. She was with Theo.

"Open your eyes!" The guard gave her lead a vicious tug, pulling her to within mere inches of him.

When she complied with his wishes, he seized the back of her neck and forced her head downward.

"On your knees."

Slowly, Vivienne sank down on to the rocky ledge and tucked her legs beneath her. She heard a helicopter pass overhead and wondered if the passengers could see her. What must she look like to them, on her knees with her wrists manacled behind her back, and her waist length black hair falling haphazardly to hide her face? The erotic picture her mind conjured up caused deliciously hot sensations to percolate through her body.

The stones bit into her knees; little pieces embedded themselves into her flesh.

The guard thrust his cock towards her.

"I've heard you give a fucking good blow job, so get on with it. What are you waiting for?"

Slowly, she raised her head. All at once she wanted nothing more than to feel that fine, thick cock between her lips, to run her tongue over the raised veins and taste the salty liquid. With a fire raging in her belly, she opened her lips in total compliance.

"No!" Without warning, he seemed to change his mind and with a hand on her shoulder he shoved her away. She almost fell as he stepped backward. "You're not fit to lick my boots, never mind my dick. On your feet again, Slut, now."

Vivienne closed her mouth. She felt cheated, her sense of being double-crossed greater than her humiliation. With a fiery urge in her loins, her quim leaked sweet juices down her legs. She shook with unspent arousal.

"Please," she whispered, "I need to come."

His hand dealt her a vicious blow to her face that lifted a red patch on her cheek.

"I was told about you and the Silence Rule! And as for that other little matter - no can do."

Suddenly, hindered by the manacles that imprisoned her hands behind her back, she couldn't steady herself and lost her footing as she scrambled to her feet. His hand shot out and made a grab at her slender arm, his hard fingers biting into her flesh as he helped her regain her balance.

"Steady. I wouldn't want to lose you over the side - you're far too tempting a titbit." He ran his hungry eyes over every inch of her body, lingering a moment on the conspicuous weals. He pinched her hardened nipples, then tugged on the rings. "These rings are big, but I'd have given you bigger ones."

Vivienne drew in a ragged breath, fighting the urge to tell him to keep his filthy hands to himself.

"They were all right about you, you were made to be abused; your body cries out for it. I've seen you when you've been punished; how your eyes glitter."

She ignored the silence rule.

"Then you're one of the guards from the hotel."

The guard turned her round and pushed her shoulders so that she staggered backward against the rock face. Vivienne screwed up her eyes in pain as she fell against a craggy lump that dug into her back and obliged her to thrust out her belly invitingly. The guard rubbed the bulbous head of his penis over the bushy mass of curly hair that covered what she'd once, so long ago it seemed, considered her private place. He kicked her feet apart so that her legs were widely and uncomfortably splayed open.

There was a crevice in the rock. He reached his hand inside and took out a heavy black casket from which he removed two chains, which he fastened to her ankle bands before securing them to iron rings that were embedded in the sheer rock. Next he released her hands. But before she had time to enjoy her freedom he attached other chains to her wrist bands, then fixed them to iron rings above her head.

Finally, he removed the lead and fitted a chain to each ring, anchoring them to rings in the ground, several feet apart. She was now secured in a classic X with her ponderous lower lips held apart, leaving her red slit grotesquely exposed.

He gave a cruel laugh that chilled her to the bone.

She gasped with shock as he once again thrust two fingers into her. He slid them in and out a couple of times, then extracted them just as suddenly, leaving her bereft.

"What a sticky, wet pussy ! Even now you want to be fucked. I hate to disappoint you, lady, but it'll be some hours yet before you're serviced."

With a sudden flourish, he ripped off his mask.

"Nathan!" Once the bombshell had been dropped, her jewel bright green eyes filled with anger. She cried out in terrible disbelief. "You bastard!"

"You've only got yourself to blame. Perhaps you should have stayed in that night and let me tie you to the table." He gave another laugh, blew her a kiss, then left her alone and naked to bake in the sun.

***

It was hours since Nathan had gone; it felt like a lifetime.

Vivienne prayed to any ancient gods that were listening for a cooling breeze as the sun beat down on her restless body, warming her hard, exposed clitoris.

She fought fiercely against the bonds that kept her securely bound to the rock face. Her sensual, feline body arched and writhed in a way that any onlooker would have found highly erotic.

It was a useless struggle, as it was designed to be. But shame, along with fading memories of the self-assured woman she'd once been, not to mention her frantic need to come, urged her on.

Her golden-toned body, bruised, branded and bearing the telltale, criss-cross markings of sadistic pleasure, was flushed pink with arousal. Keyed-up as never before, she trembled in both terror and joyful anticipation.

All at once, Vivienne became aware of movement below her. If she arched away from the rock face she could just make out a sort of flat terraced area that had been cut into the rock. She noticed that there was a small group of people gathering. Was Theo among them?

"Ah, Andromeda...."

She turned to see Theo slowly walking towards her. Dressed in a white linen suit that emphasised his olive skin, he carried a long, curled whip in one hand. His coal black eyes glittered and the stray lock of hair flopped against his forehead as he walked.

Without another word he unzipped his fly and took out his already engorged penis. Then he shook out the whip and began to beat her. The long, braided lash snaked round her breasts making them rock on her chest. Vivienne screamed in agonised relief as the bitter caresses of the whipping tore relentlessly at her writhing body. Joyfully she gave herself up to the rising tide of her orgasm as her master flogged her. She was going to come without permission, she knew it and didn't care. It would earn her further punishment, but she could see from his eyes that he wouldn't be disappointed this time. He wanted to punish her cruelly, and with all her heart she wanted to provide him with the pleasure that would give him.

End

And now for the opening of next months title "SISTERS IN SLAVERY" by *Charles Graham.*

CHAPTER 1

"You're quite sure about this, Miss Osborne? There is no chance that it could be just a simple computer error?"

"Absolutely none, sir. I've checked and re-checked the figures. It has to be a deliberate fraud and the amounts involved are huge."

"Yes, I see. I can hardly believe it. And from what you have told me, some of my senior executives must be in on it."

"I'm very much afraid that at least some of them must be, sir. The scale and complexity of an operation of this size couldn't be hidden unless there was collusion at a very senior level."

"No, I imagine not. This has come as a great shock to me, you know. A great shock. To think that some of my colleagues have abused their positions to do such a thing....Are you absolutely certain of your findings? Certain enough to go to the authorities?"

"The evidence is incontrovertible, sir. I have dates and figures which prove it beyond any shadow of doubt."

"I see. Well then, I have no choice. Does anyone else know what you've found?"

"No, sir, not another soul. I've kept it strictly private, under lock and key."

"Good. It's too late to do anything this afternoon, but I will arrange a full meeting for 8.30 tomorrow evening. We'll keep it quiet for the moment. Can you be ready by then?"

"Yes, of course, sir."

"Very well, then. Bring everything you have to the main Boardroom tomorrow and when you have presented your results, I shall take the necessary action."

"Yes, sir. I'll be there. Uh..just one thing, sir. It might be quite..uh..unpleasant..."

"I'm sure it will, Miss Osborne. But don't worry, I'll make sure that Security is present to deal with anyone causing trouble."

"Thank you, sir. I'm sure that's a wise move. Good afternoon, sir."

"Good afternoon, Miss Osborne. I'll see you tomorrow."

As he lowered the phone back into its cradle, Andrew Morrison, European Chief Executive of Shimatsu Electronics, frowned angrily.

Damn the woman, he thought to himself, why couldn't she have kept her interfering nose out of things that didn't concern her.

How the Hell had she managed to stumble across the "black" file? It was supposed to be top secret, secure against any normal investigation.

Mr Shimatsu would be furious, hc thought grimly and his neck would be on the chopping block, unless he could find a way to suppress the evidence that would blow the Company apart.

Not only his neck, either.

The blasted woman had been right, the operation did require collusion at the highest level and he, Crespi and O'Keefe, two of the other Executive Directors, were all in it together with Shimatsu himself.

If the story got out, they were all finished and Morrison knew it.

He forced himself to control his anger and concentrate.

The evidence had to be suppressed, to disappear, until every trace of the massive fraud could be buried so deeply that no-one would ever be able to find it again.

That wouldn't be easy, but it could, eventually, be done.

Which left the problem of Miss Osborne......

He lifted the phone to his secretary, "Beth, get me Miss Osborne's personal file please and tell Mr Crespi and Ms O'Keefe to come in to see me in an hour."

Five minutes later, he was on his direct line to Ozeki Shimatsu and the millionaire owner of the Company was furiously demanding to know how the disaster could have occurred.

"Dawnelle O'Keefe is responsible for security, isn't she?" the Japanese hissed venomously, "This is all her fault and I do not tolerate failure or stupidity in my employees."

Morrison knew better than to argue with his boss, but tried to soothe the angry Oriental, "I know, sir," he began, "But I'm having a meeting with Carlo and Dawnelle as soon as I come off the phone and I'm sure we can work something out."

"You'd better!" Shimatsu snapped, "If the truth comes out, my loss of face would be unacceptable. Who is this Osborne woman? What can you tell me about her? Is there any lever we can use against her to ensure she keeps quiet?"

Morrison consulted the personnel file, "She is twenty three and single, sir," he reported, "Next of kin is a sister who shares her home. No other relatives. Honours Degree in Business, specialising in Accounts and Auditing. Five foot five inches tall, one hundred and fifteen pounds, blonde hair and blue eyes and she's been with us just under three months."

"So," Shimatsu replied thoughtfully, "She is new to the Company. That is good. It is unlikely she would have any close friends or colleagues who would miss her if she were to suddenly disappear, then. On secondment to Head Office, perhaps?"

"Sir?" Morrison frowned, wondering what was in his boss's mind.

"Yes. That would resolve the situation very satisfactorily. You will arrange for the record to show that she has been transferred here and I will do the rest. Set it up at once."

"But sir," Morrison protested, "She may not want to transfer to the other side of the world. What if she refuses?"

A low, cruel chuckle came down the phone line, "I suggest you don't give her that option."

Morrison took a deep breath, "You mean...kidnap her?"

"I prefer to call it...an enforced transfer," Shimatsu replied coldly, "One that will save your neck, Andrew."

"What will you...do with her when she gets there?" Morrison asked nervously, "You won't...won't...?"

"Dispose of her?" Shimatsu finished the thought for him, "No, Andrew. That would be both dangerous and a waste. She will be kept quite safe, but in no position to harm our financial arrangements. As far as you and the world are concerned, Miss Osborne will simply vanish without trace. These things happen, particularly out here and I can assure you that any investigations that may follow her disappearance will discover nothing. Just another example of a foreigner succumbing to the allure of the..ha..mystic East, as you

Europeans call it."

Morrison bit his lip, "Are you quite sure there'll be no come-back?"

"Quite sure. We will all be safe to carry on making ourselves very, very rich."

"Well..OK then," Morrison agreed reluctantly, "But how do you suggest we get her to you? And what about her sister? She's bound to ask questions and stir things up?"

Shimatsu laughed evilly, "Think, Andrew. Use your brain. We air freight components to you and you send the containers back with export goods, don't you? I'm sure you could find room for a passenger inside one of them."

"That's right," Morrison agreed, "We do it every day. It's routine. No one takes any notice. Not even Customs."

"Correct. As you say, it's routine. And, of course, if one can travel that way, why not two?"

"The sister, you mean?"

"Why not? Then there would be no one to ask awkward questions."

"It would work."

"Yes, it will. Problem solved."

"I'll do it," Morrison said firmly, "The damn girl shouldn't have stuck her nose in. It's her own stupid fault anyway. I'll fix it with Carlo and Dawnelle and we'll do it at the meeting tomorrow."

"Good. The quicker, the better. I'm relying on you, Andrew. Don't let me down,"

Morrison knew he was being warned and hurried to reassure his boss, "Don't worry, sir. I'm not going to let one woman stand between us and all that money."

"You had better not! Now, let's get down to details......"

For half an hour, the two men immersed themselves in times and dates and flight plans, covering every contingency until the plan was perfect.

"Very good, Andrew," Shimatsu said finally, "I knew I could rely on you. Just one more thing, I want Dawnelle O'Keefe to travel with our two..ah..guests in the container."

"Dawnelle? What for?"

"For two reasons. One, to make quite sure that nothing goes wrong and two, I want to review our computer security with her. This breach of the "Black" file shows that access control is not as strong as it should be and I want to be absolutely certain that the error is put right."

"All right, I'll tell her."

"Good. It's quite some time since I had the pleasure of Dawnelle's company. I look forward to renewing our acquaintance. Goodnight, Andrew."

Andrew's two partners listened in consternation as he relayed the bad news to them, "So that's the situation," he said, "And this is how we're going to deal with it."

As he told them of the plan he had thrashed out with Ozeki Shimatsu, the wiry, dark haired Carlo Crespi frowned, "It's risky, but better than bribery. That would leave us open to blackmail for the rest of our lives."

"I agree," Dawnelle O'Keefe paced up and down the office, her long red hair shining, "But what I can't understand is how she got into the file in the first place."

"Because you screwed up," Carlo snapped, "It was your job to make sure the file was secure and you blew it."

Dawnelle turned on him furiously, "Shut up!" she yelled, "You don't know anything about it, you little jerk. I designed the security system and I know it was unbreakable!"

Carlo shot to his feet, his face white with anger, "Unbreakable, you silly bitch? Then why are we in this mess? This is all your fault, you stupid cow!"

At nearly six feet tall in her high heels, Dawnelle towered five inches over the dark Italian and her face twisted in fury as her right palm described a swift arc to crack against Carlo's swarthy cheek.

The powerful slap sent the smaller man reeling and Andrew leapt to his feet, coming between his two feuding partners, "Enough! Sit down, both of you! Fighting between ourselves isn't going to solve anything."

For a moment, the two glowered at each other, but then each regained control of their anger and took a seat.

"That's better," Andrew said, "Now, let's forget about whose fault this is and concentrate on how we're going to sort it out."

Slowly, tempers cooled, but it was still a very tense atmosphere as plans were made to kidnap and freight the two Osborne sisters.

Carlo, it was agreed, would arrange transport by container, Dawnelle was to bring two Security staff..ones who could be trusted to keep their mouths shut..to the meeting, while Andrew undertook to falsify the paperwork to cover up the girls' disappearance.

As Dawnelle strode stiffly from the room, refusing to even look at Carlo, the Italian's eyes glittered with anger.

"She is a bitch, that one," he muttered under his breath, "But one day I will teach her not to slap me!" and his lips twisted in a thin smile.

Maxine Osborne stared at her reflection in the long mirror, checking her appearance for about the twentieth time as she prepared for her crucial meeting.

"What do you think, Melissa?" she asked for the third time, "You don't think this red scarf is too much, do you?"

"You look great. Stop worrying."

Maxine looked across at her sister and saw a virtal duplicate of herself.

They were twins, Maxine the older by four minutes, the two inseparable from birth and their bond strengthened by the death of their parents in a car crash when they were eighteen.

Near identical in looks, their characters were distinctly different.

Where Maxine was reserved, hard-working and serious, Melissa was high-spirited and outgoing, a lover of partying and dances, acquiring and then dropping boyfriends without a care while her sister was more discerning.

Both had had lovers, Maxine rather fewer, but had always managed to avoid entanglements with their sibling's partners and the inevitable difficulties that would have caused and were completely at ease with each other.

Maxine looked at her reflection again, examining the tailored navy blue suit which adorned her well proportioned figure, the gleaming white blouse hugging her firm breasts, the ruffled scarlet scarf at her throat and the black stockings and mid-heeled shoes beneath the skirt which ended a demure two inches above her knees.

"Yes, you're right," she agreed finally, "It's fine."

"Told you," Melissa said casually, "You'll knock then dead. What about me, then? Will they like this down at the Club, do you think?"

Melissa looked at the tight white sweater emphasising the thrusting globes of her sister's bra-less breasts, then lowered her gaze to the skin tight black leather micro-skirt and high heeled thigh boots she wore.

"I should imagine it'll be a riot," she smiled ruefully, "How do you get away with it, Melissa? I wouldn't dare go out in public dressed like that."

"It turns the guys on," Melissa chuckled, "I haven't had to buy myself a drink for months."

"I bet you haven't. But what do you do if they get, you know, pushy?"

"I can look after myself," Melissa replied confidently, "A guy only gets what I want to give him. I'm the one in charge, not them and that's the way I keep it."

Maxine shook her head, smiling, "Oh well, fair enough. As long as it stays that way."

"It will. I know what I'm doing. Come on, sis, time we were going."

As she drove towards Shimatsu Electronics, Maxine said, "Shall I drop you off at the Club, Melissa?" but her sister shook her head, "No. It's too early, yet. I'll wait in the car until you're finished and you can drop me off then."

"Are you sure? I might be a long time, you know."

"That's all right. If I get bored, I'll find a taxi.

"OK. No problem."

The huge building was in darkness apart from the top floor and as Maxine entered her access code on the panel set into the armrest of her car's door and the high double gates swung open, she pointed upwards, "That's where my meeting is. If it goes well, it could change my whole life. I could really go places."

Maxine was quite right....but not in the way she fondly imagined!

She drove around to the back of the building and parked, then got out and straightened her skirt, "Wish me luck," she said and Melissa smiled, "Good luck," then settled back in her seat and turned the radio on as her sister walked away.

Riding up in the lift, Maxine took a deep breath, "This is it," she murmured, "I'm on my way," and as she stepped out and walked to the polished doors, she gripped her notes and evidence firmly in her right hand.

The doors swung open to her knock and she walked in.

The Boardroom was vast, a fifty-seat conference table stretching before her and at the far end, three people sat waiting as two burly, uniformed Security Guards escorted her towards them.

"Good evening, Miss Osborne."

"Good evening, sir," she replied to Andrew Morrison, the only one she recognised.

"Sit down, please. This is Ms O'Keefe and Mr Crespi, two of my senior Directors."

The two Directors didn't smile and Maxine grew a little nervous as she took her seat.

"May we see your evidence, please?" Morrison asked and Maxine handed it over.

As the papers were passed around, the faces of the three Directors darkened, "Is this everything you have?" Crespi snapped suddenly.

"Yes, sir," Maxine answered, "As you can see, it's quite clear cut."

"Yes, it is," Ms O'Keefe confirmed, "Who else knows about this?"

"No one, madam. Just us."

"Are you sure?"

"Yes, of course. Just the four of us."

"Excellent!" Morrison nodded meaningfully, then snapped his fingers, "Now!"

The two Security Guards reacted like lightning, each seizing one of Maxine's arms and twisting her slim wrists behind her back, forcing her to bend forward in her seat.

Taken completely by surprise, Maxine had no chance to resist and before she knew what was happening, a pair of handcuffs were locked tightly on her wrists.

Recovering her wits, Maxine cried, "What are you doing? Stop! Let me go!" but the men ignored her and snapped a second pair of cuffs about her ankles, securing her before she could begin to fight.

"What's happening? Take these things off me!" Maxine wrenched and kicked in her efforts to free herself, but the steel circlets were locked and much too strong for her to break, digging into her soft skin as she fought in vain.

"Don't be stupid," the redheaded woman sneered, "You can't get out of those so you might as well shut up and listen while we tell you what we're going to do with you."

The cold contempt in the woman's voice sent a horrible chill through Maxine and she redoubled her efforts to escape, "Help!" she yelled at the top of her voice, "Help me somebody! Call the Police!"

A hard hand clamped over her lips, thumb and fingers digging into her cheeks, so that her screams died to whimpers of pain.

"Much better," the speaker was Morrison and Maxine stared wildly at him as he smiled cruelly, "If you continue to scream, you will be gagged, but if you're sensible and keep the noise down, you won't be. So, are you going to be sensible?"

Maxine trembled in despair as his eyes stared at her, then managed a small nod.

He nodded at the man squeezing her cheeks and his grip slackened.

"Wh..What are you doing?" Maxine groaned, "Why have you tied me up? What have I done? Let me go. Please?"

"I'm afraid we can't do that," Morrison replied calmly, "You see, you have caused us something of a problem and we can't afford to let you go."

"But why? What have I done?" she stared at the three people before her, "You have to let me go. You can't do this to me."

"Oh, but we can," Dawnelle O'Keefe said spitefully, "You shouldn't have been so damned nosy and now you're going to find out what happens to people who mess with us."

As the redhead glared at her, Maxine shivered, suddenly realising what was going on.

"You're all in on it," she said slowly, "You're the ones working the fraud!"

"Congratulations," Dawnelle sneered, "Finally worked it out, have you? Yes, that's right. We've got a nice profitable little scheme going here and we don't intend to let you louse it up."

Maxine's blue eyes opened wide and she stammered, "Wh..What are you g..going to d..do with me?"

Carlo Crespi chuckled, "We're going to send you on a little trip," he grinned, "Air freight! Somewhere where what you know won't hurt us."

"It's all arranged," Dawnelle told the frightened captive, "You'll be going tonight...and you won't be coming back!"

"No!" Maxine screamed and fought madly against the steel cuffs binding her limbs, "You can't! Please, no! Let me go! I won't say anything, I promise! I won't tell anybody about the fraud!"

"No, you won't," Dawnelle was thoroughly enjoying Maxine's horror, "Not anybody who'll take any notice."

"Gag her," Andrew ordered and Maxine's eyes bulged in terror as one of the Security Guards produced a roll of wide, black industrial tape and moved towards her.

"Stop!" she cried, "Please!"....then she remembered Melissa.

"You won't get away with this," she said desperately, "I didn't come here alone! My sister's down in the car and she knows I came here. If you don't let me go, she'll go to the Police and you'll all be arrested!"

Her last-ditch effort to avoid being gagged failed and as one Guard held her head still, the other lifted her hair out of the way and wrapped half a dozen turns of the adhesive tape right around her head, compressing her cheeks, sealing her lips and hiding the lower half of her face.

Maxine whined in futile protest, but could not speak at all and her terror grew as she learned their power over her.

Handcuffed at wrists and ankles and now gagged as well, she could do nothing to help herself and her mind reeled to the awful knowledge that she could not prevent them from putting her in a freight container and carrying out their plan.

Melissa was her only hope and she could only pray that her sister would call the Police in time to save her.

To her sheer, stark terror, Maxine heard Andrew Morrison give orders to the two Guards, "Her sister is waiting in the car park. Go down and tell her that her sister wants to talk to her up here. As soon as she's safely inside the building, cuff her and gag her then come back up to fetch this one."

The two men nodded and hurried out and Morrison turned to Maxine, "Bringing your sister here was an unexpected bonus for us. She was the only one who would have missed you and raised the alarm. We assumed you'd be alone and that we'd have to go and fetch her from your house. It gives us lots more time."

Maxine whimpered in anguish, realising how carefully the plan had been laid.

Unknowingly, she had played right into their hands.

Melissa would have no reason to be suspicious and once she had been captured and tied up, there would be no one to rescue either of them.

They would both simply disappear!

Stunned by what had already happened, it had not occurred to Maxine to wonder where she and her sister were going to be sent or what was to be done with them when they reached their destination.

That oversight was remedied in the most terrifying way as Carlo Crespi suggested a way to pass the time gained by not having to search for Melissa.

"She is a pretty girl, isn't she?" he murmured softly, "And as she's going to become a slave on Mr Shimatsu's island anyway, I would like to see more of her."

Andrew and Dawnelle looked at him, then looked at Maxine and their lips curved into cruel smiles.

"Yes. Why not?" Andrew agreed and Dawnelle nodded, her eyes gleaming in anticipation.

The three partners rose from their seats and as Maxine saw the lustful expressions on their faces, she screamed into her gag and shook her head frantically.

As the redhead watched, the two men seized Maxine and lifted her writhing body onto the conference table, Carlo pinning her shoulders and Andrew her ankles, holding her face down and helpless.

Dawnelle raced to a cupboard and came back with a pair of sharp scissors and as Maxine screamed and fought vainly against the hands holding her, the tall redhead slit up the back of Maxine's suit and blouse, the material falling away to reveal her pale flesh and the dark blue lace straps of her bra, suspender-belt and panties.

"Turn her over," Dawnelle ordered and as the men complied, Maxine wept in shame as the redhead snipped through the front of her bra and cut the straps of her panties, sweeping the flimsy scraps of fabric aside to reveal Maxine's bare breasts and sex.

Naked apart from her suspender belt, stockings and shoes, Maxine shuddered as Dawnelle and the two men stared down at her, their greedy eyes drinking in the soft curves of her displayed form.

"Mmm," Andrew Morrison nodded appreciatively, "Lucky old Shimatsu. I wouldn't mind having her as a slave myself."

Maxine moaned in terrible despair as his words confirmed her fate.

As impossible as it seemed, they really did mean to transport her to the Far East, where she would be forced to become a white slave!

Dawnelle O'Keefe reached out and Maxine shrieked in futile denial as her defenceless breasts were captured and the redhead's slim fingers caressed and stroked the twin half moons.

Maxine gasped as unwanted arousal coursed through her, but could not stop the instinctive responses of her body as the fingers rose to her tawny nipples, toying with the delicate buds until the crinkled flesh engorged and stiffened to stand erect and quivering to every touch.

Horribly ashamed of her own weakness, but quite unable to resist the insidious arousal, Maxine flushed a bright scarlet as her tormentor giggled with delight, then sneered, "Huh! A randy little bitch like you will be easy to enslave. You're already gasping for it and I haven't even begun, yet!"

"It looks as though that's not the first time you've done that, Dawnelle," Carlo Crespi observed casually.

The redhead glared at him and snapped, "That's nothing to do with you. My sexuality and preferences are my own business, so keep your nose out of my affairs."

"Oh, I'm so sorry," he apologised sarcastically, "Touched a nerve, have I? Didn't mean to pry, Dawnelle, I was just impressed with your..ah..technique. It doesn't bother me if you prefer women to men."

Dawnelle reddened and opened her mouth to deliver a stinging retort, but Andrew cut in before she could begin, "I'm sure Carlo didn't mean anything by it, Dawnelle," he said smoothly, "Let's not argue between ourselves. Not when we have such a delightful captive to amuse us and a second one on her way. Why don't we take full advantage of our good fortune. I have an idea. The Despatch section uses strapping, doesn't it, Carlo? Would you mind fetching some up?"

Carlo chuckled and let go of Maxine's shoulders, then hurried out.

Andrew stood back, "No need to hold her any more," he said to Dawnelle, "She's not going anywhere," and he lit a cigarette calmly.

On the Conference table, Maxine sobbed bitterly as she tried to come to terms with the shocking callousness of what had been done to her and the terrors which still lay ahead.

With a convulsive wriggle, she managed to roll over, but her effort to hide her nakedness came to nothing as Dawnelle picked up the scissors and proceeded to slice the ragged remains of Maxine's once-smart suit from her body, finally stripping the handcuffed blonde down to suspender belt, stockings and shoes and chuckling, "I'll leave her those. She's more naked with them."

It was true and Maxine trembled wildly, knowing that the little she still wore only emphasised her nudity and the picture of helpless eroticism she presented.

There was no doubt in her mind that her captors were going to take her and her eyes filled with hopeless tears, because there was nothing she could do to prevent it.

Even more frightening, was the thought that her torment was only beginning and that, once delivered to Shimatsu's island, escape would be impossible.

As a slave, she would be completely at the mercy of total strangers and she had no illusions about what would happen.

Maxine knew she was pretty and was well aware of the desirability of her curvaceous body.

Men found her attractive and she had always considered that to be a bonus....

Until she had been bound and gagged and stripped, her body suddenly the plaything of men..and a woman..who saw her simply as a slave to be used for their pleasure in any way they desired!

Appalled by her thoughts, Maxine fought her bondage with every atom of her strength, her muscles cording beneath her sleek skin as she struggled to escape the awful fate looming over her, her body writhing and twisting in a grim battle she feared she could not win.

The return of Carlo underlined her utter defeat and she slumped trembling in her bonds as she was forced to accept her helplessness.

The strapping Carlo brought was made of plastic, two inches wide and immensely strong, usually used to band and secure crates for transport, but, as Andrew had calculated, it could be used for other purposes....

Against the strength of the two men, Maxine knew that resistance was useless and lay still, conserving her energy as strapping encircled each of her ankles, knees, wrists and elbows, the ingenious one-way plastic buckles allowing the straps to be drawn taut on her flesh, but preventing the straps from loosening.

On her induction tour of the Company, she had seen the strapping being used and knew, with a sinking feeling in the pit of her stomach, that it could not be released and would have to be cut from her when she was set free.

If she was set free....

Turned onto her back and slid to one end of the conference table, she gulped as her legs were pulled apart and her left knee and ankle strapped to the heavy table leg.

The instant her left ankl cuff was released, she kicked out viciously with her right leg, tearing it loose from the men's grip and feeling her shoe connect solidly.

Andrew reeled back, clutching his stomach where Maxine's shoe had landed, but her pleasure at fighting back was short-lived, Carlo rushing forward to seize her flailing leg and yank it cruelly to her right, opening her wide and holding her as Dawnelle attached the strapping to secure her in a merciless spreadeagle.

Flat on her back and unable to see down past her own naked breasts, Maxine trembled in fear as she realised that her assault on Andrew, though deeply satisfying, had achieved nothing, except angering her captors.

She was even more helplessly bound and had given them a reason to punish her!

Too late, she wondered whether it might have been better to give in peacefully, but what was done, was done and she had no choice but to put up with any consequences.

Andrew straightened slowly, rubbing his stomach and he scowled malevolently at the spreadeagled blonde, "Right," he grated slowly, "So you want to play, do you?" and he grabbed a strap, "Sit the bitch up," he ordered, "I'll teach her not to kick."

As Dawnelle and Carlo raised Maxine's torso, he reached behind her and threaded another strap through the straps already encircling her elbows.

Then, with a powerful pull, drew the strap taut.

Maxine hissed through her nose, shoulders straining back as her elbows were forced together until they met at the middle of her back, her breasts thrust forward lewdy by the remorseless tension and her arms a single, quivering column.

Maxine's distress was clearly evident, but Andrew was in no mood for sympathy, "Lay her down," he said, "I wasn't going to tie her that tightly, but it's her own damn fault."

"Quite right," Dawnelle agreed forcefully, "Slaves have to learn to obey. If I had my whip with me, I'd give her a real lesson!"

Carlo and Andrew stared at the tall redhead in amazement and Dawnelle gave a weak smile as she realised what she had said.

"Oh," her cheeks burned with embarrassment, "Well, anyway," she tried to cover her confusion with a facade of toughness, "Yes, I do have a whip and yes, I do punish a slave if she steps out of line. I'm not ashamed of it. Slaves need to be reminded of their duties sometimes."

Her eyes glittered as if to challenge the two men to say anything and Carlo chuckled softly.

"I see. That explains a lot of things. I agree with you, Dawnelle. And do you have a slave, at present?"

"No, not at the moment. And it's none of your business."

Carlo grinned, "You seem to know a lot about slaves and whips, Dawnelle. Ever been on the receiving end yourself? Maybe I could help you out there, if you enjoy that sort of thing.."

Dawnelle stared at him contemptuously, "Not if you were the last man on earth," she told him icily and for a couple of seconds there was complete silence in the room as the two glared at each other.

"Uh, well, we don't have a whip," Andrew said. "So we will just have to manage, won't we?" and he moved quickly to stand between Maxine's gaping thighs, "As she kicked me, Carlo, you won't mind if I go first, will you?"

Carlo broke his staring match with Dawnelle, "Please yourself," he said shortly, "I can wait."

Maxine shook her head, pleading mutely for mercy, but was ignored and her body gave huge jerks as Andrew's fingers explored the parted folds of her labia and slid into her sex to send uncontrollable stimulation crashing through her belly as he forced her to respond to his touch.

Gasping and moaning, Maxine's eyes bulged with anguish as her belly grew slippery with her juices despite everything she could do to resist the sexual heat he imposed upon her.

Fully aroused himself, he unzipped his trousers and Maxine

screamed in a mixture of horror and enforced desire as his rigid shaft thrust deep into her belly, penetrating her with brutal ruthlessness.

His hands gripped her hips and he lunged massively, grinding his pelvis against her, relishing her wide-eyed terror as he took her with no thought or consideration of her wishes or pleasure, "Bitch!" he snarled, "You won't kick me again, will you, eh?" and he laughed aloud as she shuddered to the jolting impacts of his masculine power, her tightly bound body able only to take whatever he gave.

His thrusts grew faster and harder and Maxine wailed in surrender as Dawnelle's fingers tugged and rolled her erect nipples, the added stimulation triggering Maxine's climax.

Her spine arched, pressing her breasts upwards and deeper into the redhead's grasp, while her belly juddered and pulsed to the release of explosive gouts of love juices that swamped her in liquid pleasure and she screamed in despairing ecstasy into her gag as blistering heat raged through her body.

Feeling her climax around and over his embedded shaft, Andrew gave a deep groan and his seed jetted in torrents into Maxine's pounding belly, his release heightening and increasing her sexual passion as she surrendered to his total domination of her body.

Sated, he slid from her even as her orgasm shook her belly with spasms of undiminished power and her eyes widened with the knowledge of her own submission as she pulsed and quivered before his cruel gaze, unable to control the fury of her need or the shameful intensity of the lust still burning brightly in her body and which her orgasm had only served to intensify.

For the first time in her life, Maxine's cool reserve had deserted her and she was helpless before the savagery of her own unmasked passions, unable to control, or even understand, the sexual frenzy which had, and was still, engulfing her!

She whimpered in horror, frightened of herself, frightened of her captors...but even more frightened of what her passion revealed about her.

To be continued.........

The cover photograph for this book and many others are available as limited edition prints.
Write to:-

Viewfinders Photography
PO Box 200,
Reepham
Norfolk
NR10 4SY

for details, or see,

www.viewfinders.org.uk

TITLES IN PRINT

Silver Mink

ISBN 1-897809-22-0 The Captive *Amber Jameson*
ISBN 1-897809-24-7 Dear Master *Terry Smith*
ISBN 1-897809-26-3 Sisters in Servitude *Nicole Dere*
ISBN 1-897809-28-X Cradle of Pain *Krys Antarakis*
ISBN 1-897809-32-8 The Contract *Sarah Fisher*
ISBN 1-897809-33-6 Virgin for Sale *Nicole Dere*
ISBN 1-897809-39-5 Training Jenny *Rosetta Stone*
ISBN 1-897898-45-X Dominating Obsession *Terry Smith*
ISBN 1-897809-49-2 The Penitent *Charles Arnold**
ISBN 1-897809-56-5 Please Save Me! *Dr. Gerald Rochelle**
ISBN 1-897809-58-1 Private Tuition *Jay Merson**
ISBN 1-897809-61-1 Little One *Rachel Hurst**
ISBN 1-897809-63-8 Naked Truth II *Nicole Dere**
ISBN 1-897809-67-0 Tales from the Lodge *Bridges/O'Kane**
ISBN 1-897809-68-9 Your Obedient Servant Charlotte *Anna Grant**
ISBN 1-897809-70-0 Bush Slave II *Lia Anderssen**
ISBN 1-897809-74-3 Further Private Tuition *Jay Merson*

*UK £4.99 except *£5.99 --USA $8.95 except *$9.95*

All titles, both in print and out of print, are available as electronic downloads at:

http://www.silvermoon.co.uk

e-mail submissions to:
Editor@Silvermoon.co.uk

TITLES IN PRINT

Silver Moon

ISBN 1-897809-16-6 Rorigs Dawn *Ray Arneson*
ISBN 1-897809-17-4 Bikers Girl on the Run *Lia Anderssen*
ISBN 1-897809-23-9 Slave to the System *Rosetta Stone*
ISBN 1-897809-25-5 Barbary Revenge *Allan Aldiss*
ISBN 1-897809-27-1 White Slavers *Jack Norman*
ISBN 1-897809-31-X Slave to the State *Rosetta Stone*
ISBN 1-897809-36-0 Island of Slavegirls *Mark Slade*
ISBN 1-897809-37-9 Bush Slave *Lia Anderssen*
ISBN 1-897809-38-7 Desert Discipline *Mark Stewart*
ISBN 1-897809-40-9 Voyage of Shame *Nicole Dere*
ISBN 1-897809-41-7 Plantation Punishment *Rick Adams*
ISBN 1-897809-42-5 Naked Plunder *J.T. Pearce*
ISBN 1-897809-43-3 Selling Stephanie *Rosetta Stone*
ISBN 1-897809-44-1 SM Double value (Olivia/Lucy) *Graham/Slade**
ISBN 1-897809-46-8 Eliska *von Metchingen*
ISBN 1-897809-47-6 Hacienda, *Allan Aldiss*
ISBN 1-897809-48-4 Angel of Lust, *Lia Anderssen**
ISBN 1-897809-50-6 Naked Truth, *Nicole Dere**
ISBN 1-897809-51-4 I Confess!, *Dr Gerald Rochelle**
ISBN 1-897809-52-2 Barbary Slavedriver, *Allan Aldiss**
ISBN 1-897809-53-0 A Toy for Jay, *J.T. Pearce**
ISBN 1-897809-54-9 The Confessions of Amy Mansfield, *R. Hurst**
ISBN 1-897809-55-7 Gentleman's Club, *John Angus**
ISBN 1-897809-57-3 Sinfinder General *Johnathan Tate**
ISBN 1-897809-59-X Slaves for the Sheik *Allan Aldiss**
ISBN 1-897809-60-3 Church of Chains *Sean O'Kane**
ISBN 1-897809-62-X Slavegirl from Suburbia *Mark Slade**
ISBN 1-897809-64-6 Submission of a Clan Girl *Mark Stewart**
ISBN 1-897809-65-4 Taming the Brat *Sean O'Kane**
ISBN 1-897809-66-2 Slave for Sale *J.T. Pearce**
ISBN 1-897809-69-7 Caged! *Dr. Gerald Rochelle**
ISBN 1-897809-71-9 Rachel in servitude *J.L. Jones**
ISBN 1-897809-72-2 Beaucastel *Caroline Swift**
ISBN 1-897809-73-5 Slaveworld *Steven Douglas**

*UK £4.99 except *£5.99 --USA $8.95 except *$9.95*